Strange Attractors
A Story about Roswell

by

Mark Todd

Cover design by Kym O'Connell-Todd
ktodd@hughes.net

"Alien head" cover art image courtesy of
FreeDigitalPhotos.net

ISBN-10: 147938559X
ISBN-13: 978-1479385591

For Trent and Clayt

CONTENTS

ACKNOWLEDGMENTS

Gratefully, I had many eyes scrutinize this work. I'd like to thank biologist Peter Gauss for his help in keeping my genetics and virology accurate. Also indispensable were beta readers Kara Dalky, Matt Davis, and Ange Tysdal – all of whom offered insights that made this a better story. A special thanks to beta reader T.L. Livermore, who told me the original short story deserved a novel. I want to thank Rebecca J. Vickery and Caleb Seeling for giving me valuable insights about the pacing and characterization flaws they saw in earlier drafts, as well as John Barnes, Barbara Chepaitis, and Russell Davis commenting on the novel during the home stretch. And finally, my deepest thanks go to my wife Kym O'Connell-Todd, whose professional and critical eye always urged me toward "one more rewrite." Always good advice, and taken right up to the moment of letting the story go.

CHAPTER ONE

Conti

Monkeys don't drop out of the sky. They crash.

Just as they should. But Major Conti knew he had to find the monkeys first – and so he sat in the transport that lurched across open rangeland, struggling to keep its driver-side wheels in a cow trail.

Conti knew the cross-country trek jostled the two corpsmen who rode in the canvas-covered bed of the truck, but he couldn't help that. The major signaled his driver, Corporal Thurman, to brake to a stop when the truck topped a promising ridgeline, and the officer swept the terrain through field glasses for a sign, any sign, of the latest crashed monkey.

Conti swore as he leaned back against his own sweat-drenched khaki shirt, sticking to the truck's bench seat. He signaled Thurman to change course along a dry creek bed that angled more to the south. When they passed under an anvilled thundercloud, the shadow blunted some of the usual July heat – but not for long. Never for long. Within minutes, the sun reappeared and glared off the cracked green and brown paint of the transport's hood. Conti ran his fingers through the close-cropped white hair that sprouted over his head, and he felt the moistened grit that came away under his fingernails.

He squinted as his eyes scanned the ground from truck to horizon, from horizon to truck, trying to will the crash site into view. The major assumed they were on private land by now, but the terrain made it hard to tell. When they encountered the sagging wire of a three-strand fence, Conti rapped on the rear wall of the transport's cab and ordered the corpsmen riding in the back to hop out and cut the barbed wire. No telling where the gate stood. And ranchers in the area were all used to seeing military vehicles trespass on ranch lands. Locals knew better than to interfere. They could damn well do their part by keeping quiet about the military goings-on in the desert landscape. So what if ranch hands had to repair a bit of fence now and then? What the hell, the Army was fighting to keep the country free from the Red Menace and safe for democracy – even there among the sage and scrub brush of a New Mexico wasteland.

"Where is it?" Conti asked aloud, realizing as he spoke that neither he nor the corporal had exchanged a single word over the past hour.

"You'll find it, sir. Always do." Thurman grinned at his commanding officer but returned his gaze to the rough terrain directly in front of the transport.

Yeah, he always did. But Conti was more worried that a local would come upon the site first and start asking questions.

They spotted the crash site just before sunset. Winds had carried the pod further from the military reservation than the staff meteorologist had predicted, but there it was at last, TS-11. The pod lay broken and crumpled against a weathered sandstone rock formation. Conti jumped out before the truck came to a complete halt, and he picked his way past the twisted limbs of waist-high cactus to get to the wreckage.

As he approached, the major studied the childlike corpse of simian Test Subject No. 11, strapped into the broken rigging. Although he expected the autopsy to confirm his observations, Conti knew from the results of TS-09 and TS-10 that the chimp had died long before it crashed. Conti glanced at the modifications they'd made to the latest pod and made a mental note to strengthen the struts and shock-absorbers. Of course, the chimp's body would show massive internal trauma when it impacted the ground at a velocity exceeding a hundred miles per hour, but these were secondary considerations for the TS-11 experiment. Conti was anxious to get the test subject back to the Army airfield installation so he could examine the level of gas saturation in the tissues. If the experiment had worked, the ascent would have slowed the animal's motor functions by the time the balloon reached 20,000 feet, but by then the oxygen mask began delivering an adjusted gas mixture that kept the chimp's lungs from failing until the pod approached 38,000 feet. After that, of course, a high-altitude trigger had released the pod to return the completed experiment back to earth, slowing only enough to test the seams on a prototype parachute.

"Let's get the specimen and rigging loaded," Conti announced as he motioned to the two corpsmen standing behind him.

At the same time, Thurman backed the transport closer to the impact site. Conti stood aside as his recovery team placed the chimp in a body bag and then collected the broken parts of the pod and blown-out chute. Behind the crew, Conti watched the orange clouds to the west drain color as dusk claimed the site of the recovery.

Conti settled back into the seat as Thurman concentrated on the terrain ahead. It would be easy in the fading light to overlook the ruts that passed for the road they'd followed earlier, so the major didn't distract the transport driver.

Conti looked out the window at the darkening landscape and smiled. He claimed, on occasion, that his work had turned his hair the premature white that covered his scalp, but that was nonsense. All the men in his family had white hair by the time they were in their mid-twenties. But it made for a good story on base. Conti the mad scientist and his secret experiments. Still, it was a helluva job for a biologist, and an unlikely one. As the war had drawn to a close two years earlier, Conti had jumped at the chance to transfer to Army R&D. The European Theater was tightening its grip on the Axis of Evil – Hitler committing suicide, Mussolini dangling from a public rope – and Japan would soon surrender. But by then, most soldiers just wanted to finish the war in one piece. When the head of R&D approached him to join the new Space Biology program, Conti figured the transfer increased his odds of making it home alive. Only later did he wonder why R&D showed interest in his academic background.

At some level, Conti assumed somebody had finally looked at his personnel records and noticed the doctorate in biology. What's a guy with that kind of smarts doing in the field? Let's put his talent to better use. That's what they'd probably said. Before he knew it, Conti was state-side again and assigned to high-altitude testing – at least nobody was shooting at him. When the war did end, he knew he wouldn't opt for a discharge. Thousands of soldiers returned home, hoping to rebuild lives that a world at war had interrupted. The competition for jobs in the public sector was fierce. But R&D promised Conti a promotion to the rank of major if he re-enlisted, and they told him there was a different kind of war on the horizon – the Cold War, though it took a few years before they gave political stalemate that name. And they told him he would have a chance to help save the world from the Communist threat. Conti hadn't been that hard to convince.

When the orders finally came down, Army R&D sent Conti to the Southwest, where they attached him to a facility responsible for testing the extreme limits of pilot endurance –

only they didn't use humans in their tests. Conti's mission for the Space Biology program began to take shape: How far could they push the human body before a mission was at risk? What physical extremes made pilots unreliable? These were the questions Conti was supposed to answer, and primate testing was an approach that didn't risk military personnel – at least, not prematurely. Best of all, they gave him a budget, left him alone, and told him to improvise.

Thurman down-shifted, grinding gears as he forced the stick shift into low once they found the parallel ruts that passed for a road into the rangeland. All the while, Conti's eyes traced the silhouettes of the yucca plants that staked the edges of the light cast by the headlamps. The major shook his head at no one in particular. Ranchland. The occasional cattle they saw throughout the day looked as scrawny as the starved POWs he'd seen overseas. Except the only confinement these cows knew was the thousands of acres they foraged in search of isolated blades of grass. He wondered if the crashes ever fell close enough to scare the stock. Had the ranchers noticed their herds scattering into the hinterland since Conti had started the simian experiments? Not that there was anybody to complain to. No one on the airfield installation would have even acknowledged the testing. There seemed to be an unspoken code of conduct at the installation, an understanding that anybody working under classified assignments helped bring them one step closer to ridding the world of the Red Menace.

Conti glanced at his watch and swore when he realized how late it was going to be when they returned to the airfield. He knew that Elsa would have waited – was waiting now, in fact – not knowing that he wasn't going to make it to the movie. It was a John Wayne film, *The Angel and the Badman*, and she had turned down the invitation to see the movie with the other WACs stationed at the installation. Untidy wisps of her long, blond hair would be working free from the regulation bun she wore, lifting in the slight breeze that always stirred about sunset. She was probably tapping a foot and looking up and down the street, waiting for him to appear at that very moment. How often had he stood her up in the past month? Three or four times, at least.

She had said yes to the picture show in a weak moment, and he had taken advantage of her, he knew. Elsa, along with the rest of the country's female population, had a screen crush on the Duke, and Conti knew she had been waiting for weeks for the film's release. She'd said she was still mad at Conti, but she agreed to meet him at the movie theater – her way of putting some distance between them after The Incident.

It had become a matter of trust, and she'd tired of his evasions about what he did for the Army. She told him that she had thought their relationship was going somewhere, but not if he insisted on keeping secrets. He took her to the lab one evening for the night feeding – something he did himself so that the chimps were more manageable, more cooperative when he strapped them into the pods.

"Oh, they're so cute!" she said, and she walked over to one of the cages. "What's this one's name?"

"TS-11," he replied as he pushed lettuce and fruit through the tray at the bottom of the enclosure.

Elsa frowned. "That's so cold. I think you should give them names." She cooed at the primate like it was a puppy. And the damned thing responded by twisting its head down and looking up at her with large, brown eyes. "I think I'll call you Lars. Yes, from now on, you're Lars." She glanced up at Conti, adding, "After my uncle."

Elsa Lundgren had told Conti she was a Minnesota farm girl, hailing from hardy Norwegian stock that had settled in Blue Earth County after they had passed through Ellis Island in the early 1900s. Although she was a second-generation American, she was also proud of her Scandinavian heritage. Conti had often heard her talk of her relatives, of the tales they told of the Old Country, but Lars was a name that hadn't come up.

"No point in naming them, Elsa."

"Why not?"

"Because they won't last that –. " *Long*, he was going to say, but stopped.

He hadn't really been honest with her about the chimps, only that they were used in testing. But it was too late to back-track now, and before they had left the lab, Conti had confessed what would happen to Lars. The argument that followed turned into The Incident, and Elsa refused to talk to him for days afterwards. Agreeing to go with him to see the Western had been an encouraging signal for rekindling their relationship – or so he'd hoped. It was going to be touchy now to explain why he had stood her up at the movie house.

The truck lurched into a rut, jarring Conti out of his memory of the last evening with Elsa. He sighed, wondering what he could possibly say to woo her back again. It wouldn't be that he was bringing Lars back to the airfield in a body bag after a "successful" test.

Two hours later, Thurman guided the transport onto the paved highway that led to the airfield, and Conti noticed his driver start to relax. The corporal began to tap the heels of his palms on the steering wheel, an irregular motion that punctuated the unspoken words his lips mouthed. These were signs that told Conti his driver was building up to a conversation. It was almost as though Thurman was rehearsing his opening lines. Conti didn't have long to wait.

"Did you hear about the civvie pilot up in Washington State, sir? The one who saw all those flying disks?" Thurman kept his eyes on the road and continued to punctuate words with his hands as they struck the steering wheel when he spoke.

"Just what was on the radio." Actually, Conti had received a classified report on the incident, and a request from his superiors to assess the possible ballistic effects on human pilots within those disks – assuming the reported disks were real. The unspoken context, of course, was trying to decide if the Russians had been planning a new trick. But Conti knew better than to share with Thurman what he'd learned from the communiqué, let alone that the military was worried about the implications of the anomalous sightings.

"Well, the news said the guy saw this string of lights tracking him," Thurman continued. He worked the stick-shift from one lower gear to another as they approached the gate to the airfield installation.

"Yeah, I heard that."

"But then they flew past him at twelve-hundred miles an hour."

"Nothing flies that fast." The secret report on what the pilot had observed seemed far-fetched to Conti, and he figured the guy had more likely seen a reflection off the aircraft's window. The report quoted the witness as saying he saw the craft make sharp right-angle turns at high velocities. Conti had prepared a brief, suggesting the craft – if the lights turned out to be craft – could only be unmanned. No humans could withstand the stress caused by such a sudden shift in vectors.

"And he said the disks skipped along in the sky like saucers skimming across water. Flying saucers, ha-ha. Don't that beat anything you've heard, sir?"

"Yeah, it does." But by then Conti wasn't listening. He had monkeys on his mind.

It was several days and a few chimps later, and Conti had just begun the first stroke of a Y-incision into TS-14's thorax when the door to the lab opened. He half-turned, expecting to chew out whichever member of his team had walked in unannounced. But Conti was surprised to see a man dressed in street clothes stroll – no, swagger – into the lab.

"Who the hell are you? And how'd you get in here." The

man must have some kind of clearance to get that deep into the facility, but there were protocols. Mr. Plain Clothes had just violated one of them.

"All it took was this," the man said as he flashed CIC identification, but the motion blurred any chance for Conti to catch the name.

The man planted himself on top of Conti's desk in the corner like it was his own. Conti knew that the Counterintelligence Corps had virtual carte blanche to look into anything that interested them, and there seemed to be more of them showing up at the installation in the past few days. Not that Conti would have noticed, but Corporal Thurman had mentioned – was it a couple of days ago? – that the airfield had a lot of new faces, some in uniform but others in street clothes. Thurman said they had to be CIC. In fact, one of them had stopped Thurman the day before, and the corporal described the way the man asked questions. More like an interrogation than a conversation. Conti had dismissed Thurman's remarks because their presence didn't concern the TS project – at least, not until now. Unlike Thurman, the intrusion didn't spook Conti; it irritated him. He hadn't spent much time around CIC, but what he remembered was that everything was like a game to these guys. They seemed to get their kicks by talking in riddles. Conti didn't have time for this crap.

"I've come down to see first-hand what you do," the CIC figure said as his eyes probed the lab.

"Uh-huh." Conti turned back to the chimp and continued the incision.

"So that's a TS."

Mr. Plain Clothes knew project terminology, which only appeared in Conti's written reports, but Conti tried not to show his surprise. Besides, the comment sounded more a statement of the obvious than a question, so the major didn't reply. Maybe the man would take the hint that he was busy and go bother somebody else.

"And do you train these monkeys?"

Conti set the scalpel on the autopsy table and turned toward the desk. "They're chimps, not monkeys. And yes, they're trained to be cooperative."

"Which means…?"

"They climb into the pods, leave their oxygen masks on, that sort of thing." Conti stared at the intruder. "Why are you here?"

The CIC officer – if he were counterintelligence, Conti knew he would be an officer – ignored the question, and countered, "So, could you train one to fly a jet?"

"We have pilots for that, last time I looked outside."

"Yeah, but if you wanted to."

For just a moment, Conti conjured up the image of a chimp in a flight suit, sitting in a cockpit full of dials and gauges and batting the joy stick back and forth between its prehensile feet. "It would never happen."

"You're sure about that?"

Conti didn't like his smug visitor, and he certainly didn't have time to walk him through chimp behavior. "Look, you've obviously read my reports. You know what I'm doing here. And I don't have time for this. I have work to do." He turned back to the autopsy table, determined to get on with his dissection.

And that's when it came, words snapping like a bullwhip flogging motes of aimless Southwestern dust. "Not anymore. Not here. You're being transferred into CIC, and you're off this project."

Conti dropped the knife when he wheeled to face the CIC officer again. "What? You must be joking."

"We need your skills elsewhere." The guy didn't move off the desk, and Conti could hear the smirk in his voice. "We're moving you over the hill to the 509th."

Conti knew the 509th was stationed at Holloman Army

Airfield, across the Sangre de Cristos from his own lab facilities, but a vertical mile of mountains was no hill. And to move him there was irrational.

The CIC officer continued, "Don't worry. Think of it as another promotion."

Conti fumed at the way the CIC officer seemed to enjoy delivering the message. "But my work…"

"New application."

"This makes no sense. The 509th is a bomber group. They don't do research."

"They dropped the Big One and ended the war."

Conti had heard the scuttlebutt, but it was one of those things that nobody talked about – something in the category of neither-confirmed-nor-denied. But here was this guy talking out loud about the classified military use of an A-bomb. Conti didn't know how to respond. What relevance did a tactical air field – distinguished or not – have to do with his research?

The CIC officer stood. "It's an important installation. Top security. But there've been . . . intruders. Fly-bys near the base. And they're not ours."

"I still don't see what – "

"We're going to shoot one of them down, and we need someone to examine the pilots. But it has to be someone on our team. Somebody inside CIC. Somebody with your expertise."

Conti stared blankly as the man pointed at the dissection table.

The CIC officer continued, "The craft are so small, the pilots can't be much bigger than that monkey. That chimp."

"You – you think someone has trained chimps to pilot these craft?" Conti breathed a mental sigh of relief. "Look, it can't be done. Chimps aren't smart enough. Maybe these craft are unmanned."

"No. The guidance is too sophisticated, too . . . unusual."

"And you think the Russians have created a craft and crew that – "

"Not Russian."

"Who then?"

"That's what we're going to find out." He walked toward the door. "And you're going to help. Start packing."

And then the CIC officer was gone.

Morgan

Morgan Johanssen tried to pull the long teeth of the comb through her hair, but when she hit an almost impenetrable snag she stopped and pursed her lips, piping a stream of breath between her lips in frustration. She didn't hold out much hope. She'd forgotten to buy a bag of water softener salt – again – which she only remembered when the shower head rained down enough iron-enriched water to fortify an armored car. As she tugged against resistant strands of long blond hair, she sighed and resigned herself to the reality that it was going to be another bad hair day. She wouldn't have minded so much except that she was sure to see *him* on swing shift today.

How lame is that for a thirty-something? she taunted herself. She worked at the tangles with fierce persistence and then walked over to the closet to dress.

She'd tucked her white blouse into the red skirt she'd laid out the night before, then tugged on the matching jacket. Before she headed toward the door, she returned to the bathroom to swab her lips with a light coat of lipstick, lying to herself that she'd always meant to start wearing a gloss – to protect her lips from the high-altitude ultra-violet rays. It was just that she never seemed to remember – well, not until she'd met Grant. Today would be different. Besides, she felt like she needed to compensate for the hair.

Taking one last glimpse in the mirror, she raised her

hands in a gesture of defeat at her reflection and headed out the door. Morgan recalled the way her dad used to tell her that she "cleaned up good" when she wanted to. It was just that back when she lived at home – God, how many years ago was that? – she never much cared how she looked. Besides, she now had a scientific image to maintain. Biotech companies didn't expect their virologists to look good; they just wanted results. A haggard and disheveled appearance meant you were thinking about work. But these days Morgan had begun to take a second look at her appearance, and she shook her head as she pulled open the door on the old barn where she kept her car. *Come on, Morgan, 'fess up. It's only been since you started working swings that you started wearing skirts again.*

She grabbed her asthma inhaler and walked out the door. Climbing into a her Honda Civic, she backed out of the barn and got out to close the sagging wooden door, careful not to let her skirt touch the side of the car. She loved living in the country, but the dirt and occasional mud that came with the scenery wouldn't mix well with the monoclonal antibodies she wanted to culture in the lab that day.

As she turned the car down the gravel road, she let her gaze sweep across the little house and broken corrals that surrounded her home. It always brought a smile to her face to see the place. Not exactly a dream home by most people's standards, to be sure, but then Morgan had never really shared much in common with others. The old ranch house fit her perfectly, once she'd had it repaired. And at least she had electricity. She liked the way the day's work tended to slip away as she drove home the thirty miles that separated her from the labs in Denver. And besides, nobody ever dropped in unannounced – assuming they could have even found the place without directions. Assuming anybody would have wanted to visit her in the first place.

The tires hummed as they floated over file miles of washboard ruts and roadbed to connect to the access ramp of I-25 North. She accelerated to seventy-five and set the cruise control. Before long she could see the downtown skyline of the Mile High City in the distance beyond undulating hills of prairie grass. The city's center looked like a lonely colony of tiny buildings, skyscrapers that poked like toy blocks above the plains. From the interstate, she could see how the land sloped the twenty miles to the west of Denver and met the Front Range, the first wave of the Rocky Mountains.

Morgan glanced at the digital readout in the dash and decided she would make it in plenty of time for the doctor's appointment. Maybe even have time for a bite of lunch before she was due to log in at Contitech. It seemed a shame that her appointment was downtown. She was going to have to back-track to the south side of town to get to the biotech facility. But it couldn't be helped. And she knew if she cancelled again, the doctor might scratch her off his client list. It wasn't like she wanted to even be there, but she knew she'd already waited too long to ask for help. She had promised Conti that the final phase of the transgenics project would be finished the week before, and it wasn't like her to miss a deadline. And now there was no way she could hope to be ready, at least not for another two weeks. This had to stop. Of course, medical research had rhythms of its own, which she could live with – they all did. But this was different. She hadn't told anyone about the real cause of her delayed progress, and it had been easy to hide since she was holding the ball on this one for Conti. Lots of researchers contributed pieces, but he had insisted that only she should know how to connect the dots that made sense of it all. And she reported only to Conti.

To tell the truth, she wasn't sure yet where Conti's latest "Baby" was heading. He was legendary for coming up with ideas out of the blue and, to the delight of his board of directors, turning them into corporate margins that soared higher every fiscal quarter. The current Baby was a government contract, and the heightened security issues had shut her out of the highest level discussions with the feds who funded the work. Old cronies from after the war, he said, and just smiled that sly, white-haired alpha wolf smile of his. She'd never understood why everybody else at the lab hated to be engaged in the boss's pet projects. She thought he was sort of sweet, in an I'll-devour-you-whole sort of way for those who didn't perform up to his expectations. But Morgan had seldom seen that side of his personality – and never had it been targeted toward her. It was as though she could do no wrong. A couple of times she thought she'd caught him looking at her. Not with that predatory look she sometimes got from other men on those rare occasions – well, they used to be rare, before Grant – she dressed up to present findings to the board or to some special client. Instead, Conti's gaze had said something else to her, like she reminded him of someone from the past, someone he might have cared about. He'd hinted as much the first time they met when he asked if her accent was Minnesotan. It was, of course, to Morgan's chagrin. She'd tried for years to eradicate that Minnesota "O" from her speech, but it persisted. Conti had told her he'd always found Midwesterners to be down-to-earth, dependable. And then he said that she reminded him of a Minnesota woman he used to know. But that's all he'd ever said. Now *there* was a story worth hearing, but one she knew she'd never learn.

When she thought about her relationship with the boss, she and Conti did make kind of an odd couple – the snarling old white wolf and the cub, his anti-social protégée. No wonder workers cut a wide swath around them whenever they strode down a corridor debating whatever happened to be the experimental challenge of the day.

Morgan exited the interstate where it snaked around the downtown district and threaded her way to the parking lot that flanked the Towers, a pair of stylish old office buildings that were now connected at the third floor by an enclosed catwalk. When she stepped out of the car, she froze for a moment. Maybe she was giving up too soon. After all, asking someone else for help just wasn't like her. This was Morgan Johansson, Wonderworker. No equation too thorny, no pressure too high to … what, keep her from appointed rounds? She was beginning to sound like a mail carrier rather than a researcher. Morgan visualized walking through the doors to the professional building, a technique in her bag of tricks that had often helped her will herself through tough-going before. See the terrain, calculate the obstacles, and then there were fewer surprises. But nothing in her experience was anything like the conversation she'd likely have somewhere on the other side of the door before her.

She became aware that people passing on the sidewalk had begun to cut a wide swath around her. She overheard one woman arguing with a boy about his nose ring. To Morgan, he looked too young to be wearing some sort of metal booger attached to his nose.

The youngster whined, "Mom, it's the new millennium. Everybody wears them."

The new millennium, Morgan reflected. *Right, or a few years into it. And here I am still trying to get my act together.*

The woman and boy had also stopped to stare at Morgan, and then Mother seemed to tug Nose Ring Boy on down the street and away from the crazy lady who paced back and forth in front of the office building's door. Or had Morgan just imagined the woman's reaction? *Huh, maybe that's the point, Morgan.* She shrugged, reminding herself that this was only a consultation, not the end of the world, and heaved the front door open. By the time the elevator delivered her to the fourth floor, she had tried to place in perspective the night terrors that had plagued her all that week. Seemed silly now in the sunshine on the street, the bustle along the corridor. But that false sense of security had been the route she'd taken too many times in the past few weeks. She couldn't wait – Conti's Baby couldn't wait – and so she turned the gilded knob of the expensive deep-red mahogany door, cringing that it had come to this.

Old English letters beside the office read: Dr. Lamont Thornton, M.D., Ph.D., Jungian Analyst.

Conti

Conti's day at the 509th began with a briefing, just like the previous two mornings since he'd arrived. The CIC staff gathered in a barracks near the tarmac of the main runway, and Armand – the plainclothes noncom Conti had met the previous week – reported to the gathered men that radar blips had once again appeared near the bomber base during the previous night. What's more, they appeared over the installation's guided-missile launching sites. And once again, fighters failed to visually confirm any of the radar targets.

On this, the third morning, Armand scowled at his small brigade of CIC operatives as though it was their fault that the fighters hadn't found an enemy to engage. And the enemy they were, Armand announced.

"They've penetrated our military airspace without authorization, and we will assume hostile intentions," he said. "The airfield is on highest alert, and we have the full cooperation of the base commander to bring this situation under control."

To Conti, it all sounded a bit too personal. He had heard that Armand served as base intelligence for the 509th during the war. In fact, Armand had been here when the base received its orders to launch the first nuclear bombing mission against Hiroshima. And Conti figured that Armand was feeling protective of *his* bomber base.

But Armand wasn't alone in his zeal. Over the past forty-eight hours, Conti had witnessed the arrival of dozens of officers and enlisted men. As soon as they got off the transport planes, some of the newcomers changed into street clothes and disappeared into the community. Others formed into on-base retrieval teams ready for deployment at a moment's notice. Yeah, Conti thought, somebody wants these intruders bad, but it's not just Armand. To tell the truth, Conti was curious about what they would find as well.

As Armand's briefing drew to a close, he gave his CIC team a penetrating look and said, "We're at full deployment now, and we're ready for them. Let's just hope they come back tonight." It seemed to Conti that Armand sounded anxious that they might miss their chance.

When he dismissed the briefing, Armand asked Conti to remain behind. As everyone else left the barracks, Armand asked, "Is your lab ready?"

Armand had seen to it that all of Conti's equipment was flown in, and the major had spent the past two days creating a make-shift facility. They had set him up in the airfield's hospital morgue, or what passed for the morgue. It was a cramped space at best, but serviceable. Hospital staff had stacked several metal morgue trays to one side and built a wall of cardboard-boxed records to the other side, creating a wide corridor down the center. It was clear that the room hadn't seen much use as a morgue, but it had made a helluva storeroom. By the time soldiers had unloaded Conti's boxes and cabinets into the morgue, it was all Conti could do to squeeze around his own wheeled autopsy table. Conti wasn't going to have to step far to get from the table to the instrument cabinet to retrieve a fresh scalpel blade.

Was his lab ready? Conti shrugged a response to Armand's question and then added, "If there's anything to examine." He still wasn't convinced that these craft had pilots – if craft existed at all. Except for nighttime lights in the sky and a few targets on radar screens, no one had actually seen anything that could be described as a craft. Thunderstorms had filled the past few nights with electrical storms, and the major couldn't shake the notion that what a few edgy officers thought they had witnessed could just as easily turn out to be natural phenomena. Besides, Conti reasoned, who could survive the G-force of a hair-pin turn at a thousand miles an hour? It just didn't seem likely.

Armand nodded absently as Conti assured him everything on the medical side of things was ready, but it was clear the man's mind was racing ahead to the next item on his mental checklist. Before the major could finish his report, Armand had excused himself and was through the door.

Outside the barracks, Conti could hardly tell anything was out of the ordinary. Military personnel went about the business of maintaining an Army airfield – even if it was a high-security nuclear bomber base. Aircraft mechanics sauntered in and out of hangars performing routine maintenance inspections on the behemoth B-29s that served at the core of the installation; patrol jeeps and sentries swept the area at regular intervals; and trucks ferried soldiers from one nondescript detail to the next. Standard operations. But under the façade of normal routines, Conti sensed something more, something that signaled a certain edginess. He witnessed a reminder of that tension as he headed back toward the hospital, walking past a line of men who unloaded crates of canned food through the side door of the mess hall. Even though he was fifty feet away, Conti could overhear the soldiers complaining about the high alert status and the cancellation of the evening's celebration.

That's right, Conti realized, it's Independence Day. Only two years had passed since the end of the war, but people still treated the holiday as a patriotic remembrance of the nation's triumph over the forces that had threatened the nation's freedom. But so far as the base was involved, the lights in the sky had interrupted this summer's festivities. The heightened alert status meant that fewer – if any – soldiers were likely to receive off-base passes. In fact, security would curtail traffic between the airfield and local community. The few days Conti had been at the 509th had given him no opportunity to visit the town, but he now remembered that Corporal Thurman had suggested he visit a little hole-in-the-wall barbecue shack off Main Street the first chance he got.

Suddenly, Conti could think of nothing else he wanted more than a greasy side of pork ribs. But that would have to wait. He smacked his lips and shrugged to himself, quickening his step back to his morgue-turned-lab.

As he entered the hospital, he nodded to one of the nurses he'd met on the first day at the base – what was her name? Conti was bad at names, but he avoided looking at her name tag and strolled down the hall. Funny that he could remember from their short conversation that she liked to read mysteries – she had a dime store novel tucked under her arm as she had returned from break – but she could be an Ethel or a Jane or a Lois for all he knew. Names never stuck for Conti until the third or fourth embarrassing time he asked. He stopped in front of the lab door, which was under lock – Armand didn't want hospital personnel nosing around – and fished the key out of his pocket to let himself in. Everything was in order, checked and re-checked, so he slid himself into the narrow slot before the tiny desk he could call his own, and waited. A fish without water, that's what he felt like. Everyone else seemed to have a job to do, but his would only begin when, or if, Armand had his way and was able to shoot down one of those lights in the sky.

He wished they had installed a telephone for him to use. Over the past two days, he had tried to call Elsa time and time again. But it was always one of the other WACs in her bungalow who answered, and always with an excuse why she couldn't come to the phone. Conti felt bitterness well up inside. It wasn't supposed to be like this. Other people had happy lives, happy loves, and he felt cheated by the failure to bring any sort of closure to The Incident. He recalled when she had questioned whether or not their relationship was going somewhere. He knew the answer now, and it hurt like hell.

Conti pulled out the top desk drawer, extracting the log he planned to use for preliminary notes on his new assignment. The log was empty, of course, and it might be a long time before he had a chance to make any entries. He closed the logbook and stared at the metal autopsy table that stood against one wall.

It could be a long wait.

Morgan

Morgan tugged at the hemline of her skirt, which had ridden up half the length of her thigh when she took a seat in the inner office. Dr. Thornton sat across from her, glancing over the notes his secretary had recorded about Morgan Johanssen, the public person.

Maybe Morgan should have waited to wear the outfit for her second day on swing shift at the lab. The department store clerk had assured her the weekend before that her new skirt was cut in the latest length, tasteful but flirtatious. At the present moment, however, a flirtatious skirt seemed altogether the wrong impression she wanted to communicate. That was for later, for the Man-Who-Never-Gave-Her-a-Second-Look. *Way to go, Morgan, your shrink* – she inwardly cringed as she used the term, but that's what he was, her shrink – *is going to think you're trying to come on to him on your first visit*. She was surprised that the thought even occurred to her. Maybe it was her defenses rising, or a sudden sensitivity that she was talking to someone trained to interpret her every word, her every nuance – certainly a red come-on skirt that felt like it inched up her leg each time she fidgeted against the clinging leather of the armchair.

From time to time, his head tilted up or down, as though he were struggling to find the right focal length for the tri-focals that balanced across the bridge of his nose. At last, he looked up, and to Morgan's relief, looked her in the eye rather than the thigh. "You're an educated woman, Dr. Johanssen."

"Morgan. Nobody's called me Dr. Johanssen since – well, nobody calls me that." She hastened to add, "It's not that I don't appreciate the title, or the time that it took to get it, but everybody where I work is a doctor of one sort or another, and if we all called each other Dr. This and Dr. That, the day would be over before – " Morgan stopped short when she realized that she was rambling. What had gotten in to her?

"Morgan then." Thornton nodded, and continued to glance at his notes from time to time as he spoke. "And I see you did post doc work at the University of California." He smiled. "That's my school. And then you worked for NIH."

"Yes, the National Institutes of Health. Oh, you'd know that. You're an M.D."

"Most people don't realize that we're medical doctors."

"It was on your door, and besides, I've been reading up on psychiatry." Morgan broke eye contact – what would he think that meant? – then forced herself to look at him again.

"A little self-help?" His smile seemed genuine, and Morgan could discern no condescension in his face.

"No. I wanted to know what to expect when I came in here."

He pressed his lips together and arched approving eyebrows. *Well, score a point for Morgan. He likes people who do their homework*

"And what brought you to Denver?"

"The usual. Contacts. The head of Contitech knew Daniel Gajdusek at NIH."

"Daniel Gajdusek? The Nobel laureate?" Thornton let the notes sink to his lap and his head tilted up once, twice, trying to find that magic focus though his glasses as he looked at his client.

"Yes, it was Gajdusek's work on slow viruses that brought me to NIH."

"I know his work on Alzheimer's and other dementias. Morgan, you travel in cutting-edge circles."

You don't know the half of it, Morgan thought. *If you did, I'd have to shoot you. Or maybe not. You could maintain doctor-client confidentiality, right?* But all she said was, "Anyway, Conti – the head of the lab where I work – he knew Gajdusek, and before long he'd talked me into working for him in the private sector."

"More lucrative, I'm sure."

"I guess," Morgan lied. The money was good, and among other things, it let her buy and fix up her little dream home. "But that wasn't it. The head of the lab is a driven man, and I liked where he was driving."

Thornton nodded again. "So, let's talk about why you're here. Not in Denver. Why you're here today." Thornton settled back in the chair with a familiar motion that he must have performed hundreds, maybe even thousands, of times. "Tell me about your night terrors."

So much for small talk. Morgan felt the breath hanging in her throat. It was a hard thing to admit out loud, but that was why she was there, right? She blurted out. "I'm having these – these visitations. Sometimes in my dreams. At least, I'm pretty sure they're in my dreams."

"And why do you say you're only pretty sure?"

He didn't bat an eye. Training, she guessed. But then, he did say he worked with dementias. Severe loss of memory, thinking abilities, perception, judgment, attention. Maybe her case was going to seem mild compared to his usual fare. Maybe not.

"Well, sometimes when I wake up, or recover, after these…episodes, well, I'm not in bed. I'm where I thought I was in the dream."

"Any history of sleep walking in your family?"

"No, not that I know of. But it's not like sleep walking. I looked that up." She offered him a sheepish grin. "There's this little boy."

" – in your dream."

"Yeah, and he always starts by telling me he's amused, but

he never smiles, never laughs. And he – he shows me things. Things about my work and all the awful stuff that could happen if I finish the project. It's like he knows all about what I do."

"In your dream."

"Yes, and …" Morgan stopped short as she realized he'd repeated himself. "What's your point?"

"Just that you're couching your language as a product of the unconscious mind, of a dream state. Sometimes dreams have a way of presenting our life back to us in symbolic ways that, upon reflection, tell us what we already know. Look, Morgan, I'm happy to work with you, to develop a series of progressive sessions for you, but you're an intelligent woman. Dreams are a wonderful, if mysterious, function of the brain."

"So I've read." Her tone had hardened.

"Hear me out. I see on the form that you've opted to pay for these sessions without using the health insurance I'm sure a biotech company offers."

"That's right."

"And why is that?"

Morgan stared at him for several seconds. "Because, well, … I don't know, because it's personal, I guess."

"But the dreams are about your work." He glanced at his notes. "Your work for Contitech. And, as you just told me, about all the awful things that might happen because of your work."

"Dr. Thornton," Morgan bristled, "that's not what I said. It's what the little guy in my – " She wouldn't say it.

"In your dream, Morgan. It's what a figure said in your dream." He paused as though he were waiting for the conclusion to sink in. "Who is really doing the talking in a dream?"

Morgan didn't answer. He'd made his point.

But then he continued, "So you're researching slow viruses. Slow viruses," he repeated the phrase as though he were savoring it. "The causative agents in human neurodegenerative diseases, right?"

"Like Alzheimer's."

"Yes, and AIDS. Diseases that take years to detect. Only now you're doing it for money rather than humanitarian reasons. Morgan, do you suppose you might be feeling guilty at some level about your new career? Before you spend a lot of your own money on letting me listen to your dreams – and I'll do that, if you want – maybe you should spend some time thinking about whether or not you're happy in what you're doing?"

Morgan nodded, not because she agreed with him, but because she could see his line of reasoning. "You have no idea what we do at Contitech, or whether it's serving the public good."

"Fair enough. But I don't need to know what Contitech does in order to tell that I'm looking at a young woman who has night terrors about her work. You don't think there may be a bit of guilt?"

"No, not guilt. And you're overlooking something I said earlier."

"And that was?"

"I said that these visitations were sometimes in my dreams, and they are. But not always. Sometimes they happen when I'm awake. And – " She almost started to begin with the phrase, *I know this is going to sound crazy*, but then she thought better of it. " – the little boy's still there, and he's showing me the future."

Thornton arched his eyes again, but this time Morgan didn't think it was a sign of approval.

Gamma-Ori

Gamma-Ori felt more than saw how people stared at him

as he shuffled along the corridor. Even though he was only ten years old, his engineered body had reached maturity. He knew, however, that the stares he felt were not from his height; they were caused by uneasiness about the way he looked – his disproportionate, elongated limbs, his bulbous head, his large eyes. But Gamma-Ori had never questioned why he had been made the way he was. His entire life he had spent with the other novitiates of the Order of Orion, and all second-generation Oris looked this way. In fact, it was only through their distinct mental signatures that one Ori could tell another apart. It had been like living in a dorm with a dozen identical twins.

Gamma-Ori wanted to reassure the Commoners he passed in the outer halls of the temple that despite his modified appearance he was still human, but he knew that it was forbidden, without permission, now that his abilities had begun to augment. Especially now that the Priesthood had called him to take his place among the Translators. But Gamma-Ori didn't envy the Commoners the differences between their bodies and his, and certainly not their speech and tongues, and he would gladly sing into their minds the story of how human he really was if only they would ask him. Instead, they looked away, which saddened him. He tilted his head forward to hasten his shuffle toward the room just ahead.

The autonomous life sensor that lived in the portal leading into the room must have already received the news of his Calling because it greeted him by name and granted him access without an ident. In the direction of the Live-in by the portal, Gamma-Ori managed a slight smile with the mouth indentation that still adorned the lower part of his face. His "mouth" served no purpose, of course, but part of his childhood training included daily exercises to work the residual muscles that still formed inside his cheeks – the facial expression, he'd been told, was one that reassured most Commoners. Maybe the life sensor that lived in the wall would feel reassured as well.

The opaque membrane that sealed the entrance dissolved, and Gamma passed through the portal. Before him sat a single figure in the center of the room. Theta Sag, one of the Appointed Ones from the Order of Sagittarius. Although this was their first encounter, Gamma recognized his new mentor from a resonance of thoughts that radiated from the priest's mind. The Sag was reciting notes to the desk's memory cells, but he looked up and smiled, motioning Gamma to sit in the empty chair beside his own.

"It's all right; have a seat," the Sag said, although Gamma sensed these words more strongly as thoughts rather than sounds.

I am your obedient child, Gamma sang into the Sag's mind, but only deep enough to register as a kind of whisper in his mentor's thoughts. Then Gamma bowed his head.

But Theta Sag raised his hand to stop Gamma-Ori's gesture of ritual obedience. "None of that. There'll be no ceremony between us if I am to instruct you."

The Sag radiated chords of genuine warmth, and Gamma knew at that moment he was indeed fortunate to have drawn such a mentor. His Ori brother, Beta, had shared sorrowful songs of encounters with his own mentor, an instructor who also did the bidding of the Priesthood, but without conviction or joy. Theta Sag was not like such priests, Gamma could tell.

As he watched the Sag priest, Gamma was puzzled by the flutters that interrupted his mentor's thoughts until the priest removed the wearable stimulation band that fitted over his temples. Gamma knew the stim-band fed virtual images into the Sag's brain from the Live-in that grew inside the desk. It was a new experience for Gamma. He had never sat in the presence of someone using a wearable, and Gamma was tempted to take a deeper hold into his mentor's thoughts to see how it affected his new mentor's mind. But since such a sharing was permitted only by invitation, Gamma decided he would have to learn to compensate for the flutters without strengthening his read on Theta Sag's mind. While the Sag finished reciting his notes, Gamma practiced editing the flutters from the word-streaming thoughts of Theta Sag.

After a few minutes, the Sag slipped the stim-band from his head, and Gamma noticed that the flutter ceased at the same time. Theta Sag turned to hold Gamma with a direct gaze. "Welcome, young Ori. I look forward to our time together, and I hope we'll be friends."

Gamma wanted to bow his head again to show respect, but he didn't want to contradict the Sag's instruction against formality, so he simply lowered his eyes. Gamma could detect a slight sadness from his mentor, but again the Ori didn't want to intrude into the source of the emotion. In recent months, as the growth strengthened in his own brain, Gamma struggled not to violate others' privacy. But the access was so easy – so automatic – that Gamma found he had to make a conscious effort not to read what others thought. Gamma had to admit that he was tempted now and then, nonetheless. He liked this new mentor, and he wanted to sing away the sadness that colored the thoughts behind the words. Still, the young Ori recognized that would be a breach of the trust between them. He resisted the impulse as the Sag continued to speak.

"Did you know we share a passion?"

Gamma looked up, wondering what a lowly Ori could share with one of the Appointed Ones. And then the answer arose through his mentor's word-streaming thoughts as he began to speak again.

"We both love stories. And we both love telling them to others."

Gamma knew the Priesthood had generated the Oris for a special purpose – one that he would learn when he completed his initiation – and the priests had engineered several Oris with the gift of storytelling. But it surprised Gamma that a priest from the Order of Sagittarius would be able to sing stories. Had his mentor been engineered as well?

You have the same gift?

"No, not a gift, not like yours. But I love to tell stories anyway. That's why I asked to instruct you."

Gamma was happy to talk about his first gift, the gift that was the reason the Priesthood had generated him. *I love to sing stories, but . . .*

"But what?"

I have to be careful now. Gamma hesitated, and then remembered that he was permitted to speak of such things to a mentor. *Now that a new gift grows in my head, my songs are too strong for — for some.*

Gamma had been so surprised, and dismayed, when he'd sung into the mind of the Commoner who had tended the Ori dorm. The old man had fallen to the floor, his mind unable to separate the song from reality, Gamma realized too late. No one had scolded Gamma, but they had taken the Commoner away. Later that week, Gamma received the news that it was time for him to begin his instruction.

"Your powers, your gifts, are growing, especially now that you have received a Call. And do you know why you need a mentor?"

Because I must learn to interpret my Call.

"Yes, young Ori. The Call is a great honor."

Gamma sang — though softly — the mantra he and all the Ori brothers had learned as novitiates. *The Call helps reiterate the past for the sake of the future.*

"Well, of course, but that's an answer that anyone can give." The Sag's face remained steady, reassuring, but Gamma detected a flash of disappointment ripple across the margin of his mentor's thoughts before he continued, "What else can you tell me? Now that your Call has begun, don't you sense something more?"

Gamma paused for a moment, trying to guess rather than read the response that his mentor wanted to hear. Then he ventured, *I see flashes of the Call inside my head sometimes.*

"Yes, although colonizing would be a more accurate way to describe it. You were engineered to accept colonies of ideas and images that are developing throughout your brain, placed in those parts of your brain where memories develop naturally. Gamma-Ori, you're growing knowledge and talents – " that sadness again " – beyond your years. But the brain has to learn how to connect these memories in order to make sense of them. It's like reading about a boy who can walk. But the words that you read would make no sense unless your memories can tell you what walking is like. Do you understand?"

Gamma-Ori shook his head and sang, *But I already know how to walk.*

The Sag sighed, and at that moment Gamma slipped and read his mentor's thoughts more deeply: *This youngster can never have more than a childlike grasp of the adult world.* Gamma heard these thoughts, but they were puzzling to him. Here was the source of his mentor's sadness, it was clear, but Gamma couldn't understand why this would affect Theta Sag. Gamma was happy to serve the Priesthood; it was his calling, his joy, his gift.

The Sag then said, "Yes, Gamma, you know how to walk, but if you didn't know how, the words would make no sense. Don't you see? It's only an example. There are other things, unlike walking, that you don't yet know. But the knowledge of these things is forming memories inside your brain. And it's from our conversations that you will learn how to associate these colonies into meaning. Doctrinal meaning."

Meaning from the adult world?

A faint surge of surprise crossed Theta Sag's face. "Yes, something like that."

It pleased Gamma to see his mentor smile, and the Ori knew at that moment he would do whatever it took to help lift the sadness from Theta Sag's mind.

Conti

Conti could hear the telephone ringing inside his room, but he fumbled his keys and didn't make it inside in time to answer. He stood staring at the black phone, wondering if he should call the switchboard to see who had placed the call. When it began to ring again, Conti grabbed the receiver off the cradle and identified himself.

"Conti, where were you?" It was Armand, and his voice sounded nervous, or maybe it was excitement. Conti hadn't made up his mind which mental state described the noncom best.

Conti didn't care for Armand's familiarity, and the man had several times referred to Conti without the prefix of "major." It wasn't that Conti minded so much when they were alone, but Armand would slip and call him just plain ""Conti" in front of enlisted men as well. The intelligence work had seemed to disconnect the CIC officer from military protocol. But considering the circumstances, Conti decided this time it would be ungenerous to harbor a grudge.

"I was at the mess and just got back," Conti replied. Then he added, "Has something happened? Have you – have you shot one of these things down?"

"No. But things are starting to happen. Get over here."

"Where's 'here'?"

"The control tower."

In the background, Conti could hear other excited voices.

"I'll be right there." Conti replaced the receiver and headed out the door.

He could have called for a driver to deliver him to the control tower, but Conti decided to walk the twenty minutes rather than wait for a jeep to come pick him up. It would amount to the same time. As he cut across a field, he could hear the crackle of sun-burned grass under his shoes. It might only be midsummer, but all things green had long since surrendered to the heat. In the fading light, he headed toward the airfield lights that surrounded the control tower and radar facilities. Conti saw flashes of lightning to the northwest of the military installation. He'd lived in the region just long enough to realize that the storm clouds could be five miles away or fifty. There was no way of telling. The high desert plains made distance a tricky thing to reckon by the naked eye. On a clear morning, before the winds whipped dust into the atmosphere, he could even make out the blue peaks of the Sangre de Cristo mountains seventy-five miles to the west.

Another flash assaulted his vision, outlining a huge thundercloud that must have filled a third of the sky. Just as quickly, the sky turned dark again, hiding the giant electrical storm. The sudden darkness reflected Conti's gut feeling. They were on a fool's errand, and he could already hear the tone of Armand's debriefing the next morning, reporting how, once again, the fighters had been unable to acquire targets that corresponded to the radar blips. Conti was beginning to hate summer thunderstorms.

As he approached the control tower facility, he saw a line of Jeeps parked near the front door. Beside the vehicles stood about two dozen MPs, smoking and talking among themselves. They straightened and saluted as Conti passed them to enter the facility. When Conti had arrived at the base, Armand suggested he change into civvies, but Conti liked wearing the uniform. Rank had its privileges, and he saw no reason to abandon the edge it gave him. Of course, that wasn't the reason he gave Armand. Instead, Conti had countered that his role in the mission was medical, not recon, and besides, he'd blend in better in the military hospital by wearing a uniform. Armand hadn't pressed the issue.

When Conti passed inside the front door of the control tower, the guard on duty also saluted and then directed him toward a narrow hallway. Conti had no trouble finding the room; all he had to do was follow the voices. He opened the door to a darkened room where he saw the green glow of a radar screen lighting the faces of Armand, the radar operator, and a handful of CIC officers, including Harlan Williams, a hard-nosed CIC Washington type that Armand had introduced at the briefing that morning. All the men huddled around the console.

Armand looked up from the screen. "It's about time. Come over here and look at this."

Conti made his way around the console and peered over the shoulder of – was his name Michaels? – anyway, the CIC officer in charge of the immediate-response dispatch team. Conti guessed the MPs out front belonged to Michaels. When Conti had joined the others, he stared down at the console, watching random patterns pulsate, change shapes, or dance across the screen with each radial sweep of the radar's display. The sight made the hair on the back of his neck stand up.

"Well, I'll be! Are those the craft?" Conti asked.

"No, sir," the radar operator said. "Thunderstorms. Standard echoes."

The screen continued to light in odd, ragged patches as everyone looked on. Time and again, the radial sweep on the screen renewed the signatures of thunderstorm patterns in the vicinity, and each time on a different part of the display. However, Conti noticed that the patterns never fell directly over the center of the screen, which represented the source of the radar – the building where Conti and the others now stood. The meteorologist who used to advise Conti on when to launch his balloon experiments has once told him that storms almost never came across airfields. He explained that the heat from the runway tarmacs was great enough to deflect local weather patterns. In fact, a storm would more likely split in two and circle an airfield rather than pass overhead. Conti realized he was observing the truth of that observation now. But after a few minutes of watching the phenomenon, Conti had had enough.

"So what are we looking for?"

It was Armand who replied. "Give it time."

No one needed to explain to Conti what the next sweep on the screen revealed. As if on cue, a pulsating blip traced an arc moving across one quadrant of the screen. Conti also didn't need the controller to tell him that what he was seeing was not a thunderstorm echo.

"There!" Armand exclaimed, touching the screen's surface with his forefinger and following the arc. "That's what we're looking for!"

Conti stared in disbelief. He'd seen radar displays before, but he was no expert in the technology. And he certainly couldn't explain the behavior before him. Still, if no one else was willing, Conti resolved to be the cautious one of the group. "Could that be some sort of freak lightning?"

The radar operator responded without looking up. "No, sir. That target appears to be solid."

"But – but the length of that arc? How fast was it going?"

The operator's gaze was still fixed on the screen along with everybody else's when he replied, "About a thousand miles an hour."

Conti didn't know what unnerved him more – the impossible velocity or the matter-of-fact tone of the operator's voice. Everyone in the room seemed mesmerized by the display.

"Could be Russian," Williams, the Washington new arrival, offered. "Maybe slipped through our radar defenses from South America."

"No, sir. Trajectory's wrong," the controller said. "The vector is from the north."

"Okay. Through our defenses out of Canada."

"Why would the Russians do that?" asked one of the other staffers standing at the back of the huddle. "This is insane."

Williams glanced back in the direction of the voice. "To take photos of top-secret military installations. We do it. Why wouldn't they?"

"One thing's for sure," Armand added. "It isn't ours; it's invading our military airspace, so we can assume it's an enemy aircraft. I'm calling the base commander and ordering an intercept."

But before Armand could reach for the phone, the next sweep on the console display showed the arc moving into the opposite quadrant of the screen, where it disappeared for just an instant. Conti found himself relaxing; it must have been an aberration, a flux in the radar reading. Without warning, the quadrant where the arc had disappeared suddenly expanded into a bright flash that only slowly dissipated on the screen.

Conti realized that he had been holding his breath for close to a minute, and so had everyone else.

Armand was the first to speak. "What just happened?"

The radar operator swiveled in his chair and looked up at the CIC officer. "It crashed."

It only took a split second for Armand to react. "Can you pinpoint the location?"

"About thirty miles northwest, sir."

"Thirty miles," Armand repeated and then turned toward his crew. "We can get there before anyone knows what's happened." He leaned over the shoulder of the controller again and said, "I need those coordinates. Now!"

It was clear that Armand sensed that his moment had arrived. He turned toward Michaels and, in a voice filled with triumph, said, "Michaels, locate and secure that crash site."

"On my way," the captain called out over his shoulder as he headed for the door.

Armand faced Conti, a smile spreading across his face. "Let's go find out if monkeys can fly."

Although he hadn't served in the African Theater during the war, Conti thought now that he had a clear idea what a desert invasion must have felt like. He rode in the jeep with Armand and Williams, leading a convoy of two-ton trucks and flat-bed wreckers down a country road. They hadn't seen the light of a ranch house in over an hour, so he knew they had to be in the middle of nowhere. That was good news. It meant that no civilians had likely stumbled on the site ahead of them. With any luck, they'd be in and out before the local hicks had finished their morning chores.

Michaels had been one lucky son-of-a-bitch. In the dark, on uneven and uncertain terrain, the captain had located the crash site in only four hours. Of course, he had coordinates, which is more than Conti had ever known when he'd searched for his own downed pods. Still, for Michaels and his retrieval team to pinpoint the site in the middle of the night was no small feat, and Conti had to grant that the captain had operated with as much skill as luck.

The thunderstorm had long since broken up, and the night air was thick with the smell of fresh rain. Despite mixed aromas of ozone and wet sage, the ground was already dry except for the occasional trapped puddles in the ruts of the dirt road the convoy negotiated. Conti knew that arroyos crisscrossed much of the New Mexico terrain, channels where sudden torrents of flash flooding could carry water miles from where the rains had fallen. He hoped they wouldn't turn a bend in the road to encounter a rushing wall of water, but there was no way to avoid the danger. The mission's clock was ticking.

The sliver of moon had gone down hours before, and the stars popped out against dark sky all the way to the horizon. Not bright enough to read by, but close to it, Conti mused.

Just over the ridgeline ahead, Conti began to make out a dim glow. A trick of light? Or maybe the wrecked craft was burning. But when they topped the ridge, Conti saw that Michaels had set a ring of Jeeps in a semi-circle that pointed toward a broad, low rock outcropping that formed one wall of a ravine. The Jeeps' headlamps were all shining toward a single dark object at the base of the rocks. As their own Jeep approached, Conti could just make out the silhouettes of some of Michaels' MPs, who had fanned out to form a sparse and ragged picket line outside the circle of vehicles.

The convoy had two trucks loaded with reinforcements, and Armand motioned for their own Jeep's driver to pull off to the side. Armand jumped out and flagged down the trucks carrying the soldiers, instructing the drivers to drop off the troops so they could fill in and enlarge the circle of MPs. It was clear he wanted the site completely surrounded.

Only then did Armand let himself turn and study the site at the bottom of the ravine. Michaels had joined them and reported in.

"It's an aircraft, all right, but hell if I can figure it out."

"Have you inspected it yet?" Armand's voice sounded anxious to Conti.

"No. All we've done is secure the perimeter as best we could. Besides, it's your baby. I figured you'd want to ..." Michaels' voice trailed off as though he were letting Armand finish the sentence however he wanted to.

"Yeah, probably better to wait to see how hot it is," Armand said in an even voice, but Conti knew damn well that Armand would've had Michaels' balls for breakfast if the captain had done more.

Armand waved in a team of men dressed in hazardous material suits and carrying Geiger counters to check for radiation. Anything that could travel at a thousand-plus miles per hour might have a nuclear propulsion system, the CIC team had conjectured, and they were taking no chances. Besides, the 509th made sure that all its personnel knew about the consequences of exposure to nuclear material.

While the radiation sweep proceeded, Conti pulled a set of field glasses from the Jeep and tried to get a better look at what was in the ravine. Although the shadows cast by the headlamps distorted any real detail, Conti was sure that he could see a triangular-shaped craft.

"I thought these things were supposed to be disks?"

Armand stepped up and Conti handed him the binoculars. "Un-uh," Armand replied. "It was the newspapers that said that."

"But the reports of – " Conti could hardly get himself to say it " – of flying saucers?"

"This is more consistent with what I expected. Pilot reports usually describe a deltoid shape – like this one." Armand passed Conti the field glasses again. "Looks like Geiger counters aren't showing much of anything. The hazard team is giving the all-clear. Let's get down there."

The CIC personnel made their way down past the scrub brush and into a depression that led toward the craft. Conti realized that they were walking in a trench gouged by the craft as it had impacted the ground and careened toward the ravine wall. Scraps of debris littered the trench, but nothing he could identify.

Although Conti had heard the stories, he had to admit that he'd always figured that whatever pilots and civvies had reported couldn't be what lay before him. The reports had to be atmospheric aberrations, lights reflected off of windows. Hell, they had to be swamp gas – anything but this. As they approached the craft he noticed the skin didn't reflect light; something about the surface absorbed the direct glare of the headlamps.

By now the retrieval team had begun to close in as well, and men swarmed toward the craft from all directions as best they could, considering the uneven terrain. Armand had already given the signal to start collecting the larger pieces of debris before the trucks moved into position, and Conti was struck by the nonchalance of the men around him. As they moved along the trench or beside it, they knelt and picked up foreign-looking objects – small, frail sparring, wiring, pieces of what looked like foil. Behind him, he could hear the voices of signalmen and radio operators as they relayed instructions to coordinate the activities of the military operation that had descended on the scene. Didn't these men realize the importance of what they were witnessing? Of what they were handling? Of course, they did, Conti reasoned. They were as awe-struck as he was, and they were coping the best way they knew how; they were doing their job and likely trying to turn off the part of their brains that tried to make sense of the object at the center of all the lights.

"Come on, Conti," Armand said and motioned for Conti to keep moving. Only then did Conti realize he had stopped.

He could make out a rupture running the length of the craft on one side. The craft should have broken up on impact, but it hadn't. The scene looked less like a crash than a forced landing – despite the depth of the trench leading up to the craft's final resting place. The rift in the side was what did it for Conti. It somehow made the craft tangible, real. Somewhere in the back of his mind he still hoped that what they would find was a downed airplane, a secret experimental project not unlike the one he was performing – what? just a week ago? But no, this was no military artifact. This was ... alien. There, he admitted it to himself, but that didn't make him feel any better.

"Conti, get over here!" Armand had already joined the men in hazardous material suits who stood beside the craft, and Conti somehow found the feeling in his legs and began to walk forward again.

In the shadows cast by scrub and sage, he could just make out a small figure lying on the ground, motionless.

"What – what is that? Is that a person?" Armand's voice was almost hushed and no longer held the confidence he had blustered up to this point. Conti could hear a tenor that betrayed the man was more than a little unnerved.

When Conti drew up beside the craft, he realized they were way out of their league. Despite the lights, he couldn't make out much detail about the figure on the ground before him. It was monkey-like, yes, but something about the proportions suggested it was more humanoid than simian.

Before he could respond to Armand, he heard a soldier on the other side of the crash gasp and call out, "Oh my God! There's another one over here, and it – he's alive. I – I think."

Armand and Conti exchanged a quick glance and scrambled to the other side of the craft. The soldier stood, holding the hood of his hazard suit in his hand. He pointed out past the craft toward a depression swallowed by shadow, some thirty feet away.

"I saw s-something move out there," he stammered.

Armand blew a disgusted sigh from his nostrils. "I don't see anything. You probably just saw a raccoon or – "

But as he spoke, he leaned his head forward and peered in the depression. He and Conti saw it at the same time. Something was moving, or crawling, away from them.

"Get a light over here!" Armand called out, and moments later two soldiers shined flashlights toward the hollow in the ground.

This time it was Conti who headed toward the figure that struggled to pull itself out of the light. Conti realized as he drew nearer that the figure's movements were not methodical; they more resembled the jerky reflexes of trauma. He had occasionally seen it in some of his simian subjects – those that had survived touchdown. Survived, but not for long.

As Conti knelt by the small figure, he felt a wave of sadness. Not his own, but somehow the sadness of the person – no, the creature – on the ground.

"Get a medic over here. Now!" Conti shouted over his shoulder to Armand, although Conti wasn't sure that a medic would know what to do. Conti sure as hell didn't. The creature seemed to be wearing some sort of flight suit, but Conti couldn't see any signs of contusions, no obvious blood stains. Without thinking, he said to the figure, "It's alright; we're getting help."

Conti had the impression that it understood him but couldn't decide how he knew that. Just a gut feeling. As he waited for help, the figure gripped Conti's arm and shifted its torso over so that its head faced the major.

Again, a wave of sadness overwhelmed Conti, and he sensed that the creature was mourning the loss of its other crewmember.

And that's when it happened.

A collage of images began to assault Conti's brain. Horrible images, one after the other in a jumbled sequence. It was as if Conti was watching a movie inside his head, but the story didn't make sense because the reels were all mixed up. Something about the future, something that was going to happen. Something was killing off all the people – no, first it killed off the birds, and in the end, all living things. Everywhere the images showed a swelling devastation caused by . . .

While Conti tried to make sense of the maelstrom of pictures flashing inside his head, he heard a scream, long and ragged. Just as he lost consciousness, he realized the scream was his.

CHAPTER TWO

Theta-Sag

Theta Sag paced the narrow breadth of his private chamber, but his mind focused on the outer meeting room where he would meet his young pupil during the next hour. He knew the catechisms with Gamma-Ori had reached a critical juncture, a point where heresies could emerge if the Sag didn't craft his words carefully.

When the Order of Sagittarius had generated the first series of Oris, the problem had taken a different turn, a darker one that Theta pushed from his mind. Those earlier clones had proven too independent, too uncontrollable. They lacked the imagination of the second generation, to be sure, but they were less prone to confabulation. Although the Ori-1s were mature enough to grasp the larger picture, the trade-off had been the rigidity of their perspective. At least the molecular assemblers that colonized those earlier brains with memory presets never led to ... well, unexpected leaps of logic. This newer generation was an altogether different story, and they connected the dots too quickly for Theta Sag's liking. And if a precocious Ori-2 failed to receive instruction in time, the Ori might innovate, building connections without realizing the need for guidance. Sometimes these unguided connections led to startling interpretations; occasionally they led to independent thinking. Unacceptable conclusions. Heresies.

But that was a manageable obstacle to Theta Sag. It only required a skilled – if manipulative – mentor. No, of more concern to him was the emotional growth limit they had engineered into the Ori-2s. It had seemed like a sensible compromise to most of the Sag priests. If the Oris' bodies matured in a decade, their brains could still learn, with presets, to develop skills and knowledge well beyond their literal ages. Theta Sag had been quick to champion development of the second-generation project because the arrested emotional maturity of the Oris would make them more dependent. It was essential, the Sag priest had argued to his peers, to create childlike minds that remained loyal and susceptible to the authority of their elders. How else could the Priesthood dare engineer the Oris with the mental gifts needed to fulfill their mission as Translators? How else to control them?

As Theta's thought vacillated between the lesson he would offer Gamma and the limited scope of the project the Ori-2 could comprehend, the Live-in computer that grew in the wall opposite his pallet uttered a soft phrase, something approximating an "ahem." Its programming had adjusted to the rhythms of Theta's lifestyle and had learned when to intrude and when to delay. It must have deemed it important, indeed, to interrupt Theta's agitated state of preoccupation.

"What is it, Djehuty?" Theta knew the Live-in would register the irritation in his voice and reconsider future interruptions under similar circumstances.

"I thought you would want to know." Djehuty's tone sounded apologetic, although Theta knew that the core bio components that controlled the computer possessed no more than a reptilian sense of decorum. Still, Djehuty's intuitive subroutines could create an uncanny illusion of sensitivity at times.

"I'm sorry," Theta responded before he could stop himself from treating the Live-in as though it could feel his rebuke. "What's so important?"

"Alpha Sag requests you join him in his private sim."

"Does he know I'm preparing catechism for the Ori?"

After a pause, Djehuty replied, "Yes, he does, and he still insists."

Theta sighed. "All right. I'll be there in a moment."

He crossed to the desk, picked up the stim-band, and fitted the hoop of the wearable above his ears and against the temporal bones. Without transition, Theta's private quarters dissolved as the stim-band's neurotransmitters fed signals into his brain. The simple pallet and bare floor of his bedroom changed into a garden filled with pink hydrangeas draped around the casement of a fountain. The chatter of birds filled the air and Theta turned just in time to see a flock of small red-winged blackbirds sweep past the railings that formed one side of the garden wall. Blackbirds. Now there was a sight he hadn't seen in decades. The Sim environment was carefully rendered, even down to the ants that filed past Theta's foot as he circled the fountain. It was a harmless enough past time, Theta conceded, and Alpha Sag's fascination with certain varieties that no longer existed – birds, ants, flowers – gave his superior a canvas as finely wrought as that of any painter. Theta caught the scent of orange blossoms, a new addition to the virtual scene since his last visit there, but the smell seemed a bit pungent for his own tastes. He made his way past the fountain and followed a path lined on either side with red flagstones.

As Theta turned a bend flanked by thick junipers, Alpha Sag came into view, sitting in an ornate, wrought-iron chair and writing in a leather-bound book. The older priest's habit of "writing" while he sat in his private Sim seemed to Alpha a curious anachronism. Surely Alpha Sag had rendered the virtual program to transcribe all its activities into the memory cells of his Live-in computer. Then again, the very form of the Sag's avatar was idiosyncratic and assumed the look of a man who still possessed a thick shock of coal-black hair. The face was tanned and youthful, and the sleeves of the black cassock were pushed back to reveal toned, muscled arms. Theta didn't approve of such vanities, but he would never say so to Alpha Sag. Perhaps the high priest had earned his right to pretend from time to time that he still lived as he must have before the Plagues. How antithetical that Alpha Sag had opposed Theta at every step in the Ori-2 project.

"Ah, thank you for joining me," Alpha said as he looked up from his book. The older priest motioned to a second chair that faced his own. "Come. Sit with me for a moment or two."

Although there was no love between them, Theta tipped his head in diffidence to Alpha Sag's office as head of their Order and took the offered seat. "With your permission, I can only stay a few moments. My catechism, you understand."

Alpha nodded. "Yes, with the young Ori. I know. But it was good of you to join me." The priest closed his book and hugged it to his chest. "It's the Ori I want to talk to you about."

Theta waited as the old priest closed his eyes and sat in silence. Theta was afraid that Alpha had fallen asleep. A young man's appearance with an old man's behavior – it was an unsettling image. Then the priest spoke, "I've read the summaries of your reports about Gamma-Ori-2. Very promising."

"Yes, he's talented. Perhaps the strongest candidate we've had so far."

"Have you tested his ability to tell stories?"

"Not yet, no. We're still associating his memories. Of course, there was the incident with the Commoner who tended the dorms."

Alpha's eyes opened. "Unfortunate, that. Do you think

45

that it will inhibit the Ori?"

Theta shrugged as he considered the question's implications. "Not necessarily. I'm not sure he understands how powerful his most recent gift is."

"Our gift to him," Alpha corrected.

"Of course, our gift to him. In any event, his brain was very receptive to the telepathic colony, and I have no reason to suspect otherwise for the virtual storytelling."

"And does he know why he has that gift – *his* gift?" Alpha smiled as he changed his own choice of words.

"Soon enough. His catechism should take him past the risk of heresies in a few days."

"That's fine. As you say, 'soon enough.'"

"Alpha Sag, if you'll permit me, I must be going."

"Of course, of course. The young Ori is waiting." Alpha Sag stood, an act with no effort in a virtual world, and the avatar seemed to move with more vigor. "Just one more thing …"

Theta tried to swallow what he feared was the impatience in his voice. "Yes?"

"Do you think he'll love you enough to do as you ask, when the time comes?" The tone of the old priest's question sounded casual, as though he were asking Theta to comment on the color of the rendered sky above them. But, of course, the implications of the question were enormous. And the truce between the two priests was no more than a détente. After all, it was Alpha Sag himself who had spent endless hours in debate with Theta, trying to convince Theta to end the project.

Would Gamma-Ori do as Theta asked? Could Theta bring himself to ask it? Theta studied the old priest's avatar, who was already settling back into the chair. Theta answered, "He's an Ori-2."

Alpha Sag lowered his gaze and opened his leather book. As he began to write, he said. "Not just an Ori, Theta Sag.

The Storyteller."

Theta felt a rush of anxiety course through his body. Not through the virtual body of his avatar, but the body of the flesh-and-blood man who stood in his own private quarters as the garden dissolved.

Yes, the Storyteller. The one who could save the future – and maybe the past.

Morgan

Morgan glanced at her watch and then peeled off the surgical gloves that she had worn for the past hour-and-a-half. Her finger tips looked like flesh-colored prunes, and she decided to call it a day. Or at least a break.

When she'd told Conti that she was going to start clocking onto the swing shift, he had only shrugged as though she were minding the store too closely. But Morgan knew better. The project had entered a critical stage of the gene therapy. After all, swing shift was charged with producing the virions for the final phase of Conti's Baby, and they were going to need a sizable population of RNA segments that matched the tolerances she had worked out. The genomes on each of the segments of RNA had to invade a challenging variety of cellular material if they were going to work the magic Conti wanted. Yet creating viral genomes that could replace key strands of genetic code was only the first step. Medical intervention through gene therapy was in its childhood, and Conti had charged her to find some way to leap past the current research she could draw upon. In fact, he wanted her to deliver a mature technology that produced a slow virus capable of replacing cellular genes in all animals. He was asking for no less than a trans-species viral therapy – something so far in the future that the research literature had scarcely begun to talk about it. Why not throw in the moon, while he was at it?

The wolf smiled, telling her she would find a way, and his

cub charged ahead. And in the end, it looked like Conti was right after all. Morgan might just succeed.

She didn't need to look over her staffers' shoulders as they generated test after test batch – the reports and protocols they logged each evening told her everything she needed to know. In fact, they seemed puzzled when she showed up that first afternoon. In particular, Sandy Morton challenged her about the need to supervise the later shift. Morgan knew that Sandy had served on many of Conti's special projects, and the woman wasn't someone Morgan could brush to the side. Rumor had it that she had a direct pipeline to the boss. That was okay with Morgan; she had her own pipeline, and besides, the woman was competent. *No*, thought Morgan, *be fair. The woman's damn good.* Morgan rationalized that, if nothing else, her own presence drove home the message that the evening phase of the project was important, and she was watching to be sure it was their best efforts. It was a good reason, but Morgan knew that it was also an excuse. An excuse to bump into Grant Winston.

Enter the Short, Red Dress.

It was now the fourth day of Operation Short, Red Dress, and she had only seen him twice since she had started showing up to supervise the swing-shift progress. That instance occurred in the lab commons area, which stood at the center of the Quad – the four-building complex that comprised the lab's research facilities. Contitech encouraged all the staff to take their lunch on the premises. Or put another way, the security procedures for the high-level research facility discouraged anyone from leaving until the shift was over. So, for the most part, lunch meant the company cafeteria or the newly installed food court, and for the swing shift, "lunch" occurred sometime between eight and nine in the evening. That meant that Morgan had a better-than-average chance of seeing Winston in the Commons – unless he took his meals in his office. Morgan always had.

As it turned out, luck was with her and Morgan saw him that first evening just as he was leaving the Commons. She determined to time her own arrival to coincide with his on the next day. But when he didn't show on the second evening, she wondered what was wrong. Was he out sick? Had he gone to day shifts? The answer, when she realized it, was obvious, and she had to laugh at herself: She was clocking in over the weekend. Researchers were at liberty to set their own work-day schedules, and the "weekend" could start anytime during the week. She often worked weekends, and the days ran together in an endless succession for her. Grant Winston must have opted to set his calendar to coincide with the rest of the world, she decided. As new director of Conti's Special Projects division, Morgan had staggered the personnel on her swing-shift research team so they could continue the RNA production phase on a seven-day schedule. However, most of the techs preferred the Monday-through-Friday arrangement, and she was slow to realize that some of the faces of her own techs had changed on the first day of Grant Winston's mysterious absence. At least she found herself able to concentrate as her team prepared the single-strand batches of RNA over the weekend.

However, it was now Monday, as she peeled off the surgical gloves, and it was already seven-thirty. How could she have let the hours slip by without keeping closer tabs on the time? Morgan announced to Sandy and the techs who worked under her that she was going to grab a bite to eat. The woman glanced up from her microscope and nodded. Morgan thought she caught just the faintest hint of relief in Sandy's face that she was leaving.

"I'll be back in thirty minutes," Morgan said as she pushed through the door that isolated the team from the other ongoing projects. No one responded, which didn't bother Morgan in the least. In fact, she felt a certain satisfaction that everyone was engrossed in the work at their various stations. She pulled off and tossed her lab coat on the desk in the outer office and hastened her stride down the hall. By the time she headed through the connecting corridor that led to the Commons, it was seven-thirty-five, and Morgan felt her chest tighten. Anticipation or terror? Morgan wasn't sure, but she suspected it was a bit of both.

When she arrived, Winston had just finished and was already making his way around the Commons to the other side of the food court.

Her timing still needed work; she had found herself pushing past the woman in front of her, which had earned an irritated "Hey, what's the rush?" But Morgan made it to the exit anyway, and Grant Winston stepped aside to let her leave first.

As he followed her out, she looked over her shoulder to thank him.

"I know you," he said, and smiled. "It's Marion, isn't it?"

"Morgan." She stopped, half-turning as she spoke, and he nearly ran over her in the process.

"Yes, of course. I'm Grant Winston. I think we crossed paths on …" He frowned.

"The protein project for Merck."

"That's right. Gee, what was that, a year ago?"

Eight months, Grant. Eight lonely months.

He continued, "Burning the midnight oil, I see."

"Yeah, it happens."

A chuckle. "Don't I know it. I can't wait to go back on day shifts myself. Hell on the social life."

I wouldn't know, thought Morgan, but said instead, "Maybe I'll see you more often now." She cringed and then corrected herself, "I mean, maybe we'll see each other around more often now."

He nodded. "Maybe. Well, gotta go. You take care." And he walked off toward Complex C, where, she knew, he oversaw Contitech's computer modeling division on the second floor. His office was in Suite Two, Room Seven. And his extension was 2114. Not that she'd ever visited the office or called his number.

Morgan walked down the hall in the opposite direction, beaming at herself that he had remembered her – well, sort of. And she'd obviously made enough of an impression that he recalled that they had worked together on a project eight months before. Since then, she reasoned, he must have seen and worked with dozens of people, maybe hundreds, and he still remembered her.

As she strode down the hall, Morgan wondered if she should have the dress dry-cleaned. She had worn it four days running. But at least it was working. Operation Short, Red Dress was off to a promising start. She decided to call it a night and only poked her head into her own lab long enough to tell Sandy that she was going to log out and head home. Sandy nodded but didn't even look up. The woman had a winning way about her, no doubt about it, and Morgan suspected it was one reason she had landed that swell job as overseer on swing.

Theta Sag

"Maybe you should consider a retreat."

The words were like a slap in the face to Theta Sag, but he knew that Alpha Sag had intended the suggestion as a barb.

From time to time, of course, a priest within the order did fall into the trap of thinking that the Priesthood was religious. And when that happened, the head of the Order had the responsibility of prescribing retreat. The illusion of spiritual power could turn into a strong intoxicant. But to suggest such a thing to Theta was an affront to his position in the Order. After all, it was Theta who had first proposed the method as a way to bring priests who had lost their way back into the fold. Theta had resurrected the model from his childhood recollections of attending Mass with his parents. He remembered his father announcing one time, to his mother's chagrin, that Rev. Andrews would soon be attending a retreat. When the young Theta asked his father how he knew, his father had chuckled and said, "There's just a splash of water in the wine these days, and we know what that means," and then he winked at Theta Sag's frowning mother. Sure enough, within the month Rev. Andrews was called away on retreat – or, as Theta's dad had put it, the priest had been sent away "to dry him out." When the minister had returned three weeks later, Theta watched as the pastor prepared the Eucharistic wine before the congregation, but adding only a splash of wine to the water this time. During the course of the next year, Theta and his father watched as the proportions reversed once again, signaling the priest's next approaching retreat. The cycle had become a private joke between Theta and his father, but it was years before Theta came to understand that the source of the drinking – pastoral pressures, isolation, celibacy – was indicative of a larger problem, a falling away from the Church's historic mission. And centuries had shown the wisdom of reacquainting fallen priests with their faith through retreats. In the years following the Plagues, Theta had proposed a new application for the one that the Church had perfected in past millennia.

The intoxicant for the Sag priests was less tangible than wine, but no less threatening to the purpose of the Order. Sag priests took retreat to remind them that their mission was not spiritual.

As Theta Sag heard the head of the Order propose that he, Theta, consider attending a retreat, he felt his face burn, an involuntary reaction he couldn't hide and one that he was sure gave Alpha much satisfaction.

Theta kept his voice as even as he could manage. "My commitment to the Order is as strong as ever."

Alpha Sag shrugged. "Some say your commitment is too much to the Oris. Your role may have taken on a certain spiritual quality, particularly in your role as mentor. A retreat might bring you more perspective."

Sure that an unseen Live-in was capturing their conversation on holo, Theta knew that he had to choose his words – in fact, his arguments – with care. "It's not a matter, with all due respect, of placing the Oris before the project. But this generation requires a different approach from the earlier Oris we generated."

"Yes, of course." There was impatience in the old Sag's voice. "We all understand that. But your relation with Gamma-Ori. None of the other mentors have taken so much time to prepare their charges."

"Alpha Sag, it is you yourself who've reminded me numerous times that he is to be the Storyteller. Surely, the handling of this Ori is an exception."

Alpha Sag turned his head slightly to one side even as he kept his eyes on Theta. The effect was to look unconvinced, but Theta knew that it was for the Live-in's benefit. The older Sag had no doubt made up his mind already, but Theta continued for the sake of that invisible audience who would review their conversation.

"As you said yourself, he has to love me," Theta continued, "and he must know enough to understand what is expected of him. Gamma-Ori must act without a trace of heresy in his reasoning, and do it without the benefit of our guidance at … the critical moment."

The older Sag sat quietly, if a bit stiffly. Theta had wondered why the head of the Order had requested to meet this time in person, but that was clear now. Alpha's virtual garden was capable of rendering their conversation into anything the author wanted. And the palette at his disposal could create any conversation between any individuals in its virtual environment, which made it more suspicious if Alpha wanted to maneuver a replacement mentor for the Ori. If that was Alpha's intent, which Theta suspected, then the record of their conversation had to remain above question.

"Dates are as critical as actions, Theta Sag. He must be ready to start the Translations at a time that coincides with the calculations of the Lector Priests."

The reference to the Lector Priests confirmed to Theta that the conversation was indeed for an external audience. Alpha would know that Theta worked closely with the Lectors, who had the responsibility of checking meteorological and historical records before the Translations.

"He will be ready," Theta replied, wary of the nebulous advantage Alpha was attempting to gain. "His aptitude has astonished me, and the associations he's made with the implanted memories have been exceptional."

"Then why haven't you given him the final Call?"

Theta considered for a moment how to answer. The young Ori had been ready for weeks; it was Theta who had been slow to complete the training. The last part of the Call, the instruction that would create the final association, would set the project in motion. It was like placing a single corner stone that turned an arch into a structure that could support a bridge, a ceiling, or in their case, a new direction. The final part of the Call would give Gamma-Ori the context he needed to complete the mission of the Translation and, God help them all, change the course of things. But how was it fair to send an innocent on such a mission, particularly when the innocent would have the power to destroy or inspire? No, Theta corrected himself, he would be sent to both inspire and destroy.

Theta's chest heaved through a breath that seemed to push against the weight of the world. Was he ready to transfer that weight to his young student? Theta realized that he had waited too long before responding to the older Sag. At last he said, "We'll be ready."

"You mean, *he* will be ready."

It was a slip of the tongue that told Theta just how closely the older Sag was watching him. But Theta knew now that he couldn't hide the extent to which the colonies that grew inside Gamma-Ori's brain had matured. The Ori was so close to completing initiation that there was no averting the final step. Rather than run the risk of replacement, which Theta suspected could be devastating to his young charge, Theta determined at that moment to do whatever it took to remain there for Gamma. To help him made his first Translation. Maybe an innocent could accomplish the impossible.

Theta wondered if the Order might not have benefited from a little religious faith after all.

Morgan

After two days, Morgan realized she'd put it off longer than she knew she should have, no doubt about that. And when no one could make her happy with the progress on the recombinant DNA, everyone had pleaded with her to go jump off a cliff. But, of course, they'd meant it in the nicest way.

This morning, Morgan decided to do just that.

Two miles behind her home, she looked over the edge of the cliff and guessed the drop would take her a good hundred feet straight down – if she was lucky. She reached in her pocket and pulled out her inhaler, took two hits, and waited for her lungs to clear. Damn summer pollen. She walked back from the ledge to give the trunk a good tug. Still sturdy, she decided, and attached an anchor. Next, she slipped the rappelling rope through the webbing she'd knotted around the trunk and pushed a loop of the rope through the figure-eight descender's larger hole. She then passed the loop around the smaller end before she clipped the descender to her harness with a carabiner.

The action was so methodical that she let her hands do the job without giving it much thought. But that defeated the whole purpose, she admonished herself, and tried to fix her attention on what her hands did with automatic actions.

Morgan reminded herself that whenever a problem at work got to her, she found that getting away for a few hours tended to do the trick. Well, the real trick was not to think about the problem – think about the rope, the wall. Think about falling. If she could keep her mind focused on the physical world, her brain had a tendency of solving abstract problems in the meantime. Morgan had once read that Einstein would take a nap when he faced a problem he couldn't solve by brute force of mind. But his trick was to hold a brick in his hand as he dozed off. When the brick hit the floor, he'd awaken with the solution in mind. Morgan hadn't developed as simple a gimmick as that, but then Einstein missed all the gorgeous scenery that surrounded her now. No, her trick was jumping off cliffs – that, or climbing up them. And she bet the diversion gave her an adrenaline rush that Albert never got in his lounge chair.

Keeping tension on the rope that passed through her fingers, Morgan paced away from the tree and over to the edge of the drop-off. She knew it was better to do this with a friend, but Morgan had fallen away from her circle of climbing friends in the past months. Deep down, she had always preferred going it alone anyway. Morgan had to admit that she hadn't even tried to call anyone the night before, when she'd determined to spend the morning roped up. Then again, for her the whole idea was to get away from everything and everybody. Some people rejuvenated in the presence of others, she'd read somewhere. Extraverts, the article called them. But the ones who charged their inner batteries when they were alone were the introverts. Morgan knew she fell into the second category, and wouldn't have it any other way.

She faced away from the edge and leaned out into open space – a maneuver that got her undivided attention because it was the most uncomfortable part of the descent for Morgan. Still, it was the safest way to start. She let out the rope as her legs straightened into a position that was almost perpendicular to the drop-off.

When she pushed off the edge, Morgan sprang out in a descending arc that carried her down the pitch of the cliff, dropping a dozen feet before the rope returned her to the wall. Her feet bounced off the rock, and she allowed her braking hand to let the rope slide through the figure-eight as she descended again. Over and over, Morgan recoiled off the rock wall in a series of arcs that carried her down the cliff's face. At about the midway point, she came to a halt and wrapped the rope that dangled below her twice around her thigh. The friction of the wrap held her in place while she took a breather.

Although she didn't want to worry about work, Morgan let images of Grant push into thoughts. *That's not really work related, is it?* She'd managed to run into him again the evening following her first planned encounter. Morgan had arrived at the Commons earlier that next night, positioning her chair so she could see the corridor that led from his building. Within minutes, Grant arrived and headed straight over to the new Sbarro's booth that had opened in the food court. While she was pondering her next move, Grant surprised her by walking up to her table and asking if she minded some company. Morgan's mouth must have gaped open as she stared at him because he started to move toward another table. He must have thought that she wanted to be alone, and she bumped the table as she stood, blurting out, "No, join me. Please!" She hoped that she hadn't sounded too desperate, adding that "please." After Grant seated himself, he chatted about pleasantries she couldn't now remember. All she recollected was the dumb smile she couldn't seem to wipe from her face as she watched him munch on a calzone. Then she recalled that, with an almost sheepish grin, he confessed he had remembered her name the previous night after all. He was only teasing her when he pretended to forget. She sighed as she replayed the scene in her head, all the while stomping one foot against the cliff wall before her. Bits of the rock chewed off and tumbled to the base some fifty feet below, and the sound of the pebbles glancing off the granite face brought her back to the rappel.

Morgan unwrapped the dangling rope from her leg and prepared to rappel down the rest of the cliff as her mind wandered to her previous luck with men. What was wrong with her? She knew that men found her attractive – they'd hit on her the times she'd gone to the bar at the insistence of the occasional coworker. She'd even dated from time to time since coming to Denver. But somehow the men she'd met had never looked as good after a few times out to dinner or a movie. Some were still trying to find themselves; others didn't have a job – or if they did, they soon found themselves intimidated by hers. Strangers had fewer faults than those who began to take on the quirky personalities of a closer inspection. Morgan wondered if she'd waited too long, letting her career take first priority during the years since she'd finished grad school and post-doc work. The pickings had gotten slimmer, for sure, and the thirty-somethings she'd met were often rebounding from broken marriages and carried so much baggage that she cringed at the effort they seemed to require. The last one, David, took on more the feel of a project than a relationship, and she'd sworn off men for two years after that one. Grant, on the other hand, had seemed different. More self-possessed and . . . well, intriguing. He seemed to know what he wanted and was doing what he liked. Besides, he lacked the desperation she saw in some men's eyes – that is, when he'd looked at her at all. Not that he was unfriendly, but he'd had the appearance of a man who'd figured things out. While she'd observed him during the Merck assignment the previous year, she kept waiting for him to reveal the usual quirks she'd come to expect from men. Yes, the more she was around him, the better he looked. In fact, she couldn't find any faults. No faults – the first sign she tended to show when she hurtled down the path of hopeless infatuation. Morgan smiled to herself that maybe she was making progress in her choices of men. No longer interested in those who were broken, she'd developed a taste for men who seemed unattainable. Until now. Morgan wasn't ready to call Grant an obsession, but he qualified as a full-blown fantasy. Certainly worthy of her Secrets Box. Smiling to herself at the way she'd taken some initiative with her love life again, Morgan at last decided to push Grant from her mind – at least for the time being.

She focused again on the solid feel of the rock beneath her climbing shoes. She loved the way the shoes let her caress the texture of the granite through their soft soles. Over her shoulder, she caught a glimpse of a raven that swooped by her immobile stance and then wheeled away with a loud "caw!" as if to let her know she was trespassing on its aerial turf. She smiled and bounced away from the rock face. Plenty of time later for thoughts of Grant. For the moment, she felt a swelling in her breast that told her she still needed time alone, time with the granite wall, and time to let her mind find the solution to her DNA problem.

With the sun warming her back, Morgan bounded off the rock and let herself descend along the face of the rock, promising herself she wouldn't wait this long again before she felt the pull of a rope in her hands.

As Morgan traveled along the south-bound interstate, the moon hung high in the sky and washed the hills with a luminance so bright that the occasional trees alongside the highway cast distinct, long shadows. She glanced over at the ragged wall of mountains on the western horizon and, sure enough, a lunar glow painted the peaks with the illusion of fresh snow. Not likely in late June, of course – not even in the Rockies. A lone car flashed its brights at her and she hit the dimmer switch. It was close to midnight so traffic was the exception rather than the rule, a driving condition that Morgan loved. Yeah, things were looking up. Grant had noticed her earlier that week, and Conti's Baby was running smoothly for a change. Maybe she would work on throwing in that moon for Conti as well as the completed gene therapy project.

She realized that she'd been able to concentrate more on the project ever since her visit to Thornton's office. Maybe the shrink had uncorked the bottle on her night terrors after all, and perhaps she had been harboring some deep-seated misgivings about viral transgenics. She had to admit, in any event, that she hadn't had the dreams for three nights. And no little boy had appeared to show her visions, terrible visions, of what could happen if she succeeded. Thornton admitted that first session that he was puzzled. After a few probing questions, he seemed convinced that she didn't fit the profile of a fantasy-prone personality. And he insisted that dream states could create worlds that seemed so real that she may still have dreamed it all. Including the episodes that involved the little boy during the times she maintained she was awake.

A small, dark shape – a dog or, more likely, a coyote – darted across the road in front of her and she hit her brakes. At the same time, she heard something heavy slide off the back seat and tumble to the floor. What the devil? Then she remembered that the morning after her session with Thornton, she had gone by the Denver Public Library and checked out a couple of books. More homework, but this time assigned by Thornton. He had suggested she read up on Old Hag's Syndrome and the mythology of the incubus. Both were versions of night terrors from less educated eras, he'd told her, and he was curious to see if she could identify with any of the descriptions or images in the books he'd recommended. The books had sat in her car for two days, and she'd forgotten all about them. The good night's sleep she'd had that night had reassured her that all she'd needed was to confront her fears. Maybe she would even cancel the session she'd scheduled for the following week. *Morgan, you just needed a good talking to, so you could get control of the situation.* All the same, she promised herself that she would at least take the books into the house when she got home. But she had some different reading in mind for that night.

As she pulled off the exit ramp, she smiled to herself. Thornton had asked her if she ever felt anxious about living alone in the country. She was quick to dismiss that explanation. The isolation felt more like an extra layer of security to Morgan although she knew from first-hand experience that not everybody felt that way, not even her own mother. The summer after she'd moved into the house, her folks had come to visit for a few days, and every night her mother had made the rounds to lock all the doors and windows, which surprised Morgan. Her mother only stayed four days instead of the promised week, and she'd never come back for another visit. Still, the country had always seemed to Morgan a safer place than a suburban neighborhood. In fact, the only people who had ever come by uninvited were an old couple – lost tourists – and they seemed relieved to find a place to turn their motor home around, so they could look for a campground closer to the highway.

By the time Morgan pulled her car into the old barn, the moon was overhead, and she didn't need the porch light she'd left on that afternoon. She walked into the house and threw the library books on the living room table. Then she popped a frozen dinner into the microwave to heat while she changed. She slipped off the skirt and held it up before her. It did show signs that a good dry-cleaning was in order, and Morgan decided to go back to the department store that coming weekend to get a couple more outfits. When she heard the microwave dinging, she flung the skirt on the bed and glanced at the bedside table. Then she grabbed The Box out of the drawer and headed back out to the kitchen. Fishing a fork out of the dishwasher, she grabbed the heated tray and walked out into the living room, where she sank into the sofa.

She swallowed mouthfuls of the chicken entrée – "a zesty meal sure to please the whole family," the carton promised – without tasting any of the bites. Morgan was playing that evening's encounter with Grant Winston in her head over and over, and then she began to plan how she could appear casual when she met him "by chance" the next night. Was there some aspect of their recombinant RNA cloning that could benefit from Grant's computer modeling expertise? She shook her head as she munched on the tasteless chicken. She had already considered and discarded that angle in her research – and without giving any thought to the eligible Dr. Winston. Besides, Morgan couldn't bring herself to waste project time on a dead end, even if it gave her the pleasure of his company. No, it had to be something better than that. *Come on, Morgan, you're a creative gal.* When she realized she was stirring an empty TV dinner tray with her fork, she decided she'd have to sleep on that one. Maybe the answer would come to her in a dream. Worse things had happened lately – a lot worse.

She leaned forward and picked up The Box from the table before her, deciding it was time to reward herself. After all, the RNA cloning was back on track, and she had a feeling she'd have good news to report to Conti in a matter of days. She turned the box over in her hand. It was an old tin that used to hold cough drops, and part of the "s" and most of the "u" had all but worn off the Sucrets label. The irony hadn't escaped Morgan that the word now came close to looking like "Secrets." How long had it been since she'd opened The Box to study its contents? Not that long ago, she conceded. When she'd made the decision to log in during the swing shifts, as a matter of fact.

Morgan pushed her thumb against the lid's rim and popped it open. Inside were two pieces of paper. The first was a business card, worn to the touch, but the simple lettering was still clear and legible. It was the standard card that Contitech produced for all researchers and admin personnel. Clean, elegant, no-nonsense – designed to communicate the confidence of the bearer. In addition to the standard contact information printed in a smaller font across the bottom, the card displayed at the center the featured name of the employee. In this case, "Dr. Grant Winston, computer modeling." She studied the card as though she were looking at it for the first time, the displayed name a kind of unspoken mantra.

Next she pulled out the only other item the box held, a folded note, this one bearing the printed heading, "While you were out ..." and below that, a hasty scrawl in blue pen that read, "Call me when the results are in, and I'd be happy to discuss them with you.

–Grant."

The results had come in eight months before, and they met briefly to finalize the study that Merck had commissioned from Contitech. And that was it. Done. And she now held in her hand all that was left of the beginning of her relation with the affable Dr. Grant Winston. Each returned to their separate duties for the biotech firm, and Morgan waited for him to call her – after all, he had, at the end of that final meeting, suggested they maybe they would see each other again. Morgan looked at the handwriting on the note, allowing her eyes to follow the jerky strokes that formed each word. Months ago, she had found a slim volume in a used bookstore on handwriting analysis, and she set about trying to learn as much as possible about the man from the handwritten artifact. The sample wasn't really long enough, she learned from the book, to do a thorough analysis. His script slanted neither up nor down, which only indicated that the lettering couldn't determine if he was optimistic or pessimistic. One of his i's was dotted, but the other one wasn't. The tails to his final letters showed none of the telling exaggerations that could provide the clues the book urged her to discover. In the end, the only thing she learned was enough to make her self-conscious about her own writing, but that held no surprises. She discovered she was obsessive and meticulous – but what research scientist wasn't? That sort of profile came with the territory and fit anyone who lasted longer than six months at Contitech. The book also suggested that she had anti-social tendencies. Also no big surprise since she lived in the middle of nowhere and liked it. The down side, of course, was that she lived by herself.

When she'd exhausted the handwriting analysis angle, she next turned to the semantics of the words themselves, as though they were ancient Egyptian hieroglyphics that begged to be deciphered for their hidden meaning. Her gaze couldn't resist connecting two phrases in particular: "Call me ... and I'd be happy." Was there a code buried in the note? Perhaps at heart he was too shy to initiate a relationship, and he had phrased the language to encourage her to read between the lines – or at least to connect the key phrases. In the end, she couldn't bring herself to make that call. It didn't seem to be in her social repertory. But now, eight months later, Morgan was determined to carry their relationship to the next level.

She refolded the creases in the note and placed it alongside the card in the "Secrets" box while she waited for Part Two of the ritual. Part One had been Reward; now came Punishment. It didn't take long, and Morgan felt it welling up from deep inside her.

She was a grown woman – in fact, just over thirty – and she was acting like an adolescent. Why did she do this to herself? She should throw away that damn silly box and get control of herself. At some level, Morgan feared that she was reacting to her mother's recurring hints that Morgan's biological clock was running down, that she needed to be thinking about a family and children. Morgan had always laughed at her mother's innuendoes – that or tried to change the subject. But lately, Morgan was finding it harder to shrug off. Talk about a late bloomer.

No, Morgan, you're not going to do this to yourself this time. You've decided on a course of action, and you're going to stick to the plan.

She tossed the box on the table in front of the sofa, an action she visualized as flinging aside a crutch she no longer needed – for now. And that's when her eyes fell on the two books she had retrieved from the back seat of her car.

If nothing else, the books might take her mind off a night of the usual recriminations. She grabbed the book on sleep paralysis first, which had a section on Old Hag's Syndrome. Thornton had questioned her closely about any history of narcolepsy in her family. The disorder, he told her, described a condition where people suffered from sudden or uncontrollable drowsiness. Morgan couldn't recall getting sleepy without good reason – maybe from pulling all-nighters at work, but not much else. But when she mentioned that the episodes sometimes caused her to feel paralyzed, he asked if she'd ever been diagnosed with hypothyroidism, hypoglycemia, or epilepsy.

"No," she said. "Why do you ask?"

"They can be common misdiagnoses for narcolepsy because the symptoms are the same."

Morgan frowned, "But I told you, I don't get drowsy. And besides, I told you it happens when I'm awake, too."

Thornton scrunched his mouth like he didn't seem convinced. "A person can be awake and still experience paralysis due to narcolepsy. Although ..." he hesitated, "it usually lasts for only a minute or two as you wake up."

"But I see the little boy before I go to bed, and sometimes when I'm in the middle of reading or working on reports."

"You could have drifted off. Maybe you just thought you were conscious."

It was Morgan's turn to be skeptical. "No. It doesn't happen like that. It's happened when I've been walking outside – not sleep walking." She shot him a look meant to say, *I would know the difference.*

"Any anxiety or fear?"

Gee Doc, she wanted to say, *why would seeing a strange little boy appear and start talking to me about how my work was going to end the world – why would that produce anxiety?* But she didn't. Instead, she only commented, "No more than expected."

She had to admit she was painting herself into a logical corner. *If it's not always a dream, then I'm either seeing things – that, or I'm having a paranormal experience.* Morgan couldn't accept either explanation.

Thornton had written the terms "Old Hag" and "incubus" on a prescription pad and handed it to her. Then he told her to look them up to see if anything she came across seemed to fit her situation.

As she sat on the sofa at home, she leafed through the sleep paralysis book until she found the section that discussed the Old Hag Syndrome. She started to read the first page, which explained that the experience consisted of waking up and sensing that someone else was in the room, someone who didn't belong. The victim then realized she couldn't move; she was helpless in a room with an intruder. That much seemed a pretty close fit to Morgan's own experience – so far as the dreams went. But the account was a far cry from her encounters while she was awake. And since the two situations in her experience were the same, both sleeping and awake, the sleep paralysis angle didn't wash. She read on for couple of more pages, learning that the so-called "Hag" was a folk rendition that attributed the intruder to a witch. It was sounding less and less like Morgan's problem.

She reached toward the table and switched out the sleep paralysis book for the one on mythology. This time she turned to the back of the volume, looking for an index. Sure enough, the end pages held an entry for "incubus." When she flipped to the page listed, Morgan's eyes grew wide. On the leaf opposite the entry for the incubus was a black and white reproduction that sent chills down her spine. She glanced at the caption under the picture of the painting: "*The Nightmare*, by Henry Fuseli (1741-1825)." Then her eyes returned to the composition, which contained three figures. A woman lay prone, her hands draped off the end of her bed and her eyes closed. Above the bed, the head of a horse with bulging white eyes emerged from the darkness and looked on while a small creature – some sort of demon with the face of a grotesque bird – squatted on her chest. The image struck some deep, indescribable chord in Morgan, especially the little figure sitting on top of the sleeping woman. Not only the birdlike features of the creature, she realized, but also its size. If the demon had stood up, it would be about the height of her own little visitor. Why would that bother her so much? Nothing else in the painting bore any similarity to Morgan's experiences.

She forced her eyes away from the reproduction to the words of the entry, which read not so much as a narrative as it did a dictionary definition: "Incubus, Latin for 'nightmare.' A male demon. His female counterpart is called a succubus. Legend has it that they were fallen angels. Superstitions traced back to the Middle Ages describe the incubus as a demon who seeks sexual intercourse with sleeping women. The belief was used to explain the birth of deformed children."

Quite enough of that, Morgan thought to herself and snapped the book shut. She uncurled her feet out from under her and stretched herself up into a standing position.

She turned off the lights and headed toward her bedroom, remembering how she'd tossed the skirt and jacket on the bed when she arrived home. Maybe she should straighten them out and then evaluate whether to take them to the dry –

Morgan stopped cold in the doorway. At the foot of the bed stood the little boy, wearing a yellow t-shirt with horizontal red stripes. It looked just like the shirt her little brother used to wear when she was a kid. In fact, it even had the same ripped seam on one short sleeve, where Jonathon had torn his shirt on the playground slide at their grade school. Of course, it couldn't be the same shirt; then again, there shouldn't be a little boy in her bedroom either. But there he was.

"I'm amused," he said, but his face remained somber, his

eyes wide and searching her face.

A feeling of calmness washed over Morgan; the sensation felt out of place but persisted. As her breathing slowed, Morgan let her eyes soften to take in the short figure in front of her. *He's just a little boy, not a demon.* But even as she thought this, some part of her brain told her that she should be afraid, that this wasn't like finding some expected caller who'd dropped in to see her – this was …unnatural. Morgan started to ask him what he was doing there and then realized that she couldn't speak; she couldn't move her body at all. *Sleep paralysis. I must be sleeping.*

The little boy walked up to her and took her hand. "There's something I want to show you, but it's a secret. Just between you and me."

That's when Morgan felt herself lift off the floor. Her first thought was that it was just like the scene from Peter Pan, Wendy and the other children gliding up into the air as they sailed through the night to Never-Never Land. She had loved that story when she was a little girl. *I'm just like Wendy,* she thought, except her room had no window that led to a stone-encased balcony. Instead, they headed toward the bedroom wall without windows, but this didn't concern Morgan. Stranger things happened in dreams, she observed with a certain detachment. About the time they should have collided with wainscoting and plaster, they passed through the wall as though it were no more than a permeable membrane. *Yes, this must be a dream,* she assured herself. Soon they were floating over the fence, and Morgan found herself looking down, thinking that she must find time to fix the broken slats that passed below her. The idea nagged at the back of her mind that she must have fallen asleep on the sofa, and she really should get up and go to bed. But the idea of getting to fly like Wendy, to be Wendy – even in a dream – was so magical that getting undressed and going to bed could wait. And then she looked ahead.

A sleek, black craft no larger than a child's tree fort

hovered without sound about ten feet off the ground in front of them.

CHAPTER THREE

Theta Sag

Theta walked alongside his Ori charge as they passed ever deeper into the Inner Sanctum. It would be Gamma's first glimpse of the vehicle he would use during the Translation, and Theta could sense the youth's excitement.

After his confrontation with Alpha Sag, Theta had taken a full week to explain the truth about the mission. At least, the truth up to that point. But Theta had not burdened Gamma with the history of the Order of Sagittarius. Although the young Ori's mind was facile when it came to facts and quantitative analysis, he was still engineered for naiveté. He'd be able to understand the politics of the Order no better than the Commoners, nor would he understand how the Sagittarian base of power gave order to the chaos that was left in the wake of the Nanoplague. No, it was better to let both Oris and Commoners assume that the Order operated from a spiritual core that gave "priests" the power to act without question, sometimes in inscrutable ways. Technocrats masquerading as a theocracy, Theta often called them behind sacred doors. And through this guise, the Priesthood had come to function as one of the few stable organizations to emerge after the Nanoplague had run its course.

Actually, most nanocolonies had reached an unstable dormancy of their own accord once their initial programmed mission had taken its toll, but isolating rogue outbreaks would always be a high priority. Population densities across the continent – across the world, for that matter – has so diminished that new contagion had become a secondary concern. But news of occasional outbreaks meant the plagues continued to ravage pockets of humanity, reducing the number of people that remained. It was also a reminder that the nanos were there to stay, a fact of life and a part of the new ecology of the planet.

That much everyone knew – the role of the Priesthood in preserving order and giving what hope they could. But Theta saw no advantage in telling Gamma-Ori about the origins of the Order, even if he had been at liberty to repeat the tale. Of course, Theta himself had been a mere child at the time, and he'd learned the secret of the Sagittarians only through initiation – passed on to him and others along with the vow of silence on the topic. The tradition was oral, and so cloaked that initiates heard the account in a hall purposely constructed without Live-ins grown into the walls. Theta himself had delivered the tale more than once to new initiates within the ruling class of priests. As he walked along the corridor with Gamma-Ori, strains of the story came to mind unbidden, like a mantra that reminded him why they were here now – even if Gamma would never really understand his part in that role. Perhaps it was just as well for the young Ori.

Theta consoled himself that the task before Gamma didn't need to be burdened by knowing about the particulars of the Order during those first months when the Plague began to alter life on the planet. It wasn't important to Gamma's mission, and Theta had omitted the part that recounted the story of the cloistered group of scientists who had survived the initial pandemic of the plague. They consisted of astrophysicists, engineers, and biologists – all part of an underwater colony in training for the first permanent off-world settlement. But the dreams of planetary colonization evaporated as that most fragile of human ecosystems, public infrastructure, collapsed in the weeks that followed the first wave of the pandemic.

As the Nanoplague ravaged life outside the colony of scientists, governments around the world began to topple as cultures and civilizations came to a standstill. The effects of the plague were common knowledge – to Gamma and anyone else. That part of the history was accurate, describing how the virile nanos struck with a baffling precision. Individuals with colds and flu symptoms died worldwide, as did many of the planet's old people. But not everyone in those categories, which was puzzling. On the farms, ducks and hogs died, along with most domesticated animals. And then, without warning, the nanos shifted their focus and jumped from the animal to the plant kingdom. It was as though they had developed a new agenda of their own. The scientists who survived postulated that the nano swarms had self-organized around a new mission, and the plague shifted to seek out any genetic marker that showed evidence of transgenic tampering. Crops engineered for greater productivity all withered and died, leaving indigenous varieties that couldn't hope to keep pace with the hunger of the world's peoples. The resulting famines eliminated three-quarters of the human population the first year. But the effects reached much deeper. The ecologies of the natural world suffered the same puzzling consequences that had affected human populations. Elk and deer became extinct and co-dependent predators soon followed. Everywhere, new ecologies struggled to find a balance that the nanos would tolerate, and the biosphere oscillated for decades before a new equilibrium asserted.

What he hadn't told Gamma was that when the scientists of the colony emerged from their underwater sanctuary, many of them died as well. But they had been spared the initial chaos of the surface, and perhaps even more, they had been spared the loss of hope. Within a decade, the scientists had isolated themselves to seek solutions for restoring order. In fact, the greatest secret of the Sagittarians was the semantic mistake that propelled them into power. Word of their zeal for order spread through the struggling human settlements that remained, and people began to shorten the way they described the group. The scientists who sought to return order to the world became The Order. It was a short step to begin thinking of them, by association, as a kind of priesthood. When their ranks began to swell, creating the planet's only post-apocalyptic brain-trust, it was the astrophysicists in the original group who suggested the categories, designating each technological research group with the name of a constellation. The irony wasn't lost on them that a cluster of scientists should be regarded as the spiritual core of an emerging culture, and the surviving populations had begun to look to the Order of Sagittarius for guidance and hope. The Order began to adopt religious terminology as a kind of code language that lended well to their emerging position during the tenuous conservation of the human species. Perhaps just as important, the religious veneer brought them an authority that needed no defense from outsiders, the class of people those within the Order began to refer to as Commoners. They must have been heady days as Commoners began to build settlements near the Order's facilities. The general population depended on the Order for the technology the priests had salvaged from the early years of chaos, and in return, the Commoners provided labor for cultivation and building projects. The arrangement possessed an uncomfortable similarity to feudal societies, but Theta had to admit that those early post-apocalyptic days were not all that different from the Dark Ages. And once the Order had reestablished lost or dormant technologies for the benefit of all, they had found it too difficult – perhaps too intoxicating – to surrender the power they had acquired.

In some ways, the scientist-priests may have been right to retain their control. After all, other competing models had surfaced through the years – alternative experiments in power and control – but most were not as benign as the Order. To give up control, in the minds of many of the priests, was the equivalent of abdicating responsibility. Alpha Sag, for one, had championed the movement to retain control, and he had managed to persuade his peers of the wisdom of preserving the power of the Order. His argument had won him much support – so much so that he now assumed the position of "High Priest," although Theta suspected that Alpha had grown too fond of his own authority. It was a sentiment that Theta dared not voice. But there were other ways to oppose his influence.

Of course, Theta told none of this to Gamma. The Sag knew that the Ori's limited emotional maturity could lead him to question what the Order wanted him to do. The worst form of heresy. In the decades since those early years of the Order, their technological advances had far surpassed the pre-plague years. But then, scientists – through interconnected but scattered enclaves – now controlled much of the remaining resources of the planet. As their power stabilized, they had begun to consider the options before them while there was still time. And many scientists within the priesthood feared that time was running out with each new outbreak of the plague, further reducing the human population numbers of the planet. The Order's plans grew more ambitious. Even revolutionary. Without the weight of a spiritual mandate, even an Ori might not accept the magnitude of the project that lay before them. That, or its arrogance. But these were thoughts that Theta shoved from his mind since they verged on heresy themselves. At least, heresy as Alpha might portray such thoughts.

Theta and Gamma passed from corridor to corridor, and at each stride they drew closer to the hall that held the Translation craft. At each stage, the autonomous Live-ins that grew in the portals hailed them in a ritual voice and let them pass without asking for the customary idents. Theta had instructed Djehuty to contact these Live-ins and to have them create the protocols that would allow Gamma to pass without interference. The Sagittarian priest wanted the young Ori to be able to come to the Translation Hall freely as he trained for his mission, and so Theta orchestrated this first trip so that it would reinforce Gamma's confidence in being able to pass through the successive portals without delays – a new experience for one who had served all his life as a lowly Ori. But that time was now over.

Gamma glanced up at his mentor, and Theta smiled reassurance despite the reawakened doubts that nagged him. When they at last came into the Translation Hall, Theta led his young charge over toward two large spheres that floated just above the floor in the center of the chamber. The globe to their right was the amplification sphere. Inside, Theta knew, lay the small dark craft designed to carry the Storyteller.

"Inside this shell," Theta said as they approached the hatch on the lower hemisphere of the sphere, "is the craft that will let you translate into the past."

Morgan

Morgan's gaze focused on the way her hands overlapped in her lap. She studied how the fingers of one hand traced the contours of the other hand's knuckles, as though they were seeking some anomaly that would explain the story she had just told Dr. Thornton. She couldn't bring herself to look him in the face as she waited.

At last he said, "So, do you think you were abducted by aliens?"

There it was, out loud. Although she hadn't allowed herself to say it in so many words, she still couldn't figure out how to describe the event in terms that didn't lead her to that conclusion. At the same time, the explanation was not something she could accept.

"No," she replied, and looked up. "It was a dream. I think. It's the only explanation." *Unless I really am crazy.*

"You did say the little boy was there." Thornton's voice was soothing. Morgan imagined that he must have taken a class that taught him how to modulate his voice so that it sounded calm and even whenever his clients told him outrageous stories. The shrinks-in-training must have taken turns inventing stories that tested each other's limits. Now you try it, Thornton, try to break the calm tenor in your classmates' voices.

He prompted her, "The same boy that appears in your dreams."

"Yes, but he's never come in a spacecraft before. I don't even believe in that sort of thing."

Thornton nodded. "Let's explore that for a moment. You say you don't believe in extraterrestrials."

"That's right."

"Why not?"

It was an argument she knew well. "For one thing, the likelihood of aliens visiting our planet is slim. They'd have to come from an extrasolar civilization, and the distances are too vast."

Morgan thought she sensed Thornton shifting forward in his chair, like he was listening for a clue that would shed light on her case.

"You seem to know a lot about the subject," he said.

Morgan wondered how much she should tell him. It wasn't her reputation she worried about. After all, here she was, talking to a shrink. Her shrink. But she wasn't sure how far doctor-patient confidentiality would cover other people she mentioned in their sessions together.

"Well, I have a friend who's, well, who's obsessed with the topic. My boss, actually."

This time Morgan was sure the doctor had leaned closer toward her. "Your boss."

"Yes."

"And he's obsessed with aliens."

"Yeah, he is." She shrugged. "We all have our quirks, right? And it's not like he goes around talking about it. Nobody knows it."

"That's not quite true. You know."

"I found out by accident. When I was in his private study."

The incident occurred when she had been in the apartment that John Conti kept on the premises of the biotech facility. It was no wonder that he was an old loner; not only did he spend most waking hours at the lab, but he also slept there half the time. But the apartment was off limits to everyone at the facility. He wouldn't even allow the lab's custodial service to clean his quarters. Morgan hadn't meant to invade his private apartment. The two of them had been in the midst of one of their many consuming discussions about Conti's Baby. Without thinking, Morgan had followed him from the outer office into the adjoining apartment, where he'd searched for a paper on RNA capsids he wanted her to read from his study. At the time, neither of them realized that she was standing with him inside Conti's Cave, the name biotech staffers had long ago given to the private quarters – that legendary space where the white wolf was said to pace at night.

While Conti tried to locate the paper on a lower shelf of a bookcase, Morgan's eyes began to scan the shelf at eye level, a shelf about four feet wide and filled with books on UFOs, popular accounts on sightings, Area 51, that sort of thing. Some of the titles had a scholarly ring, but many were of the ilk she could have picked up herself at the supermarket. And then she noticed that the same kinds of books filled the shelf below that one. Her jaw must have dropped because when Conti looked up, he stopped in mid sentence. Then she realized he was trying to explain his collection. She didn't hear much of what he'd said, but from that day forward, he had often allowed himself to talk about the subject when they were alone. In fact, it seemed to her like his enthusiasm for the subject had remained bottled up for years. And for the first time, he could share it with someone else. Lucky her.

Conti would drop a word or phrase now and then and give her a knowing look when he must have been sure that nobody else in the room would understand the double-entendre. "Now there's an unidentified object worth a second look," he might say as they examined a view screen above an electron microscope. Or the time he'd referred to "Little Green Men" while everyone was puzzling over the pathogenic behavior of a slow virus they had considered for the master clone. He boxed himself in on that one when a member of her team called his hand on the allusion, wanting to know what he meant.

But Conti was quick on his feet, she had to give him that. "I mean the behavior resembles what some people believe true but nobody can prove. Like Little Green Men. Keep your mind open to the unexpected," he'd told the team member, and then winked at Morgan. Within two weeks the story migrated throughout the facility, becoming part of biotech lore and even entering the research vocabulary to describe everything from hunches to the phantom behaviors of microorganisms. If Lone Wolf Conti had said it, it must be worth preserving.

At first, Morgan accepted her boss's obsession with things extraterrestrial as an idiosyncrasy – perhaps his cosmic antidote for concentrating on the microcosmic world of viruses. But in the end she found herself countering his notions with more rational explanations. Although his fascination with UFOs didn't seem to affect his competence as a leader in biotech research, Morgan found it unnerving nonetheless. She began to debate the issue with him whenever he brought up the topic, but she couldn't shake the idea that he seldom bought her arguments. It felt more like he was humoring her.

Thornton brought her back to the reality of the session when he asked, "So what kinds of arguments do you find convincing?"

"Carter's Inequality." It was her star example, but one that never seemed to phase Conti.

"I'm not familiar with Carter, or his inequality," Thornton said.

"Brandon Carter – the cosmologist from Cambridge? Actually, I didn't know his work either." She grinned at Thornton. "Some homework I did to throw my boss off guard. Anyway, Carter's the one who came up with the Anthropic Principle."

"I thought we were talking about Carter's Inequality."

"Yeah, but you have to talk about the Anthropic Principle first."

"All right." Thornton tightened his jaw. Morgan suspected the psychiatrist was telegraphing a tell-tale sign – without knowing it – a mannerism he might have developed when he knew he was in for a digression by one of his patients. But he'd asked for it, and he was going to get it.

"It's not that complicated. The Anthropic Principle is just the idea that scientists tend to forget that they are themselves a part of any experiment." Now Thornton was frowning. *C'mon, Doc, you're a bright guy.* But she forged ahead to drive her point home. "In other words, when we set up an experiment, we begin by asking questions that are meaningful to us. And maybe the meaning doesn't have anything to do with us."

"To scientists, you mean."

"To anybody. But let's say we're talking about physicists – or cosmologists."

"Like this Carter."

"Right. So Carter says that physicists think that the universe has to be at least thirteen billion years old because that's how long it takes to make physicists."

"I'm not following."

"From the Big Bang to now. It took ten billion years for the universe to cook down the elements needed for the building blocks of life, and few more billion to wait around until life made physicists."

Thornton nodded. "Okay, that sounds logical."

"Of course it does. But it's meaningful only because we're formulating the question to get an answer that fits the experimental apparatus – which includes us."

"So you're saying that we only look for answers that fit our own conceptions of reality. I don't see how we can do anything else."

"May be, but you have to admit that it sure limits the playing field. You'd agree that the world is more than the eye can see."

"Of course."

"Take mental disorders. They can result from a rotten childhood, but can't imbalances in brain chemistry cause these disorders as well?"

Thornton pursed his lips but his eyes twinkled. "More homework? You've been reading up on me again."

She shrugged. "The point is, that's just because we've got better eyes now – microscopes. It's still no more than amplifying human eyes. We're still seeing what makes sense to humans."

"You're an articulate woman, Morgan. You've made your point. Okay, so what about Carter's …"

"Inequality. Right. Well, maybe we assume there's intelligent life out there because we're intelligent, and the universe is a big place that could hold other intelligent forms of life like ours. Billions of stars out there, so why not?" She let that soak in for just a moment, and then continued.

"I thought you said you didn't believe in extraterrestrials?" Did Thornton think he was about to trap her in a contradiction?

Think again, Doc.

"I don't. And that's where Carter's Inequality comes in. It's a mathematical formula that calculates how life on earth was the result of an unknown number of very improbable steps – coincidences – that have to take place before you get intelligent life. And those steps have to take place between the birth and death of a sun. And since we don't know – not yet – how many improbable steps there are, we don't know how rare life is."

"But with millions of stars of there – "

"Billions."

"Okay, billions of stars, it would seem that the odds were still in favor of life out there somewhere."

Morgan smiled. "Are you saying that you believe in extraterrestrials now?"

Thornton seemed flustered for a moment, but then stated, "I'm not saying they've visited the earth, but at the same time, it seems arrogant to assume we may be unique in the universe."

If only Conti had been this easy to trap. But he wasn't.

"But that's the Anthropic argument talking. Because we're intelligent, we assume that there are other intelligences out there. But there's no reason to believe that. Nothing that supports it. Nothing, except that we're able to ask the question, so we assume that there's somebody else out there who's going to answer it. Besides, we've been sending radio signals for decades – in fact, long enough for anybody in the neighborhood to answer. Still nothing. No, there's no reason to believe that life in earth isn't unique. I'd go further: to create more than one world where there's intelligent life would be a waste of cosmic resources. And nothing that I know about the physical world is wasteful."

"So you don't believe in aliens."

"No. I don't buy it. There's no reason to believe that an uncountable number of improbable steps have led to life more than once. And no evidence to the contrary."

Except Conti did buy into it, which puzzled her. Was her reasoning flawed? Was she like a religious convert who spent her time trying to convince others only so she could convince herself? Morgan didn't think so.

"So why are you seeing … Little Green Men … in your dreams, Morgan?"

She slumped back in the chair. "I don't know." She sighed. "Maybe the cosmic joke's on me after all."

Thornton leaned back in his chair, subtly mimicking her posture – even to the way she supported her elbow in one hand while the other hand pressed against her cheek. Morgan had read about the mimicry in her research on shrinks. They sometimes used the technique to create the physical illusion of being in synch with patients. The irony to Morgan was that it seemed to work even though she suspected what he was doing. But then, at that moment she wanted all the help he could give her, and she found the effort he was making somehow comforting.

"There's something I want you to consider," Thornton said. He paused as if to give what followed more gravity. "Has it occurred to you that the UFO symbolism in your dreams – the spacecraft, the abductions – may represent Conti? After all, he's the one who's interested in the topic, not you."

"I don't see the connection."

He raised his palm toward her. "Bear with me for a moment. Granted, you're not seeing Little Green Men."

"No, it's a perfectly normal little boy – "

"That's right, but one who arrives in a spacecraft. At the same time, he's wearing clothes you remember from your childhood. A non-threatening image. And one that could only come from deep within your unconscious mind. Someone who's like your brother, but isn't."

"Okay…" She drew out the word as she tried to follow

his point.

"And he brings you a message each time."

Morgan shuddered as she recalled the awful images that the little boy in her dreams had shown her – images of a world gone awry and full of sadness, he said, because of the things she was doing at the lab.

Thornton continued, "Think about it. You told me your research has ethical implications." This time he raised both palms toward her. "I know, I know, you can't tell me. And I don't want you to. But your dreams have created a non-threatening little boy in the form of your childhood brother, yet he comes to you in a spacecraft. And he tells you that you shouldn't be doing what you're doing. Morgan, put these images together. Your unconscious mind is trying to tell you something that your conscious mind is ignoring."

She had to admit that it made a kind of sense. And it was better than any explanation she had come up with on her own. Maybe her dreams were trying to make her reexamine what she was doing. It was that, or aliens were visiting her in the night.

Besides, what else could it be?

Theta-Sag

Theta felt an almost parental pride swell in his chest as Gamma emerged from the translation craft. Of course, it had only been a test – a journey of zero consequence since it operated within the laws that prohibited paradox.

From Theta's time-locked vantage point, the translation had appeared as no more than a flutter of the craft, caused by its reemergence to temporal-spatial coordinates that were not quite a precise match with the exit point. But the craft and its crew had translated back to 2055. The Lector Priests had used a date only sixteen years in the past because it would not require much calculation to avoid the Laws of Paradox. Once the crew arrived, their objective was to navigate the craft to a predetermined time capsule some 200 kilometers distant and then to leave a discrete time marker before returning to the 0,0,0,0 point of origin. The time capsule was a test marker the Priesthood had constructed when the translation project began in the fifties. Gamma had projected a mental pitch into the capsule that triggered a change that priests examining the present capsule confirmed the moment the translation was complete. That the craft's flutter was so slight – especially on their maiden voyage – only validated that this generation of Oris would prove equal to the project. And to be fair, Beta Ori, the craft's pilot, was still in training at the same time as Gamma. Gamma's clone brother had navigated the craft to a point that was hundreds of kilometers distant and returned to a point that was so close that no one would have seen the discrepancy had they not all stared at the craft.

Gamma skipped in his awkward, long-limbed gait over to the side of Theta, and the mentor couldn't resist placing his arm around the Ori's shoulder and giving him a squeeze. Gamma's soft, almost timid singing reached into Theta's thoughts, but Theta knew that no one else would share the melodic communication.

I'm happy you're so pleased, Theta.

Theta subvocalized, knowing that it was enough for Gamma to "hear" him. "Yes, I'm pleased, but feel the joy for yourself as well. This is an important step."

Theta Sag felt a genuine affection for his protégé – something that the mentor couldn't have faked anyway. And as it turned out, something that was essential. Theta was sure that his sympathy for the second-generation Oris was the only reason that Alpha Sag had agreed to the match in the first place. These Oris, with their engineered predisposition for sensing other's thoughts, would be almost impossible to control if they didn't feel a connection with their superiors.

If Theta felt sympathetic, he also recognized that part of his feelings resulted from the failures the Sagittarians had experienced with the earlier Ori prototypes. And the regrettable termination of the Ori-1 generation. Theta had to share responsibility in that – all the Sag priests did. The earlier clones had proven capable – too capable – of performing independently, but the real reason they had failed in their mission resulted from the Priesthood's arrogance. Something else all Sag priests had to bear. How could the Sagittarians have ever thought that they could send envoys to interact directly with the past? And how slow to understand that they couldn't contradict the Laws of Paradox. Yet the Ori-2s held the promise of transforming failure into hope. That is, once the Lector Priests had discovered the loop-hole in the Laws.

Theta looked down at his young charge and thought to himself, *And you will succeed. You'll be the one who reiterates the past for the sake of the future.* The phrase was no longer an empty mantra ingrained into the Oris' training, and Theta had hope this time that it would actually happen.

Gamma's large eyes looked up at Theta, as though the Ori were trying to understand Theta's hope. Had the Sag failed to mask his feelings? Sometimes he wondered if Gamma read him at a deeper level than Theta preferred. It was a risk, of course, when they enhanced the Ori-2s with trans-mental powers. Perhaps the Ori only sensed the emotional content of the moment.

Beta soon joined them, and Theta watched as the clone-brothers faced each other, their heads bobbing silently even as their hands reinforced a silent conversation with one another about their excitement. It was a strange scene, Theta thought, like seeing a holo-vid without sound enhancement. Even though Theta stood between the two Oris, he had no sense of the verbal communication that passed back and forth from one to the other. Before long, Beta joined his own mentor, Epsilon Sag, for a debriefing that Alpha was sure would address the slight flutter the return translation had produced. Theta subvocalized for Gamma to accompany him back to his own quarters to talk about the mission to come, and a Storytelling exercise he wanted Gamma to try. It was a risky technique, perhaps even dangerous, but Theta felt confident Gamma's gift would be equal to the task.

As they walked the corridors that led through the temple complex, Theta wondered why Gamma hadn't asked his mentor about the particulars of the mission. Had the Ori intuited them from Theta's mind already and so didn't need to ask? Theta thought not. More likely, Gamma had contained his ten-year-old curiosity as an exercise in self-control – something that Theta had urged him to practice. The youngster may not have possessed emotional maturity, but his rational mind was so acute that he would have understood the value of developing such restraint. And Theta had often stressed the importance of spending their time together focused on relevant issues that pertained to the Ori's instruction.

Even when Theta had first explained the nature of the project, Gamma had shown remarkable self-discipline, in Theta's opinion. In fact, Theta was surprised that Gamma seemed so matter-of-fact at the prospect of translating into the past. Perhaps Theta underestimated the world in which the Oris lived – in which they all lived. To Theta, it was an extraordinary endeavor, but Gamma had only nodded at the announcement, as though Theta were explaining that the journey would take them into the streets of the nearby community of Commoners. It was possible, of course, that Gamma had already heard the news from Beta; the two had become very close indeed since the Sagittarians had chosen the pair as the crew for the project.

When Theta had announced the particulars of the translation, the mentor was at first relieved that his protégé had asked few questions. Theta was not a physicist and, truth be told, he understood only the broadest concepts of the process himself. His own strengths to the Order were in spinning narratives that supported the Priesthood's agenda, not in quantum mechanics. But the questions that Gamma had asked surprised Theta, who answered with honesty –

once he figured out what Gamma really wanted to know.

At the time, Gamma's first concern was personal.

Will you be here when I come back?

Theta had considered the question for a moment. Did the Ori understand that the actions he would take in the past could circumnavigate the Laws of Paradox and change the future? Theta knew it was possible – though remote – that events might unfold that would lead to a future from which he himself was absent, and the possibility was sobering. Yet it was a risk worth taking, to Theta's view, since he was convinced that time might be running out for them all if they continued to let the nanos decimate human numbers. But as he pondered how to respond to Gamma, Theta realized that the Ori's question had less to do with philosophical conundrums and more to do with their close relationship. Gamma's emotional insecurity was asking for reassurance that his mentor would wait for him in the Translation Hall, and Theta told him he would be there when he returned.

But Gamma's second question was more complex.

Will it hurt?

"No, not in a physical sense." Theta decided that Gamma deserved to know what to expect. "But you'll experience a momentary sense of loss. A loss of self."

Gamma's face showed an uncharacteristic puzzlement, so Theta continued. "You and Beta and the craft will rest inside an amplification sphere that will generate and superpose an enormous range of simultaneous time-states." Theta stopped for a moment. He was sure that Gamma's schooling had included the concept of quantum state superposition, but Theta was less sure that Gamma would know that, at the quantum level, a powerful amplifying force could multiply any particle with mass into an infinite range of time-states – the present, a time in the future, a period from a century ago. The amplified time-states would exist superposed, simultaneous, and waiting for the trigger that would collapse them into a single chosen state. The theory had developed in the late twentieth century, of course, but it wasn't until the Sagittarians had harnessed the power of bio-computers that they became capable of identifying and collapsing a predetermined set of particles as large as a craft and crew. Once the Sag priests had achieved the computing power, they could amplify as many superposed time states as necessary until they identified the time destination they wanted, and then they directed the collapse of the other time-states into the one – the translation to the past. The craft itself retained in a mini-amplification generator the data it needed to reconstruct the time-states that allowed them to return.

Theta decided to shift the explanation into a narrative metaphor, which made him more comfortable. And the metaphor would place their discussion in more familiar territory. "Think of it as a story that has many possible endings. You hold them all inside your head until you've chosen the right one. And then you express the one that fits. Outside the amplification shell is a huge, interconnected complex of Live-ins that keep track of all the endings, all the time-states for you and Beta and the craft, and when they have the right set – the ones that correspond to the right time in the past – they collapse the superposed states and you translate into the past." Theta knew that the Line-ins had to identify and isolate those precise time-states that experienced time dilation but no other gravitational effects, but including that information seemed to Theta more like flaunting what little understanding he had about the process. It was irrelevant to the instruction. "Does that make sense?"

Gamma nodded. Once again, Theta marveled at the nonchalance of the Ori in the face of such a staggering technological achievement. Instead, Gamma repeated his original question.

But will it hurt when I lose myself?

"It's not that you'll lose yourself, not really. All these states are still you. But it's like the time, ages ago, when people sometimes lost limbs – have you studied this?"

Gamma shook his head.

"Well, there was a time when surgeons would remove an arm or a leg because of infection or damage. They lost the limb and – "

Why didn't they just grow a replacement? Gamma shuddered as his residual mouth tried to work itself into a frown.

"It was before they had such technology, so people had to learn to live without the limbs. But sometimes, they thought they still could feel them – they could feel a phantom limb, the loss they felt was so strong. In a sense, they expressed the grief over the loss of the limb by maintaining it was still there. And that's what you'll feel at the moment of translation."

But you said I won't really lose myself.

"That's right, Gamma, you won't. But when the superposed time-states collapse, some part of yourself will sense that all the other states are no longer there. For a few moments, it will feel like something's missing, like the phantom limbs – except that you'll be whole. Everything that is you will still be there. Except it will be a you that exists in the past."

The loss syndrome had been a common complaint by the earlier generation of Ori time travelers; it seemed to be an unavoidable consequence of translation, but the Oris had learned to tolerate the side-effect. Gamma would have to develop a similar tolerance as well if he were to make the many journeys that the Lector Priests had prescribed for the reiteration.

As Gamma accompanied Theta back to the mentor's quarters to debrief the first translation test, Theta noticed that his protégé seemed to wince every so often when they passed a Commoner in the corridors. These foreigners to the temple complex were lay brothers, of course – individuals from the nearby community who served as either liaisons to the

Priesthood or else laborers who attended to the domestic needs of the temple. But the Oris lived cloistered within the complex, out of view from the outside world, and Commoners unaccustomed to their sight sometimes found it difficult to hide their reactions.

Theta observed his pupil's behavior, and the next time Gamma winced as a Commoner met them, Theta subvocalized, "Does it bother you so much that you're different from others?"

Gamma's head bobbed down to balance his forward steps, but he flashed his mentor a timid glance as his thoughts stretched into Theta's own. *But I'm not different. I wish they understood that. I'm just as human as they are.*

Theta felt as though the floor of his heart had given way. He realized that he had ceased to see the Ori's long, disproportionate limbs as unusual. And although the Sag gen-engineers had designed the Ori with a larger head to sit atop the small torso, these alterations were necessary. The cranium needed the greater capacity to accommodate the gifts, but the body was another matter. The amplification chamber could work with greater efficiency without the unnecessary mass of larger bodies in a larger craft. And the Sagittarians had engineered the Ori shape to withstand the stresses of that craft's gravity-well propulsion system. All these deviations from the normal human shape served the Oris in their mission to the Priesthood. Theta wondered why no one had given much attention to the psychological effects the Oris felt as a result of their altered appearance. Their engineered maturity – or lack of maturity – had advantages, but their ten-year-old bodies also had ten-year-old psyches poised to experience adolescent insecurities. So long as they remained cloistered, the Oris felt no difference. But the more they interacted with others, they were bound to feel growing pains – emotional growing pains.

Theta wished he could comfort the young Ori, but he wasn't sure how. "Gamma, you're right, they don't understand. But what they think doesn't matter. Never forget that the Priesthood engineered you for a special purpose, a purpose you're about to fulfill." Theta reached out and gave Gamma's childlike shoulder a gentle squeeze, hoping the physical contact would reassure the Ori the way that Theta knew his words had failed to do.

When at last they reached Theta's quarters, the two went straight into the study, where Gamma dropped onto the bench beside Theta's desk. Theta arranged himself across from his pupil and said, "You've had an exciting day. Don't let the Commoners spoil it for you. After all, you'll be making the world better for them, too – even if they don't realize it now."

Gamma nodded, but Theta's rationale still didn't seem like it had much effect. His pupil's moodiness troubled Theta, particularly so close to the launch of the mission. He decided to change topics and move on to the exercise.

"Let's talk about the Storytelling."

At the mention of his newest gift, Gamma's mood seemed to brighten, if only a little, and the Ori shifted on the bench to face his mentor.

"You know, Gamma, you're going to be something of a muse." Theta liked the allusion and wondered why it hadn't occurred to him before. In a sense, that was exactly what the loophole in the Laws of Paradox amounted to, and he rephrased the idea to add emphasis to the notion. "Each time you translate, you should think of yourself as a muse."

Gamma-Ori

Gamma puzzled over the phrase. He had allowed himself to sink into a sort of sadness when he had sensed what the Commoners had thought at the sight of him, and he found it hard to rise above the feeling. In fact, Gamma had become so distracted he had forgotten to read his mentor's thoughts at a deeper level – deeper than he thought Theta would approve.

Still, the Ori had decided, weeks ago, that it was the only way he could penetrate the intent of Theta's words. Gamma knew that his mentor was good-hearted, but Gamma also sensed that Theta had long used words to cloak his intentions. Sometimes it seemed as though his mentor's words formed a kind of defense between himself and others, and Gamma knew that he had to go deeper – if only a little bit – to understand what Theta had intended to tell him.

Chastising himself for the inattention, Gamma tried to recall the resonance of Theta's last words. What was it he said? "Each time you translate, you should think of yourself as amused."

It was a puzzling statement, but Gamma had learned to trust his mentor's suggestions. The Ori nodded to show that he would do as Theta wanted. Perhaps the thought was a way to help him focus on the story. Gamma made a mental note to include the suggestion, and then he promised himself to give Theta his undivided attention during the tutoring session. To do less was, after all, disrespectful, and Gamma had great respect for all that Theta said and did.

"I want us to share in a storytelling exercise," Theta was saying as he picked up a stim-band from the desk. "This is a special wearable, and I want you to slip it over your head."

Gamma took the stim-band from his mentor's hands and placed it over his cranium so that it rested just above his ears. Theta helped him adjust the band so that it fit snugly, and Gamma waited for the customary images to flood his mind. In the past few weeks, Theta had given Gamma many stim-band sims that depicted the world of the past. His mentor had told him that the sims would help Gamma understand what to expect during his translations. At first, the most surprising thing to Gamma was the birds. They actually flew across the sky. Gamma wondered if the people of the past had taken for granted such a wonderful sight. And the cities were filled with so many people going in different and chaotic directions – walking the sidewalks or crossing streets – and everywhere, vehicles traveled on a hard, smooth surface of … yes, it was asphalt, he thought at the time. It must be. Gamma had only seen the broken remains of asphalt in the rubbled causeway that still bisected the courtyard adjoining the Ori cloister. But in the sim, such paved roads were not in ruins; they were fresh and slick as a rain fell from the brown cloud that hugged the city. And the city! Brick and steel and glass all around him as he turned his head to see the 360-degree illusion created in many of the sims. Gamma had wandered from street to street and watched people pass straight through him as though he weren't there. And, of course, he wasn't. Some ancient videographer had captured most of the images, Gamma knew, and only much later had the Live-ins extrapolated the scenes to construct probable renderings of the scenes through which he moved. On some occasions, Gamma had found dead-ends, but he couldn't tell which ones had existed in the past and which ones the Live-ins had placed there to restrict the options inside the renderings.

However, this new stim-band surprised him when he received no initial images inside his head. The Ori gave Theta a questioning look.

"It's not for you, Gamma. It's designed to increase your ability to project your stories onto others. Now close your eyes. I'm going to envision a scene from my own childhood and I want you to see it with me."

Gamma did as he was told and reached into his mentor's mind to find the scene. It was an easy task for Gamma and in an instant he was standing next to a child of about ten years old. Gamma knew that his mentor had lived most of his childhood before the Nanoplagues; Theta had made an occasional comment that made this clear. But the Ori wasn't prepared for the world that unfolded inside Theta's memories.

The child turned to him and said, "Gamma you're seeing me when I was about your age."

But where is this place?

"No, Gamma, don't sing to me," the boy said. "You're in my mind, my memories. For me, it's similar to a lucid dream. But for you, it's more. Try to envision yourself talking to me just as I talk to you. You can make yourself do whatever you want to. You can look however you want."

Gamma concentrated on what it would be like to talk like others, to look like others, and then he opened his lips inside Theta's mind. "Where is this place?"

"It's my home town, and the circus is coming."

Gamma looked at the stream of faces filing past them. They laughed and talked without a care; in fact, they seemed to Gamma to possess a sort of cheerfulness that was absent from the world the Ori knew. And as they lined up along a barricade next to the street, Gamma became aware he was smelling a sudden rancid odor. Without having to seek out its meaning, he knew at once that it was the smell of popcorn – and he knew what popcorn was and what it tasted like because the memories were strong in Theta's memories. Gamma trenched for Theta's earliest recollections of popcorn, when his mother – *so that's what remembering a mother is like* – first placed the strange package in the microwave. *A microwave?* He savored along with Theta the violent popping noise, watched the bag swell, tasted the first buttery nuggets.

"Gamma, pay attention." The boy tugged him over to the line that was forming behind the barricade. "I'm going to show you something that I remember, and then you're going to take over the memory and turn into a story."

"I – I don't understand." Images were swirling over Gamma like a dust devil – *I know what a dust devil is!*

"I'm showing you a story from my past," the young Theta said, "but at any time, you can take it over and change it into any kind of story you want to tell."

"But when?"

"That's for you to decide. Now watch this."

And the boy turned to watch as strange figures in bright,

baggy clothes walked along the thickening line of people. As the figures drew closer, Gamma could see that their faces were painted to exaggerate their features, and some wore white balls over their noses. *Clowns*, Gamma thought, *and Theta is afraid of clowns.*

By now, the young Theta braced himself as the clowns approached. Gamma realized that Theta stood next to his mother, and she was telling him that clowns were supposed to be funny, that there was nothing to be afraid of.

Gamma noticed that the mother began to position herself behind her son. Soon she placed her hands atop the boy's trembling shoulders. As he wiped at his eyes with tiny fists, the young Theta's chest heaved. At first he kept his eyes on the ground, but as a clown approached he forced himself to look up as far as the baggy pants. But he couldn't bring himself to look the clown in the scary, scary face. The clown reached out a white-gloved hand and pushed a knot of strings into the frightened little boy's hand.

Theta gripped the strings with all his might, knowing that they would lead to a cluster of balloons. He could hear them rubbing against each other as they bobbed in the breeze. But he was unwilling to look up because he knew he would see the clown's face before he could discover their colors.

"Say thank you, Bobby," the mother was saying.

Bobby? Ah, the name the mother calls the young Theta.

At that moment, Gamma stepped up beside the boy. Remembering his instructions, he began, "I'm amused."

The boy shot him a quick, vexed look. "I'm glad somebody is."

Gamma was puzzled that Theta didn't seem pleased when the Ori had remembered to use the important focusing phrase. Perhaps Gamma needed to learn to say it with more conviction. Or maybe the ten-year-old Theta had surrendered into his memory. Then again, the boy before Gamma might only exist as part of the exercise. The experience was all too new for Gamma, so he shrugged off his mentor's failure to acknowledge the incantation and began to study the scene.

Gamma listened to the thoughts inside the young Theta's mind, which were saying, *I wish I could just fly away from here.* And then Gamma knew how he was going to change the story. He took hold of the hand that gripped the knot of strings, and the two of them lifted upward with the buoyancy of the balloons. They sailed high above the street, and Gamma filled the sky with balloons to blot out the clowns below them. Green, red, yellow – throngs of balloons bobbed and rubbed as they drifted in the air all around them. Gamma loved the bright colors and the sound of the stretched rubber balls as they bumped against each other. Without warning, he started to giggle, a contagious sound that soon migrated into Theta's voice as well. Gamma made the balloons form into a cobbled street of bulbous heads below their feet, and the two boys tromped from green to yellow to red to blue. At each leap forward, they bounced higher than the previous time, and before long they were sailing above the rubbery street, flying past the rubbing, bobbing bulbs.

Gamma willed the balls to float away, allowing them to see the lush green hills that rolled beneath them. These were images that would fade on the other side of childhood, Gamma realized, but not now, not inside Theta's memories. The Ori let them fly across the landscape and dropped them through tumbling somersaults of free fall as they plummeted toward the ground. It was an exhilarating experience and he let himself howl as the wind filled his mouth. Theta, too, was howling. No, he was screaming as the land rushed up to meet them.

At that moment, everything turned black, and all the glorious colors within Theta's memory folded into darkness.

Gamma was puzzled. Why had his story stopped? The exercise came to a close just as Gamma had begun to understand how easy it was to shape the world inside someone else's mind.

"Theta? Is the exercise over? Theta?"

Gamma withdrew his mind from the darkness and opened his eyes. His mentor lay on the floor of the study, unconscious, a silent trickle of blood snaking from his nostrils to form a pool around his head.

CHAPTER FOUR

Morgan

"You don't look so good."

Morgan considered the comment for a moment. It was coming from Sandy, who expected thunderstorms when the forecast called for five days of sun. Even so, Morgan scrunched her mouth. "You don't think so?"

Sandy shook her head. "You've looked better."

"Well, I haven't been sleeping well. Disturbing dreams." An understatement, but Morgan knew she'd said too much already.

"Reeeally?" Sandy drew out the word like a modern-day Cassandra, ready to predict doom from the entrails of a slaughtered goat.

"Well, I gotta go. The Head Kahuna awaits." Morgan whisked up her stack of reports and headed toward the door.

Over her shoulder, Morgan heard Sandy call out, "Sleeping pills. It's the only way to fly."

"Un-huh."

"And some lipstick, it'll make you feel like a – " But the door closed in time to muffle the words in mid-prediction.

New woman, Morgan thought. *Yeah, lately I sure haven't felt like the old one.* She padded down the hall toward the elevator. She wondered if she had done the right thing by agreeing to bring Sandy back to day shifts with her to help analyze the results of the RNA tests. It had been Conti who had suggested it, and who was Morgan to disagree with the boss? He must have seen something in her that Morgan didn't. Even though it was nice to have another professional woman around – a rarity at Contitech – Sandy was proving a mixed blessing. Each day, Morgan found herself weighing the woman's competence as a meticulous scientist against her gloom-and-doom vision of the world, which wore thinner with each passing encounter. As Morgan stepped into the elevator and pressed her thumb onto the scanner pad that gave her access to Conti's floor, she shook her head and wondered how much longer the project would take. Of course, another part of Morgan wanted the project to go on and on – or at least until Dr. Grant Winston began laying roses at her feet.

The elevator glided upward on pneumatic wings, and the tug at her stomach felt a bit like the reaction she'd had when Grant suggested they meet for breakfast that morning in the Commons. Not exactly a romantic tryst, but a beginning. No, a continuation. As she hugged the reports against her chest during the elevator's ascent, she replayed the charming look of intensity that had flooded Grant's face when he discussed becoming involved in Conti's Baby. For the third time, they had met for breakfast, and during each of these "dates," she had revealed bits and pieces of what she was doing for Conti. Grant had seemed intrigued by her work at first. But at each successive breakfast rendezvous, he had questioned her more and more. That morning he had gone further.

"I think we should join forces," he'd said.

Join forces, what a lovely idea. But instead, she responded, "What do you mean?"

Was he trying to find a way to spend more time with her but didn't know how to bring it up? How adorable.

"I mean, well . . ." Grant paused like he was casting around for the right words. "Look, I know you're the new project leader, but I think I have something to offer. Still, it would help if I understood more about where you're going. Maybe then I could anticipate problems, test alternatives, that sort of thing."

Grant had already revealed that he had proposed early on to Conti that he should head the new project. After all, they needed his computer modeling to predict outcomes, to guide the overall vision – whatever that vision was. When word got out that something new was brewing inside the boss's head, all the section heads had made their bid for the slot, Grant had told her – all except Morgan. At the time, all of her energy focused on a recombinant DNA experiment that wrestled with a virulent strand she had hoped to turn into an anti-viral virus. The irony was that her work followed the same lines as Conti's latest brainchild, a fact that Morgan couldn't share with Grant. Conti had passed over the other section heads and given her the project. Morgan suspected that Grant had taken the news hard; in fact, she could just see how he must have pouted about the decision – but in a cute sort of way.

As she'd stared at him across the table in the Commons that morning, she decided that Operation Short, Red Dress had gotten the better of him in the end. Now he wanted to join forces with her.

"You know how the boss likes to keep everybody guessing," she told him. *Was that too coy?*

"I know, but I want to be a part of this project. And I feel that I could help get this thing off the ground faster if you let me help you. What are you willing to share with me?"

The first words that came to mind were, How about sharing the rest of our lives? But Morgan decided that wasn't the best response – not yet. After all, she was savoring this, this smitten feeling, and she didn't want to blow it.

"Let me think about that." Although she knew she had

already made up her mind. And as she considered his proposition, Morgan decided that it might not be such a bad thing. Morgan pushed aside the little voice in her head that told her to think again. She reminded herself that her work ethic demanded the success of the project, and she would deliver. She always did. But why shouldn't she do something for herself for a change? Conti wouldn't approve, of course, but another perspective might prove useful – not to mention, it would be an excuse to spend more time with those puppy-brown eyes.

Grant had settled back in his chair and smiled. A becoming smile. And then he had written down his home phone number on a business card and passed it across the table to her. Her natural reflex was to snatch it up, thinking, *A new treasure for the Box.* But this time was different, she reminded herself; she was supposed to use the offered phone number. Yes, her interactions with Grant looked more promising as each day progressed.

The elevator came to a stop and the doors slid open onto Conti's office suite. She walked in to see her boss pacing back and forth in front of his desk. He had the look of a man who had miles to go before he slept, but one who struggled more with each new step. As she came closer, she noticed the lines around his face seemed deeper than usual.

She couldn't help shifting into her other role, the let's-get-down-to-business role, and all thoughts of Grant Winston melted away at the sight of Contitech's pacing alpha wolf.

"Is something wrong?" she asked.

He stopped and glanced up at her. "No, not really. Just scattered thoughts." Conti flashed a weak smile. "I can't seem to remember where I put my notes."

Now it was Morgan's turn to offer advice – not of Sandy's sort, of course, rather something more constructive. "You're working too hard. It happens to all of us."

But it was happening more and more often to Conti, and

Morgan was beginning to worry about her boss. He was her boss, yes, but it was more than that. Conti was her mentor. The one who had taken her out of the bureaucracy of the NIH and given her the wings to fly head-on into the clouds of cutting-edge research. It wasn't so much that Conti was a talented scientist – in private, she had to admit that his own work often lacked the gift of the muse – no, Conti's talent was in seeing the potential of others. He knew how to gather around him the brightest talent in biotechnology and then to give them the freedom to do their job. To be fair, Conti also had two rare gifts: he had vision and he had the ability to see his own limitations. Time and again, she had seen him bring to the table innovative ideas that could challenge his dream team. If he couldn't always figure out the shortest path between two points, he nonetheless knew where they were heading. "We're going about this in the wrong way," he might say, and he would sketch out in broad strokes the kinds of outcomes he wanted. And nine times out of ten, his hunches kept the bean-counters' ledgers in the black. But then, that's why Contitech was such a success – investment capital had a way of flowing into his hunches. Governmental and corporate concerns lined up to offer the lab lucrative contracts, but only when Conti guided the work.

He had talked Morgan into moving into the private sector by offering her the chance to turn her theories into reality. She had just proposed a series of protocols to safeguard one of transgenics' greatest demons – the danger that genetically altering an organism ran the risk of eliminating the original species. There was always the chance that humans might be upsetting the balance of things. Gajdusek, her boss at NIH, had warned her that Conti's dreams swelled so large that they tended to swallow whole all those who came in contact with them. Gajdusek and Conti had met in the Army when they had both served at Walter Reed Hospital back in the fifties. She could tell that Gajdusek admired Conti's rogue streak, but their approaches were very different. They were two kinds of doctor – one was in medicine while the other was in applied research. And while Gajdusek's pioneering work eventually led to a Nobel prize, Conti had disappeared into the private sector, where success was measured in commercial rewards. Despite Gajdusek's gentle admonitions, she fell under Conti's spell when he offered her the opportunity to take her theoretical models for controlling transgenic organisms and bringing them, literally, to life.

That was ten years ago, and now, as Morgan watched Conti slump into the chair behind his desk, she knew that her loyalty was more than gratitude for what he had allowed her to accomplish. Just as Gajdusek had predicted, Conti's dreams had indeed swallowed her whole. Only, Morgan had noticed in the past few months that Conti seemed to have lost a bit of the luster that had always driven him, and she found herself trying to protect him. He would pause in midsentence as though lost in thought, but Morgan suspected that it was less a pause and more that he had actually lost that thought. She covered for him, of course. If they were alone, she would repeat what he'd just said, pretending she was trying to follow his idea while her real motive was to lead him back to the subject at hand. If they were in public, she would finish his suspended sentences as though she couldn't contain her enthusiasm over whatever point she assumed he was trying to make. It was a taxing process at times, but Morgan had taken on the role despite herself. She could do no less for her mentor.

And here he was again, in an all-too-familiar state of suspended animation. But with only the two of them present, she realized she didn't need to cover for him.

"I could come back later, if you want," she offered.

"No. Brief me now." Conti rubbed his hands over his face as though he were trying to wash away the fatigue. Then he looked up. "You said results looked promising."

Why was he pushing so hard? After all, a slow virus would take years to test, and many years beyond that before they could introduce it into a controlled population. At some deeper intuitive level, Morgan began to suspect that Conti's Baby was more personal than he was willing to reveal. Was it possible that the research project had to do with his own failing mental acuity? She wouldn't categorize his symptoms as signs of mental deterioration – she pushed the notion of Alzheimer's away as soon as it entered her head – but she couldn't help but wonder about the similarities between the transgenic virus that was the focus of Conti's Baby and the slow viruses that contributed to the dementias suffered by older people.

"Promising, yes," Morgan began. "The tentative values suggest we may be getting very close. So far, it fits the profile for the medical intervention parameters of the project."

"And its trans-species properties?"

"The latest recombinant RNA strands have genes that interact across a number of species. Human, of course, and most of the expected ones." Morgan didn't have to list them. Potent trans-species viruses were rare, but common enough to transmit waves of flu from swine and birds to human populations each year. The struggle to find vaccines was always a losing battle since RNA strands were more susceptible to mutation than DNA, and the flu stored its information as RNA. But reverse engineering an interactive yet stable RNA virus had been the easy part, and Morgan knew that Conti wanted more.

"But will it cross species?" he asked.

"Possibly. We don't know yet. We're trying reverse transcription." That was the hard part, and still the challenge of the project.

RNA was notoriously resistant to the modifications they wanted to make, so they needed to turn the genetic material into the more forgiving form of DNA. Once they introduced the changes, they could convert the genomes back into RNA, a process called transcription. Morgan and Sandy were both confident the process would work, but it was painstaking work. When they had cloned enough gene segments to test how the virus interacted with various species of animal cells, it was back to the reverse transcription into DNA to tweak the genomes so they created the same results across species. So far, they had managed to tweak their virus so that it produced predictable behavior in human, swine, and several kinds of bird cells. But these paths followed the royal road of influenza strains since swine and birds were the human source of the flu and common cold. Still, this work was no mean feat because she had developed a consistent transgenic virus that could move with interchangeable ease among birds and swine and humans. Morgan knew their work was at least a decade ahead of anything she'd read in the published literature. But Conti's vision reached beyond their accomplishment; he wanted a robust virus that could attach itself to any animal species. How far down the food-chain did he want to go? And why?

Not to mention that he wanted it to be a slow virus. This was the most puzzling piece of all to Morgan. Medical intervention through gene therapy most often looked for fast-acting agents that could thwart epidemics. But Conti was after something else, something that could lie dormant across species, a sleeping virus that could provide immunity to counter agents that didn't exist – yet. However, Morgan knew that the virus had the potential to become its antithesis by applying the law of complementarity. It was an approach to developing vaccines she'd used many times before whenever she assumed that any problem has within itself its own solution, its complementary antithesis. But with Conti's slow virus, he had turned the approach on its head. The project she was helping him produce *was* the solution, but she knew that an enterprising scientist could invert the project's properties so that it became the problem. Which brought her to her second hypothesis about the project. If not designed to counteract dementias, then there was another, more sinister application for the shape of what they were producing. She knew that the government was funding at least part of the research, and that made her nervous. The whole thing smacked of biologicals for the military.

Against her better judgment, Morgan had intimated as much to Dr. Thornton when they had explored his pet theory – her guilt about the Contitech research. She knew that the psychiatrist had found her hints about the possible military applications of her work unsettling, but he insisted that some knowledge of her work was essential to unraveling the symbols her dreams were using to communicate with her conscious mind. There was a possibility that the symbols were predicated on more than childhood memories or recurring bad dreams. If someone, say, the military, were to engineer a biological agent to let loose on a population, then only those who'd been inoculated beforehand could escape the consequences. Were they developing a virus whose code could provide both an infection and its antidote?

Morgan couldn't decide if she was letting her imagination get the better of her. She stared at Conti, who had begun to rub his forehead again. Morgan preferred the first theory, that Conti feared dementia and had figured out a way to entangle military dollars to fund the research. Perhaps the trans-species twist was meant as a red herring that Conti had promised so the feds would support the project. In that case, the irony would be that Morgan was close to delivering that herring. But her results didn't seem to disturb Conti. Quite the opposite, he appeared elated. What was Morgan involved in, and why? More than ever, she felt like she needed to find out once and for all.

"John, we need to talk." She was playing her trump card. Although Conti had longed urged her to call him by his first name, it was something she'd never found comfortable. Maybe he was too close to the age of her father, or maybe it was the innate sign of respect she held for the man. Yet she had, on a few rare occasions, used "John" to get his attention. He looked up at her immediately, and she could tell he had returned his thoughts to the present.

"What is it?" he asked.

"I – I need to know where all this is going." She knew she was using Grant's argument, but it had worked on her – well, that plus her secret desire to spend more time with Mr. Brown Eyes. "If I understood more about the ultimate goal of the project, then maybe I could shave some time off the development phase."

He waved his hand as though he were dismissing her argument. "You know enough."

Morgan decided to push. After all, she was the favored child – everybody said so – but she had no idea how far that would take her. "I don't think I do. Maybe we're overlooking something important – how would I know?"

"Preconceptions might do more harm than good. I need you to keep an open mind." He grinned, perhaps hoping to disarm her. "And besides, what if the Little Green Men turn out to be gray? If you're looking for green, you might overlook them."

Don't worry, I see them almost every night – and believe me, they're not green. Morgan was in no mood for Conti's alien double-entendres; this was serious. But of course, Conti would have no idea how raw a nerve he'd struck, and she dared not tell him. She wasn't ready to walk away from her career – not just yet.

But she did want an answer. She decided to try again. "John, are we working on a biological for the military?"

Conti's face registered a surprise she didn't expect, and then he said, "Closer than you think."

"How close, John? I have to know or …"

"Or what?"

She blurted it out without thinking – or maybe because she'd thought about it too much. "Or I can't stay on the project."

A slow breath inflated his cheeks, as though he were weighing how much to say. "It's not for the military – even though they think it is. It's to protect us from invasion."

"I don't understand."

"I'm glad, Morgan. I'll tell you this, though. I think time is running out, and I need you to finish this thing for me. I just hope I live long enough to – " But he stopped short of completing his thought. And then he added something with that infuriating, enigmatic twinkle in his eye. "Just keep thinking about those Little Green Men."

It made no sense. Or maybe it made too much. Either way, Morgan was afraid Conti was going over the edge. Her mentor had ventured into territory that meant he was either demented or dangerous – maybe both. But one thing was certain: she knew she didn't want Conti to take her down the same path.

Gamma-Ori

Gamma sat looking at his mentor's silent form, grateful that the Sag doctor-priests had allowed him to keep vigil alongside Theta's bio-cot. The Live-ins who formed the cot continued to read Theta's vital signs even though they had finished implanting the neural colonies within his brain, colonies that would guide the Sag's physical recovery. Even at that moment, Gamma knew that Theta's brain was busy sending messages that hastened the sleeping body's restorative powers, overriding any surrender to damaged organs and broken bones. The doctor-priests told Gamma that the neural colonies were a decade-old therapy that had accelerated recovery in many trauma victims, and they saw no reason why it couldn't repair his mentor. If the mind could impose an illusion capable of creating life-threatening damage, then perhaps the mind held the key to reverse that process as well. At least in theory, they said, since no situation like Theta's had occurred before.

Gamma had listened to the thought-flow that wrapped their words, steeling himself against the aura of their emotions. They talked to him as though he possessed no more than the normal mental understanding of a child, but he read their intent deep enough to realize his own role in Theta's collapse. He had pleaded with them to let him try to enter Theta's mind again to undo what he had done, ignoring the flashes that lit their minds, flashes that betrayed the fear they felt toward the Ori. Even so, they explained that Theta's unconscious state placed him in a dreamless coma that was out of reach. Perhaps they were right; Gamma had already tried to reenter Theta's mind, but he found only darkness. When Gamma sensed guilt in one of the doctors at his unkind thoughts about *the little Ori*, Gamma took advantage of the momentary remorse to ask permission to remain with his mentor. "After the neural colonies are implanted," the doctor promised, and Gamma had sat quietly in the corridor outside the med-zone until they allowed him back in.

Although Gamma realized that his lucid journey into Theta's memories had convinced his mentor's body that it had sustained a fall from a great height, Gamma read in the doctors' minds that he may have saved Theta Sag's life in the aftermath.

At the time of the accident, Gamma had forgotten about the stim-band on his head and his mental scream radiated out across the temple complex. He was horrified to see his mentor lying on the floor and, without knowing it, he telepathed the image before him to everyone within the headband's hundred-meter range. Help came quickly, just as Theta's brainwaves started to shut down. Later, Gamma read darker thoughts in the doctors' minds as they speculated how the intensity of Gamma's stim-band might change the chemistry of Theta's brain. He heard them discuss the wave of proteins that had washed through Theta's neural networks at the time of the story time dream fall. But Gamma watched the patterns and images in their thoughts as they pondered how the experience might begin to reconfigure the pathways of Theta's brain. Gamma shuddered when he read one doctor's mental prediction: *eventual insanity.*

Throughout his night vigil, Gamma promised himself

again and again that he would never harm the ones he loved, least of all with his gift. And he did love Theta. Even though the Sag lacked the ability to project his thoughts, Gamma recognized that his mentor shared a deep love for storytelling; in fact, Gamma could sense how much Theta loved the craft when they discussed the nuances of spinning tales.

Just before morning, the Ori detected a faint stirring in Theta's mind. His mentor had begun to dream, Gamma could tell, and he reached into Theta's head just enough to see shadowy images of balloons and clowns. Though Gamma knew that his gift would have a stronger effect with the stim-band the priests had taken from him, the Ori stretched his consciousness into Theta's mind, hovering out of sight within the dreaming Sag. Gamma was determined to protect the dream-child, who once again watched circus figures pass by in the street. Without warning, the dream began to morph the parade of circus animals and clowns into a procession of priests, and now Theta was cowering before the painted face of Alpha Sag. The little Theta wouldn't look Alpha in the face as his mother stepped up beside the old Sag priest and said, "Tell him thank you, Bobby." As she repeated the command, she shook the youngster until he squirmed free and darted under the barricade and into the priestly procession. The priests tromped along together, kicking at the bobbing balloons that littered the street. All the while Gamma, who watched from afar, stood ready to stop the youngster if he showed any signs of flying – Gamma would see to it that the same scenario didn't repeat. The Ori felt relieved when the scene morphed once again, and this time without a balloon in sight. Gamma looked on with interest as an older Theta now stood not among a procession of priests but rather in a nursery not unlike the one in the Ori dorm. Theta stepped with care through the room full of toddlers. Something about the children seemed familiar. Then Gamma realized they all had the same face. It wasn't the look of his own brothers, but clearly they shared something with the Oris. What was it? As Gamma struggled to identify the similarities – no, the kinship

– he saw the children turn in unison and began to point at Theta. The Ori sensed that the pointing fingers placed blame on Theta for some unnamed act, and Theta reacted by backing into a corner of the room while the toddlers climbed to unsteady feet and thronged around him, pushing closer as Theta squatted down against a wall and drew his arms over his head. His chest heaved in and out as his breathing quickened. But the anguish in Theta's dream-self was more than Gamma could stand, and the Ori couldn't help but walk into the nursery, squeezing past the youngsters to take Theta by the hand. Gamma willed the wall to open and he led Theta away from the room and onto a plush green carpet of grass – a scene like the world Gamma had viewed in one of the sims during his training about the past. Then Gamma willed the thronging children to disappear. The dream world filled with the gentle slope of a grassy hill, below which a stream trickled through a shallow creek bed. As Gamma pulled Theta down to sit by the bank, the Ori noticed that his mentor's breathing became more regular. Gamma added a flock of birds that flew overhead, and he let them warble a staccato song, again like the sim, as the birds wheeled through the sky and came to rest on the other side of the stream. Gamma loved the sight of birds and he wished his own world were filled with them again. There were rumored sightings of small flocks from time to time, of course, flying the ancient migratory routes, but so far they were unconfirmed. Gamma hoped it was true, but in the meantime he was happy he could draw upon Theta's own memories to recreate a scene where birds could fill the sky once again.

Then the Ori smiled at his mentor, who smiled back, and they watched together as the sound of flowing water mingled with the chirps and warbles of the flock.

The next day, Theta opened his eyes. He was weak, but his body had made great strides to restore itself. When the doctor-priests returned to check on their patient, they asked

Gamma to leave the room. As he shuffled out, he saw that they huddled around the cot and donned their own stim-bands to scan the reports from the Live-ins. Out in the corridor, Gamma stretched his mind to hear the thought-flow of their talk.

This is unprecedented, said the doctor who stood nearest the closed door. *The neural colonies have performed with remarkable precision. Theta Sag will show complete recovery within a matter of days.*

That may be, but we need to understand why. The priest who talked now was the one whose face looked like a skin-sack drawn together around the folds of his mouth. *Perhaps the colonies counteracted the illusions of the accident. In effect, they've convinced Theta's body that the incident wasn't real.*

But a third doctor-priest disagreed with both of these ideas. *Nonsense. The damage was real even if the etiology stemmed from an anomalous event.*

This time it was Theta who spoke. *I'm going to be fine; I can feel it.*

Gamma agreed with his mentor, who shielded from the doctors his desire that they carry their debate to another room. Gamma sensed that the doctor-priests were more concerned with the therapy than with the patient anyway. But to Gamma, Theta was going to be fine, and that was all that mattered. The Ori stretched once more into the minds of the doctors, and sent just the ripple of a story – one that suggested they had other duties they needed to attend to. Even as Gamma sent the idea into their minds, he realized that he had never done such a thing before. Could the stim-band have started changes in his own brain as well?

Let's let our patient rest, one said, and moments later they opened the door and trooped out together.

When Gamma reentered the room, he saw that Theta's eyes were closed again. With silent steps, the Ori moved to the chair beside the cot and sat down.

"You're here, Gamma. I can feel it." Theta's eyes didn't

open. "I'm glad."

But Theta slipped into sleep almost as soon as his lips ceased moving.

The Ori composed a new story as Theta began to dream, a story about a man who sat in a pool of water fed by a stream. And as the water flowed around the man, his body grew whole again.

Theta-Sag

"Let me steady myself a bit on your shoulder, Gamma," Theta said as they walked across the room.

But the doctors said you're fully recovered. The singing thought lilted like a question rather than a statement.

"I know. But I guess it's hard for me to accept. Some part of me still feels like it's broken." Theta regretted his words as soon as they were out. He knew Gamma held himself responsible for the accident, but it wasn't the Ori's fault. Theta should have cautioned him about the strength the stimband had added to the child's gift. But then, Theta had had no idea how powerful Gamma's story would become either. "You're right, though. I'm recovered."

Maybe you feel your phantom self. Like I felt just after I translated.

"I'm sure that's it." Theta marveled at the insights his young protégé was starting to manifest. Another reminder not to underestimate the Ori. "I'm glad you brought that up. Let's talk about your translations."

Gamma contorted his residual mouth into a frown. Theta was pleased to see how quickly Gamma had managed to work facial features into the physical level of his communication. Had he frowned for effect, or was it becoming an integral reaction?

"What's wrong, Gamma?"

Alpha Sag told me that we might not continue the project, that there's not enough time to finish my preparations now.

Theta settled into his chair, trying to will himself into believing that he was whole again. Phantom self, indeed. "When he said that, Alpha Sag didn't realize you were practicing your storytelling every time I slept. But he knows now. All the Sag priests know, and they voted to continue."

Theta saw Gamma release an involuntary breath. Again, Theta wondered if the Ori were trying to telegraph through facial expressions his emotional reaction or had he begun to integrate them? The mental world of the Oris made them appear too often as somber and uncommunicative to the uninitiated, and early in their lessons together Theta had stressed to Gamma how important it was to practice appropriate body language each time he sang his thoughts. It would help him remember, Theta insisted, to project a self-image that supported the stories he would tell. Whether Gamma had internalized the body language or still treated it as an exercise, the message here was clear. Gamma had taken the news hard that the mission might be over even before it began.

Theta should have expected that Alpha would go so far as to talk to Gamma. Alpha had, of course, also worked hard to build support among the Sag priests to abandon the project soon after Theta lost consciousness. And he had summoned a council the first day Theta was well enough to attend so they could ratify the proposal. Alpha had intended, Theta was sure, to blind-side Theta with the cancelled plans. But as soon as Alpha pointed out to the group that their window of opportunity was about to close – that was the moment Theta chose to announce how Gamma's training had continued, how the Ori was indeed surpassing the original curriculum. Theta had watched the faces of the council members with close attention to be sure they understood that the Ori had healed Theta through his dream stories and, even more, that Gamma had proven himself equal to the task before him. The unexpected consequence of Theta's coma had provided Gamma with an exercise that outstripped the original catechism in both complexity and measurable outcomes. Theta had allowed the council to hear the information first-hand – not through filtered debriefing by the high priest – and if Alpha was pushing for a decision, so be it. In fact, Theta had told them Gamma was now more suited than ever before for a successful mission. When Theta persuaded the council that all would be ready, the mood in the room shifted once again; but this time the Sag council renewed their support for the project. Theta couldn't help it: He had reveled in Alpha's reserved smile at the decision, knowing that the smile had to have hidden a seething rage.

As Gamma sat before his mentor, the Ori's face tried to scrunch into a look of perplexity. *But why would Alpha Sag say that time was running out? Translation is to the past, which has already taken place. I don't understand why a few days' delay could stop us.*

"Alpha Sag was talking about the time-frame for starting the project. It's not something that concerns your part of the mission, Gamma. It's a limitation to the way time translation works."

And to the loophole in the Laws of Paradox. That discussion, however, seemed like a digression that could wait for another time. Theta wondered how much explanation was even necessary. Still, Alpha was the one who had brought Gamma into the conversation by telling the Ori that the window of opportunity was running out. So Theta plunged in.

"Time isn't as linear as it seems," Theta began. "Oh, when we think of the past, it stretches backward in a straight enough line. But beneath that line is a dynamic and random system that is anything but linear – something we all struggled to understand for a long time."

That things aren't linear.

"That's right. Humans don't live in a world that is even remotely linear. When we take the time to look around, we see that clouds, pulmonary blood flow, the surfaces of proteins, the proportions of our limbs, zigzags of lightning –

they're all created by nonlinear systems. And so is time. Do you remember the sim about the ancient Romans?"

Yes. They weren't very nice people.

"Maybe not. But they built some wonderful structures. Like the viaducts."

And aqueducts, Gamma volunteered.

"That's right. Do you recall how the aqueducts flowed straight, even over deep gorges and valleys? If you were standing on top of the aqueduct, the path would look straight. But underneath you would be a series of arches, and that's what really supports the line. Time is like the aqueduct because it seems to flow in a linear line, but what supports the line is a structure that builds up from a structure that's very different. When we try to translate back into the past, we can't follow the straight line; we have to work with the unseen structure that lies below it."

Theta watched Gamma's nod, but the Sag didn't see any real recognition in his eyes. And Theta didn't think it was just because the Ori had forgotten to telegraph his understanding. But then, why should he understand? It wasn't until the late twentieth century that scientists began to recognize the importance of nonlinear, nonintegral systems in the world around them. "You studied fractals when you learned advanced mathematics."

Gamma nodded in response, but Theta knew that the Oris didn't spent much time learning the complexities behind the theory. Only the Sag priests did. But then, understanding fractals was essential in recognizing the patterns that helped them predict the outcomes of a translation. Fractal iterations expressed random repetitions of similar patterns – the kind of complex, dynamic system that the Sag priests had come to understand as the underpinning fabric of time. Collectively, fractal patterns expressed the shapes of objects as simple as snowflakes but at the same time explained why no two snowflakes were ever the same.

Theta reached back toward his desk – a slight wince telling him to move carefully because of his recent injury, but of course, that was no longer true – and he picked up the stim-band. When he tried to hand it to Gamma, Theta saw a look of anxiety flood the Ori's face.

"It's all right, Gamma. This is just my receptor band, not the enhancer you wore before."

Gamma seemed to relax, but he took the wearable with tentative hands. Theta realized that the accident had created phantoms for them both, and Gamma would have to overcome his fear of using the enhancer stim-band the same as Theta had to accept that he was no longer injured. As Gamma adjusted the wearable to fit his head, Theta spoke to his desk Live-in, "Djehuty, generate and display 3-Ds of, first, a Lorenz, and then, a Rossler attractor. And rotate them against a transparent background."

Although Theta wore no wearable himself, he knew that the stim-band would create the illusion of a projected image just in front of Gamma's face. Of course, the image would lie inside his head, and the illusion came from the signals that the brain interpreted as coming from Gamma's eyes. Theta's command for a transparent background allowed Gamma's brain to "see" the attractors at the same time his eyes saw Theta behind the projection. Theta didn't need to see the images to know what the patterns would look like. Although generated by random numbers, the larger patterns would be predictable: the first, the Lorenz, would appear as figure-eights that grew and changed as the Live-in plotted points that stretched along never-closing filaments; the Rossler would look like a spinning top with strings that rotated through three dimensions.

"Notice, Gamma, how the patterns extend and enfold at the same time. Yet the lines that form them never trace the same path, and they never will; they never close."

Theta watched Gamma's eyes follow the evolving shapes that would be morphing before him in empty space. "These are characteristics of a nonintegral dimension," Theta continued, "and my Live-in used an algorithm for fractal, non-Euclidian geometry to create and plot the three-dimensional patterns you see."

They're beautiful, but intricate.

"I agree, they are. They belong to a special class of fractals known as strange attractors. The attractors depend on initial conditions we can set, but then they spin into random patterns – random but not unpredictable. We call each addition to the larger pattern an iteration."

Random attractors. Gamma seemed to savor the words, or test them. *Because the points attract each other in random ways?*

"More or less. Perhaps a better way of saying it would be that they're bound together by the random folding-together of a chaotic system. That's the attraction, but that's also what makes them seem so strange. But more important – and to the point, so far as time is concerned – is that from a distance the pattern has a repetitive and predictable shape. It's not that we can't say what the pattern resembles – "

Like a figure-eight.

"That's right, Gamma, like a figure eight. But we can't know for sure exactly where the algorithm is going to place the points that shape the figure eight. Because it's a random process."

Theta stopped for a moment and remained silent while Gamma, mesmerized, watched the strange attractors unfold before him. Then Theta told Djhehuty to terminate the algorithms. Without waiting for direction, Gamma pulled the wearable from his head and seemed to refocus on his mentor.

"Negative time displacement is like a strange attractor," Theta continued. "In fact, it closely follows the fractal pattern of a strange attractor."

And do I become a strange attractor when I translate into the past?

"In a sense, I suppose you do, Gamma. Or at least, you become part of the pattern because, in negative translation, you express a random point that has as much effect on the shape as everything else does – perhaps more so, since a natural algorithm doesn't generate your presence in the pattern. We do."

Gamma tilted his head to the side, a gesture Theta recognized as one of his own, one that Theta used to signal a shift to a new question. But it wasn't a mannerism that Theta had told Gamma to practice. *Clever boy. You're expanding your repertory.*

I still don't see what strange attractors have to do with what Alpha Sag said. How the window was about to close, the window for me to translate.

Theta tilted and nodded his head in two short, jerky arcs, one to either side. But the motion made him self-conscious about his own mannerisms. Would he see this one tomorrow imitated in the gestures that Gamma would use when the Ori wanted to telegraph, "It's complicated"?

"Strange attractors," Theta said, "describe how negative time displacement might look, but there's another random effect, and one we don't really understand. It's just like being able to see and, in general, predict a shape in fractal geometry, but we still never know exactly why randomness creates discernible patterns."

Gamma sat looking at Theta with complete attention, as if waiting for the connection. Theta went on, "When we guide your translation back to a specific point deeper in time, you'll actually go through a series of short jumps to get there. It's like skipping a stone across a lake, and it's the skips that show you the path where the stone is likely to land." Theta stopped, realizing that Gamma would have no idea what his analogy meant. After all, when would a cloistered Ori have had the opportunity to skip a rock on a lake surface?

Even though Gamma regarded him without showing any signs of confusion, Theta decided to use a different explanation. "Think of the way the Live-in generated the strange attractor for you. Did you notice how the pattern was changing?"

The Ori nodded.

"The reason it seemed to change was because the Live-in was creating a series of points that grew into the lines that made up the pattern. Those changes, those iterations, describe what we're doing when we plot a line for the translation – only we're doing it in reverse. We plot a series of skips that trace their way back to a specified point in time. And when you translate, you're following that trail back along the pattern of the strange attractor. The skips help stabilize your path so you land at the right point."

Theta stopped again to let the idea sink in. Gamma was trying to effect a skeptical expression, but he hadn't quite mastered the art. Although the result looked comical, Theta determined not to smile. He wanted to encourage the Ori's facial experiments.

At last, Gamma responded.

I still don't understand why the time for the translation is running out.

Theta shrugged. "Since time seems to operate within a four-dimensional fractal geometry, we have to follows its rules. One rule is spacing the skips so they lead to the right point in the past; otherwise we'd overshoot your destination. And the spacing to hit the first skip is coming up."

So the window for the translation is soon.

"Yes, Gamma. The first target, the first reiteration. And the one we hope will start to reshape the path of the line that follows."

Gamma opened his residual mouth as though he were expressing surprise, or revelation.

I never understood what the saying really means: to reiterate the past for the sake of the future.

"That's right, Gamma. Your song is a literal iteration at one level, but you've known that for some time. That's the nature of storytelling. At the level of fractal geometry, however, your mission is to reiterate a point in time, and the result will change the shape of the strange attractor that forms our past."

Can you tell me how much time we have before I translate?

"Your first translation – your first iteration as the Storyteller – begins tomorrow night."

Morgan

For two days, Morgan had felt paralyzed. Worse. She had moved through the days as though she were an automaton, performing her duties and perfecting the final phase of the slow virus. Business as usual. Except business didn't seem normal, and she knew at some deeper level that the pretense of normality made it easier for her to escape making a decision. She had avoided talking to Conti for the past forty-eight hours, but she couldn't continue to leave him messages when she was sure he wasn't available to answer the phone. And besides, she was the project leader; she had to brief him and report on the progress of Phase Three.

She had hardly slept, but not because of bad dreams – thank God for small favors. No, these days her life had become the bad dream, and she wished she could wake up.

As she drove the morning commute toward Contitech, Morgan hardly noticed the green undulating hills that opened onto the Denver skyline. For that matter, she paid little attention to the road directly in front of her. A black BMW honked behind her and then she heard the other driver's engine growl as the car changed lanes to pass. She glanced down to see that she was traveling only forty-five miles an hour. *Get a grip, Morgan.* Just as the driver came alongside her, she glanced over to mouth an apology, but the driver stared straight ahead while he held a steady upturned middle finger close to the passenger window for her to see.

She never drove below the speed limit and took it as a sign of her reluctance to clock in at work. Morgan pressed down on the accelerator – not enough to catch Mr. Beemer, but enough to ease back up to a speed that wouldn't slow the city-bound traffic. At the same time, she vowed that it was time to take action. But what sort?

She blew at the unruly bangs that had already settled onto her eyebrows and pondered her options. Morgan had to admit that she had done a poor job of cultivating friends since she'd moved to Denver, and she couldn't think of anyone she felt comfortable turning to. Oh, she had been to a party or two, but she seldom returned the favor with a reciprocal invitation. It wasn't in her nature to develop much of a social life. So who was left? She needed a second opinion, maybe even advice, but none of the choices for confidant were ideal. The only ones she interacted with these days with more than a passing nod or a set of instructions were Sandy, her shrink, and Grant. As a colleague and fellow scientist, Sandy stood perhaps the best chance of assessing what they were doing in the lab. And it wasn't a new topic for her. Almost every day, Sandy offered a new theory about the application prospects for Conti's Baby. The woman must have assumed Morgan knew more than she was telling. Although that was usually the case for a project leader, Sandy was dead wrong this time – that is, until the last forty-eight hours. Morgan shook her head. She didn't know anything for sure except John Conti seemed to be losing it. Not something she dare tell anyone else at the lab, least of all one of her subordinates. No, to talk to Sandy would open up a line of communication Morgan would be sure to regret. Sandy jumped on every piece of misinformation, built innuendo around any wisp of smoky evidence, and was a terrible gossip to boot. For a careful scientist – and she was – some part of Sandy's brain seemed to switch off if she couldn't grapple with results posted in a lab report. No, Sandy wouldn't do.

She was also quick to rule out Dr. Thornton. He already knew too much about the project for his own good. Although Morgan had been careful to talk in generalities about the slow virus, Thornton was no fool. He grasped the significance and the implications within a single session. Kicking herself didn't help; she should have known better than to talk to a good listener. As it was, he seemed preoccupied about how it all fit into the private symbolism her unconscious mind was cooking up to talk to her waking self. But still, she could see the worried look in his eyes, and she wondered if the good doctor had lost any sleep over what his mad scientist patient was working on. The shrink wouldn't do any better than Sandy.

That left Grant, but Morgan was the least happy with that option. It seemed like a helluva way to start off a relationship. At first, she thought it was kind of neat he wanted to be in on the workings of the project, but it was all he wanted to talk about. For once, Morgan had hoped to have a normal conversation about weekend plans, the coming ski season, the smog – anything but biotechnology. She had always assumed that companies discouraged inner-office romances because it muddied loyalties to the boss, but now Morgan wasn't so sure. Maybe it just drove normal, happy co-workers into overdrive when they talked shop on their nights off. And she was having a hard enough time learning anything personal about her love interest's life; to bring up her doubts about Conti and his baby – well, that would be enough to set things back until the next Ice Age rolled into Denver and clipped off its stunted skyscrapers. Still, whom could she talk to? Morgan had to admit that a section chief, and one who had headed other projects, might be the best bet if she was going to get a handle on the situation. And Morgan was beginning to feel desperate about the need to get control. Now there was a show stopper for any relationship.

Like it or not, Grant might have to put off pursuing her until she could get through this. And maybe they could grow through the experience – an opportunity to demonstrate that, together, they could weather the seasonal storms of life. Grant had asked to know more, and she would be showing she trusted him enough to let him in on … what? Their boss's immanent collapse? The development of a virus that could sit out a decade or more before fulfilling some dark military agenda?

And that was the next step. The real reason – as long as Morgan was trying to be honest with herself – the reason she had avoided Conti. He said he was ready to give her the genomes that he wanted the virus to carry. He told her he wanted to see if the RNA was stable enough to transmit the genetic information he had already prepared. The announcement had startled Morgan. All her work had amounted to creating a vehicle for some other project that Conti had completed. And now he wanted to put them together. That was a fourth phase, and it sounded like the final step. Yeah, she decided she'd have to risk talking to Grant. Maybe he could talk her down.

Maybe.

For once, she was opposite the flow of after-work traffic as she sailed along Interstate 25 toward downtown. The day had proven uneventful. Once, she'd seen Conti walking ahead of her in the corridor, but she'd ducked into the bathroom to give him enough time to outdistance her. She'd counted to fifty and then eased back into the corridor. Twice he'd left messages for her that day, and each time she'd returned his calls when she knew he was scheduled for conferences. By the time the work day had come to a close, she'd managed to maneuver through the shift without encountering the alpha wolf. But Morgan knew she couldn't keep up the evasions much longer. She tapped her fingers against the steering wheel as she realized that the cars on the freeway ahead of her had come to a standstill in the lanes heading south. And no wonder. The city couldn't seem to keep up with the population growth, and the local highways clogged with commuters when the work day was over. She took the Speer Boulevard exit and threaded her way into the one-way streets that formed the grid at the city's center. Even after ten years, Morgan still found it disorienting to enter downtown Denver. The layout of the streets sat at an angle offset by fifteen or twenty degrees from the rest of the city, as though early planners had elected to arrange the original plats without regard to compass points. However, the streets that connected to the outlying areas ran true to north and south, with right angles corresponding to east and west. But within a block or two, the downtown orientation supplanted the rest of the city in Morgan's mind. Force of habit almost brought her into the parking lot of her shrink's building, but she resisted the inclination and instead headed over to a lot closer to Sixteenth Street. It would take her ten minutes to walk to the rendezvous point, but she didn't want anyone to see them together. Her stomach began to growl, and she wished she had stopped to grab something to eat before this escapade.

Morgan grimaced. She felt like she should be wearing a trench coat and dark glasses – only it was summer and that would have made her feel even more ridiculous than she already did. She wasn't sure she was up to the cloak-and-dagger routine. She had parked so far away because she wasn't taking any chance another Contitech employee would see her car parked in even the same lot as Grant's. As she marched down the street, she found herself glancing over her shoulder more than once. Most of the time, it was nothing – a street person crawling into a cardboard box pushed against the wall of an intersecting alley or a brown-uniformed driver carrying a late pick-up package to his delivery truck.

She was headed to LoDo, one of Denver's attempts to bring commerce back to the city's once-prosperous lower downtown hub. The development still bordered a rough part of town, but fashionable shops had taken the plunge and increasing numbers of tourists believed the city's promotional brochures and had started to frequent the area. The locals had begun to buy into the charisma of the area's pubs and art galleries; even a comedy club took up residence on a corner of the one-block stretch of LoDo.

When she reached the pub, she ducked in the door. A hostess tried to wave her to a window seat, but Morgan shook her head and strode, eyes down, toward the tables in the back. She spotted Grant, right where she had suggested they meet. Against the pub's back brick wall, he was eyeing the menu of local beers. He beat her there, but then, he'd parked out front. Grant, of course, had no idea the meeting was clandestine.

She dropped into the chair opposite him, and he glanced up and smiled. Any other time, Morgan would have melted under the warmth of his disarming smile, but this evening, she had other things on her mind. And her stomach was turning over – maybe it was the topic she wanted to discuss, or if she was lucky, it was just the hunger.

"I'd about decided you were going to stand me up," he said as she settled into her chair.

"It took me … longer to get here than I thought." Morgan blew at her bangs, a habit to which she had begun to resign herself.

"No problem. Join me in a micro-brew?"

"I've never tried one." She stared at him, ruing how much she wished they were meeting under different circumstances. How many times had she dreamed of just such a tête-à-tête. The odd thing to her was how casually Grant had agreed to meet her, as though he was used to being asked out by women after work. And now it was her turn, but for all the wrong reasons.

"Let me suggest something."

Morgan nodded but it was an absent gesture, and she turned to scan the people who began to gather toward the front of the pub. She didn't expect to see a familiar face, but she wanted to be sure.

"Is someone else coming?" His voice sounded disappointed.

"No, I – no, it's just the two of us."

He smiled again. "Good. You know, I wasn't sure you were going to call me."

Before Grant could say more, a young man in a plain white shirt and black slacks approached their table to take drink orders. As Grant discussed the choices of alcohol with the waiter, Morgan searched her mind for a way to begin. She had worried all day about how to broach the subject of her dilemma, but she still hadn't come up with the right words.

When the waiter had disappeared, Grant began again. "You thought about it, didn't you?"

"Thought about what?"

"Not calling. But I'm glad you did."

Morgan frowned in disbelief. Not call? But she was quick to change her expression to reflect the business at hand. "Grant, I need your help."

"Of course. That's why I offered."

His voice was reassuring, and it gave Morgan the courage to continue. "I'm having second thoughts about the project I'm working on for Conti."

It was Grant's turn to show disbelief. "What are you talking about? Do you know how many section chiefs would sell their first-borns to be in your shoes? Let me help. There's no need to throw away your chance – our chance – to be involved on a high-level project like this."

"I'm not so sure."

"Morgan, everybody knows that Conti has pulled out all the stops for this one. And even though I know it's a hush-hush contract, the buzz is that this may be his next big break-through. You're poised to go all the way to the top with it. Don't you know it'll make your reputation?"

He stopped and waited for her to respond.

"You don't even know what the project is," she said as her stomach gurgled. She hoped he couldn't hear her unruly gut.

"But you're about to tell me. That's what this meeting is about, right?"

Morgan studied the earnest look on his face. Yes, she was going to tell him, but she didn't know how far to go – not at first. She needed a friend, an ally, and she couldn't think of anyone else she'd rather tell. But why couldn't they start through after-hours chats about a normal relationship? *Stop rebelling, Morgan. That's the way it is.*

"Have you noticed anything strange about Conti lately?" she asked.

Grant smirked. "How would anybody tell? Conti's always been strange; that's part of what makes him a legend, right?"

Morgan sucked in a quick, involuntary breath through her nostrils, and blurted out, "I'm worried about him. He's been less and less himself lately. Maybe it's stress – it probably is – but … he may be getting in over his head with this project."

Grant sat back in his chair. "Morgan, has it ever occurred to you that maybe you're the one who might be stressed." He hesitated and then added, "Maybe you're the one who feels that the project is getting over your head."

At that moment, the drinks showed up. She eyed the beer but decided not to try it on an empty stomach – she needed to be as clear-minded as possible, and she was afraid the drink would go straight to her head. Why hadn't she eaten something first? When the waiter retreated out of earshot Grant reached past his beer and placed his hand over Morgan's as he said, "Let me help. I want to. But you have to tell me what this is all about."

It was exactly what Morgan wanted to hear, the cue she had been waiting for. "What if I told you we're working on a special viral package? A recombinant RNA sequence coded to hold a slow virus."

"For what purpose?"

"That's what I don't know, not for sure. Conti hasn't told

me – at least, not in so many words."

Grant swore under his breath. "That's so typical of him. Always holding his cards so close to the vest that his own players don't know what they're doing."

"Tell me about it," Morgan said, and released a soft nervous laugh. It felt good to talk about her dilemma with someone who might understand. Maybe she'd been right to contact Grant, cloak-and-dagger antics or not.

"You said, 'not in so many words.' So you suspect you've stumbled onto something."

Morgan nodded. "The virus we've prepared is trans-species. Completely trans-species."

Grant arched an eyebrow as he turned his head slightly to one side, a mannerism that Morgan had always found alluring. She thought it gave him a certain suave, movie-starrish understatement whenever he heard something that surprised him.

"But it's not supposed to begin replicating," she continued, "until triggered by an unknown agent. Something that involves the military."

"A biological weapon?"

"I asked him that, but he said no."

"I don't understand. What other sort of agent?"

Here came the hard part. "Conti told me, well, he said it was to counteract the effects of an invasion."

Grant's reaction caught Morgan off guard. This time there was nothing suave about the way his jaw dropped. "I don't believe this," he said as he shook his head and once again swore under his breath. "I think I know what your RNA sequences are supposed to carry."

"You – you do?"

"Yeah, I do. And if I'm right, this is just the latest phase of Conti's 'Science Project' – that's what I've heard it called. Son of a bitch. Of course, he asked you to head it. You don't know the history."

"What history?"

"It goes way back – even before my time at the lab." He lowered his voice and scooted the two glasses of beer toward the brick wall as he leaned over the table. "How long have you been at Contitech? Ten years?"

She nodded as she heard another gurgle under her belt. Why wouldn't her stomach be quiet?

"Well, about the time you came on board, Conti asked me to model a special viral strand that would detect alien flu markers."

Morgan felt the blood leave her face. "Did you say 'alien'? You mean extra-terrestrial?"

Grant looked puzzled. "No. Alien, as in unrecognized, unprecedented." His eyes frowned but his mouth formed a smile. "You really are shook up, aren't you? Anyway, Conti wanted a behavior model for an RNA genome that could recognize and then develop one-time immunity for uncatalogued" – he flashed Morgan a smile – "alien flu strains. It seemed like an odd assignment since, as you know, flu strains mutate. A one-time immunity would become yesterday's news once the strain mutated. But Conti didn't seem to care about that."

She nodded. "So you modeled a vaccine to counteract a virus that behaved like flu, but it wouldn't have to be a real flu, would it?"

"No, you're right. The vaccine would respond to an alien flu, but it's triggered to react to anything that suggests flu-virus characteristics."

"Something that could be used to introduce an epidemic. A kind of invasion."

"Yeah, an invasion, that's what he called it at the time to me as well," Grant said. "Which makes me think that your slow-virus carrier is the latest stage of a very long-term plan."

"What became of your project?"

Grant pursed his lips and snorted. "Conti told us that he had to back-burner it. That it'd been a speculative venture and didn't pan out. But now I'm not so sure. It's like he didn't want anyone to connect the dots. What I can't figure out is why he waited so long, and why the rush to finish it now?"

Grant reached for his beer and drained half the glass. Morgan still hadn't touched hers.

"He told me time was running out," she said.

"He said that?"

"Yeah, that, and also something about not living long enough."

"Long enough for what? Although the guy's getting up there. What is he? Eighty?"

"Maybe a little less than that," Morgan replied. Actually, she knew that Conti was seventy-eight, but she was beginning to feel like she'd already said too much about her boss. All during the conversation, she had vacillated between relief and uneasiness – relief because she was sharing the burden of doubt with someone else, but uneasiness because she couldn't help feeling she was betraying her mentor.

Grant shrugged. "Anyway, maybe he's worried he won't live to see his baby finished."

Morgan shook her head. "No, I don't think that's it."

"What then?"

"I don't know. I had the impression he was trying to say he wouldn't live long enough to see the invasion he was talking about. But that doesn't make sense either."

"Not when he won't tell anybody what this is all about." He drained the last of his beer and said, "You want another?" even though she still hadn't tasted her first. She watched as he wiped the bar napkin across his lips and crumpled it into his empty glass.

He twisted in his chair and raised his hand to catch the attention of their waiter. On impulse, Morgan reached forward and plucked the napkin from the glass and scrunched it into her closed fist. She knew it was risky – what would he say if he caught her taking his discarded bar napkin? The thought hung in her mind as she thrust her balled hand under the table. Grant hadn't seen her, but she looked up and saw the waiter approaching with a puzzled look on his face. He was staring down at the table, as though he could see her clutching her prize underneath the table. Morgan smiled back at him but only with her lips. *Don't even think about asking me, buster.* As Grant ordered another beer, Morgan squeezed the damp paper. She tested how it compressed under the pressure of her fingers and decided it would fit just fine into the Secrets Box.

Then Grant turned back toward her and said, "What are you doing?"

Morgan felt her face flush as she opened her mouth. Had he seen her after all? "Excuse me?"

"I said, 'What are you going to do?'"

She reached into her pocket and extracted her inhaler. Too much stress always seemed to shrink her lungs. She pumped two hits into the back of her throat.

But Grant shook his head slowly. "Morgan, you poor kid, no wonder you're flipping out. He won't even tell you what this is all about. Look, why don't I make some inquiries."

She switched on her strongest anxious look as he pushed both palms in the air toward her and said, "Discreet inquiries. Maybe I can find out how long this scheme has been kicking along. I have a feeling this may go somewhere after all." He nodded more to himself than to Morgan, and then said, "I'm going to help you, Morgan. We're going to help each other. It'll be good for both of us."

"And in the meantime?"

"In the meantime, you should finish that beer. And then I'm going to take you out to dinner."

How long had she waited for him to say those words! But

why couldn't it have been the Short, Red Dress that had done the trick? Things just weren't going as she had expected. She would say yes to dinner, of course. After all, the man of her dreams was asking her out – finally.

But she realized that she'd lost her appetite.

CHAPTER FIVE

Gamma-Ori

Gamma-Ori took his place alongside Beta as the hatch closed behind them. He felt nervous and exhilarated at the same time. He was the Storyteller, and his time had come.

He watched as Beta snugged the guidance control wearable around the widest part of his own head. Almost at once, the ship seemed to come to life. Unlike Gamma's own enhancer, Beta's stim-band allowed him to communicate with the nav, propulsion, and guidance systems of the craft. As they both settled down into niches that served as their flight seats, they made sure their stretch-suits pressed firmly into the form-fitting depressions in the dais at the center of the ship's cabin. The suits allowed them to become part of the electromagnetic field of the craft's propulsion system and, as a result, radical shifts in the craft's vectors would have little effect on the two-person crew. Not that Gamma or Beta had to worry about this; their bodies had been engineered for every aspect of the translation mission. Just as their sparer mass created a quantum economy of scale for the translation into the past, the denser fiber of their bones reduced the stress they would feel from the sudden vector shifts as the craft maneuvered toward their destination. Gamma had always taken his engineered biology for granted, but now it made more sense as a function of translation.

Gamma could overhear the resonances of Beta's mind as it sang, merging the craft's systems into his own consciousness. But the Ori pilot's mental preoccupation with the ship made Gamma feel all the more alone. He glanced around at the cramped cabin, its dim lighting emanating from an undetectable source. The smooth surface of the interior had no distinguishable features, nothing to distract his vision. Gamma knew that Theta was nearby, inside the other amplification sphere that rested beside the one that held the translation craft, but the Ori wished he could see his mentor. Even more, he wanted to reach out for Theta's mind, but Gamma knew that holding onto a sense of his mentor would prove too disorienting once the translation commenced.

Gamma had little time to pine for communion with Theta. Within minutes, he felt a fluttering sensation; the humming meant that the force amplifier had begun to generate potential time-evolving states for the craft and crew. Since the superposed states existed at the quantum level, he knew that they would see nothing unusual – not at first. But at the moment of translation, Gamma braced for the loss he would feel as the present collapsed into the past.

Gamma knew what to expect when the first skip occurred – the tearing away from the Gamma-self that sat in the Translation Hall. In the test translation two weeks before, he had felt the phantom self that Theta had predicted. But this time, when it came, the experience was more disturbing. At the instant of translation, the skips through time exploded in a series of staccato moments so close together that Gamma couldn't differentiate the individual episodes – fifteen in all, he knew – while the two Oris traveled a path through the strange attractor of time. Although he had no recollection of these successive events, each skip had taken away a different version of his self, fifteen selves in fifteen skips. And as they entered their destination point in time, Gamma was left with a feeling that was almost unbearable. Grief ignited throughout his body when he glanced down at his missing limbs and torso – except Gamma could see his complete body, intact despite the overwhelming sense of loss.

As he reeled from the grief, Gamma was grateful that he didn't have to function as pilot. But he could hear Beta's thoughts struggling to vector the craft toward their spatial destination. The skin of the ship seemed to melt away as the hull became transparent, and they surged forward. The ship's propulsion manipulated the craft in the tug between the Earth's gravity well and its LaGrange points, making him feel weightless. It felt like flying, the kind of flying he had iterated through Theta's memories of the circus clowns. Except now he saw no green fields unfold below him. The indifferent light of a new moon seemed to fall short of the ground. While Beta-as-ship cut vectors that approximated the earth's curve, Gamma watched the dark skies around them, trying to take his mind off the illusion of loss. Besides, he had hoped to catch a glimpse of real birds on their first translation but, of course, it was night. Most flocks would have nested into shrubby hollows or sought other shelters until first light. Still, he knew from holo-vids that raptors hunted under cover of night – or they did in the past, which was now his temporary present. But at the speed the craft traveled, he resigned himself to the unlikelihood of seeing anything that relied on the power of living wings.

The grief began to subside, and Gamma turned his concentration to the First Iteration and its importance. Before the translation, Theta had shared with Gamma the lines of a short poem from the Twentieth Century, one he said had been written decades before the birth of the woman Gamma would sing to.

"I want you to listen to these lines," Theta had said, "and think of them as a guide to your iteration."

Gamma loved to hear his mentor recite lines of poetry. Early in their sessions together, Theta had told Gamma that poetry held the ancient roots of storytelling, that poetry used the power of words to create mental images in the minds of listeners – a useful tool that Gamma should apply to his own storytelling. Theta had recited, as part of the catechisms, poems he knew by heart. Some of the poems were long, with stories that were easy to follow. Gamma liked the one that depicted heroic warriors who struggled to reclaim a stolen wife named Helen, held behind a war-sieged city wall; another poem he liked described a journey to climb above the clouds to reach a mountain top called Snowden. But sometimes Theta recited shorter poems, ones that were harder for Gamma to find the story. His Sag mentor said these poems were written to make the listeners think, to make them find personal meanings in the lines. More than anything, though, Gamma had floated on the thought-flows of Theta's mind, relishing the love of words that his mentor brought to the poems.

An hour before the translation, Theta had recited to him a short poem, the kind designed to make the listener think.

"It goes like this," his mentor said and then began to recite.

> So much depends
> upon
>
> a red wheel
> barrow
>
> glazed with rain
> water
>
> beside the white
> chickens

Do you know what the poem means?"

Gamma had read his mentor's thoughts at a level deep enough to see that Theta envisioned the arrangement of the poem's words on a mental page, and that he considered the arrangement as important as the words themselves. But Gamma read his mentor's mind no deeper than this. The Ori knew his mentor wanted to see his pupil learn to think for himself. And Gamma had learned to enjoy such exercises.

Gamma thought for a moment, and then asked, *Will there be chickens where I'm going?*

Theta had chuckled at that. "I don't know, Gamma. But I'm sure there will be all sorts of birds for you to see. What else could the poem mean?"

The first part was easy *"So much depends on ..." That's supposed to remind me of the importance of the first iteration.*

"Yes." Theta smiled his approval. "And the rest of the poem?"

Gamma thought for a moment and then shook his head. He had seen holo-vids of wheelbarrows, but they didn't seem like anything important. And the glazed rainwater, that also eluded him.

"As Beta vectors you to your destination, think about the iteration, and what the poem could mean."

Now, as Gamma flew across the night sky in the transparent craft, he pondered the poem's words, but he still didn't know the meaning of the lines. So he turned his thoughts to the iteration he would unfold in the mind of the woman whom the Lector Priests had designated to receive his story. Although Theta had urged Gamma to approach her with an open mind, Gamma knew that his mentor held an unspoken horror of her. She was the one who had changed the strange attractor of time into the shape of their world, and Theta considered her a monster – something he would never have said to Gamma aloud. Gamma knew that no one knew much about her. There a photo and a meager statistical footprint. History, Theta had said, favors the deeds of public figures – kings, queens, presidents, heroes – but seldom records the personal life of the average person. At the time, no one suspected the role she would play in changing the shape of things to come. In fact, it had taken the priesthood many years to uncover the identity of Morgan Johanssen, and then the records were scarce. Motor vehicle registrations, university transcripts, bank card expenditures, a house mortgage – these constituted the primary artifacts from which the priests had reconstructed the woman's life. But so much was uncertain, so much unspoken in official records. Had she ever known kindness? Did she care for anyone? What events had pushed her into the role she would play? So much depended on what Gamma could discern from first-hand contact with this woman to help the priests develop a stronger personality profile. If all went as planned, the Ori would visit her again and again to sing her the songs – as many times as it took to reiterate the past for the sake of the future.

Below the transparent craft, lights from the ground began to appear before them, just a few at first, but as the craft moved forward more lights came into view. They lay in growing clusters until the ground was aglow with a complex matrix of luminosity.

The urban sprawl called the Front Range, Beta sang into Gamma's mind. *The brightest part ahead will be Denver.*

Although the exchange took less than a second, unencumbered by lips or sound waves, Gamma and Beta flashed back and forth to each other their thought-impressions about the density of the population it must have taken to create such a glow. No such concentrations of people existed in the Oris' world, and they observed the sight with awe.

Their ship streaked southward over the radiance of interconnected cities, the edges blending in ragged geometries of light and dark. In moments, the Ori travelers reached the southern boundary of the field of illumination and soon began to pass over a low range of ridges and valleys. Without warning, the craft vectored at a right angle downward and plummeted four-thousand meters to stop just above the ground, hovering in an anti-grav envelope unaffected by the Earth's pull.

Not fifty meters from the craft lay a small house surrounded by a picket fence. A dim light shone through the window. Its bottom half was open but the upper half crisscrossed the wood trim between panes, casting a shadow on the ground in the form of an elongated cross.

Beta turned his head to Gamma. *This is our destination.*

But Gamma was already stretching his mind into the house, feeling the presence of Morgan Johanssen as he began to sing.

Morgan

For once, morning traffic had been light, and Morgan had had no trouble getting downtown. After a dozen consultations with Dr. Thornton, the routine was clear. She moved toward the leather chair without instructions from her shrink. As usual, he sat reviewing notes from a chair positioned opposite hers. She wondered if the good doctor had so many patients he couldn't recall what they had discussed the last time she sat there. To be fair, she would have reread her own notes before launching into a new phase of an experiment, and she decided to be generous in her appraisal of the shrink. If Thornton was going to stir up the cocktail of her unconscious, she should be glad that he reviewed what ingredients already swam around inside her head.

He still looked at his notes as he said, "Still hard at work on the secret mission?"

The tone was casual, but Morgan suspected he harbored his own fears about what she was doing. She regretted explaining to him as much about the project as she had. Somehow, despite his protests that he didn't want to know, his questions had teased from her more than enough to characterize the gist of what she was doing. He was a skilled interrogator, she gave him that. To his credit, he had concentrated on applying that knowledge to the symbolism of her dreams, with never a mention of the potential biological consequences of the assignment if it were, indeed, driven by a military agenda.

When he glanced up from the clipboard he held, Morgan flashed him a brief, noncommittal smile in response to his question. They locked eyes for just an instant, and she knew he got the message.

"I presume then, Morgan, that your dreams continue to feature the child and the visions that accompany him." It was a statement that needed no response, and he continued, "I think we should focus on the child today. I'm beginning to think he may represent more than a simple projection of a friendly face who helps you center on an unresolved issue about your ... work. I still think that's part of it, but there may be more to the child." He looked down at his notes again as he said, "Do you know what an archetype is?"

Although he wasn't looking at her, Morgan shrugged her response and then added, "I've heard the term, but I'm not sure I know what it means."

He nodded as he looked back up. "I'm not surprised. The word's passed into popular language, and most people don't understand what it means. An archetype refers to a structure that organizes the psychic contents of our minds."

She gave him a blank stare. The psycho-jargon said nothing to her.

Thornton went on. "The human brain is hard-wired to order the world in certain ways. A child recognizes its mother because the brain is already organized to pigeonhole her as an important figure in the baby's life, and that inner recognition is because of the hard-wired mother archetype. Another example would be the Self archetype, which helps us differentiate the experiences that belong to us as individuals. We collect them into a sense of self. So think of archetypes as innate patterns, or even organizing containers inside our minds that are waiting to be filled with the contents of our lives."

"Like DNA coding, then." Morgan was searching for a referent from her own experience that could make sense of his explanation.

"Yes, but only in the sense that the possible codes are predetermined. They express specific kinds of outcomes."

"Like eye color or a tendency for a chemical dependence – maybe alcoholism."

"If you like. But an archetype would be more like a vessel that gathers the characteristics of being an alcoholic."

"So, inner patterns that help organize our experiences – "

"In a predetermined way."

"Okay. But I don't see what this has to do with my dreams."

Thornton held up his hand, as if signaling that he wasn't through. "It has everything to do with dreams. You see, the human mind sometimes tries to seal off a vessel, ignoring the importance of its contents to the overall wellbeing of the individual. When this happens, the unconscious mind will sometimes send an archetype into an individual's dreams. It may come as a person, a scenario, or an object, but whatever the form, it's the unconscious mind's attempt to get the conscious mind to focus on the importance of the archetype to the person's mental health."

"And you think my little friend is a messenger from the unconscious?"

"Yes, he may be a manifestation of an archetype."

"So what's the archetype for a child in a flying saucer?" Morgan wasn't at all sure that she bought any of this, but she was trying to keep an open mind.

"I'm not sure. There's a child archetype, the organization of psychic contents that collects what we understand to be childlike qualities. Naïveté, trust, and open-mindeness, for starters – plus whatever else you've experienced along the way and have stored as representing The Child. But I don't think it's that simple."

It sounded halfway plausible to her. But why was it that nothing was ever "that simple"? So she asked, "And why not?"

Thornton waited a beat before he said, "Jung once wrote a paper on UFOs."

Morgan must have shown a look of incredulity because she could swear that Thornton's tone sounded a bit defensive to her as he continued. "Oh, not that he believed in flying saucers – not as a physical phenomenon. Instead, he was interested in them as a psychic manifestation. He believed that, in the modern era, some people have substituted aliens for angels. In an age where science has supplanted religion, people may envision a technologically advanced civilization that's arrived to solve all our problems." He paused. "You visitor arrives in a flying saucer."

"That's right."

"But you don't believe in aliens."

"No, I don't. So what kind of an archetype are you proposing my unconscious mind is sending me?"

"I'm not sure. But I do know that the symbols the unconscious mind sends in dreams are personalized. They're a kind of private code meant just for you, and so we have to look for a way to break that code."

Morgan shook her head. "It doesn't make sense. Why an alien child – and he doesn't even look like an alien."

Thornton frowned while he stroked a forefinger from his lip to his chin. "The alien part of the dream might relate to your scientific work – or else your denial of its implications. But let's not get ahead of ourselves. Let's concentrate on the child, not the saucer. Maybe that's where the key lies."

"I've told you what I know."

"Perhaps, perhaps not. You said he gave you a nonsense

name the first time you met him in your dream."

"Yes, it didn't make any sense."

He leaned forward in his chair, a gesture that Morgan had come to recognize as a sign that he was zeroing in on something he thought of as a possible break-through. "That's what makes me think it might be important – a part of the code. What was it again?"

"It sounded like the name of that Japanese paper-folding art. Ori – ori something."

"Origami?"

"Maybe. But I don't know anything about paper-folding."

"Has anyone in your family ever learned origami? A friend?"

She shook her head.

"But you know what it is."

"Yeah, I've seen it. In movies, or maybe on a book cover in the how-to section of the bookstore. And, of course …"

"Yes?"

"Well, when I was little, my grandmother showed me how to cut out paper dolls. But nothing more."

"So it seems. But it may mean more than you know. Let's set that aside for now. Tell me again what your impressions were when you met this … Origami."

"That first time?"

"Yes."

"But we've gone over this already." She couldn't help but let a little exasperation seep into her voice.

"Bear with me, Morgan. You may think of details you missed – or see a connection you overlooked the first time you told me the story."

Morgan felt it was a waste of time and told him so, adding, "Couldn't you just hypnotize me or something? Then we'd have the dream on tape, and I wouldn't have to go through it again."

"Hypnotism has certain therapeutic uses, but I think it may be a questionable tool in your case."

Before she could protest, he continued. "A trance state can make you susceptible to suggestions, and we want to get a picture of your memories that's as accurate as possible."

"I thought hypnosis could do that."

"Not really. It makes a subject prone to confabulation."

Morgan gave him a quizzical look.

"You might add details that change the experience, treating it like a work in progress rather than a *fait accompli*. You'll just have to trust me on this one. That's why you're here, right?"

Thornton was playing his trump card, Morgan decided, appealing to his authority as the doctor. And to tell the truth, maybe she did need him to put her in her place. After all, that was why she was there. It made her wonder why she acted so resistant to going over her first encounter.

So ...," he prompted.

She forced herself to recall her introduction to Origami and began to recount the event to Thornton. She'd been reading in bed, a draft of a report that was due the next day. But it was late, and she found she had trouble concentrating on the words. In fact, she realized she'd just read the same paragraph two, maybe three times and decided she wasn't getting anywhere. When a rustle of wind came through the open window, she remembered thinking how unusual that was. Sometimes freak winds came at night, but those only came right before a storm front. And she hadn't heard anyone mention at work that the state was due for some weather.

She asked Thornton if he thought that meant anything, but he shrugged and shook his head as if to say, *probably not*, and urged her to continue.

After hearing the wind, she said, she must have fallen asleep. She remembered that her head felt heavy, like the buzz she got from drinking Long Island Teas. They tasted good, more like punch, but all the while the tea's rum would creep along the edge of her perceptions. Then all at once, it would hit her: Voices around her seemed muffled and her awareness of where she was would fold in on her. Not that she'd been drinking that night – too much reading to do. But the feeling she got, that's what it was like, she told the doctor.

"Reading about the project?" he asked.

Yes. And she could almost see Thornton connecting the dots – his own bit of confabulation, she couldn't help musing.

Anyway, she was lying in bed, heavy with that rum feeling, and that's when it began to occur to her that something was wrong. But she didn't become frightened until she realized she was paralyzed; she couldn't even move her neck. Her eyelids were open, however, and she flicked her eyes back and forth to catch as much of the room as she could through her peripheral vision. It felt like someone was in the room, watching her. Panic began to set in as she struggled to move, but none of her limbs would respond. She sensed that a person was approaching the bed although she still couldn't see him.

"Why did you assume that it was a man?" Thornton asked.

Morgan's demeanor changed to a look that said, *If you were a woman, you wouldn't have to ask that question.* Whether or not he understood her body language, he asked her to go on.

Although her bedroom was still and silent, she could hear no footsteps against the hardwood floor, no telltale swish or rustle of clothing – yet she knew he was coming closer. The funny thing was that he didn't walk into her line of sight; it was more like he, well, just materialized – a figure that grew into a solid form beside her bed. It was a little boy, and with a somber look on his face he said, "I'm amused." Morgan would have grunted a laugh had she been able to move a muscle.

For the first time that night in her bedroom, it dawned on her that she was dreaming. The whole scenario was just too weird to be anything else.

"And was he wearing your brother's clothes?" Thornton asked.

Leading the witness, Doc. No, he wasn't. Not that time. His clothing was … nondescript. But that wasn't quite right either. He seemed to be wearing some kind of one-piece jump suit. Not the rough-and-tumble clothes of a child. Instead, it was a matte gray suit, or perhaps it held a trace of sheen. But the thing that most caught her attention was the eyes, the way they stared at her with fascination – maybe even a touch of awe.

By the time he touched her hand, all of her anxiety had melted away. Then he whispered to her that his name was … well, it sounded something like Origami, but she couldn't be sure. She still felt that drugged sensation, but nothing about the boy – or the situation – struck her as odd anymore. Yeah, she decided, it was a dream. Had to be. And what happened next convinced her it could be nothing else. She felt release from her paralysis at his touch, and then he led her by the hand as they walked toward the bedroom's exterior wall. Just as they were about to collide with the rough texture of the wall's plaster, she stopped short, looking down at the boy. He smiled and pulled her forward with him, and she realized that the wall no longer blocked their way. Instead, they stepped into a scene that reminded her of a landscape near the place where her grandparents used to live – wooded, lush, and filled with the piping of birds.

She'd never seen so many birds, certainly not in one place. They chattered down at them from swaying tree branches as they flitted from limb to limb. But some of them seemed out of place. There weren't any peacocks in the Minnesota woods, at least not in the wild. But here they were, strutting between the trunks and alongside – white chickens? Barnyard fowl just didn't fit the scene, and she found herself glancing around to see if there was a farmhouse nearby. Maybe they'd found a hole in their wire pen and escaped the care of a nearby farm. But no, the birds were standing by a lake that looked just like the one where her grandparents lived. She even recognized the angulated rocks that jutted up near the water's edge. She couldn't recall any farms in the area, at least none that raised birds. Next, she turned back to face the lake. Breathing in the stench of rotting logs, she felt a certain nostalgia for the many times she'd stolen away to walk the shoreline and skip rocks across the lake's surface as a teenager. For some reason, she found herself playing and replaying the rock-skipping memory through her mind's eye. Then she looked up in time to see ducks begin to land in the marshy reeds, and she listened to the splashes their wings made as they settled into the water. At any moment, she expected to hear her grandfather's shotgun and see his old yellow lab come dashing from a thicket to pounce through the reeds as he retrieved the limp bodies of green-headed Mallards.

But the little boy was tugging at her and pointing at the clearing where the chickens had pecked at the ground beside the strutting peacocks. To her surprise, they now lay still and lifeless. She recoiled and turned toward the lake's surface, but it also lay littered with the floating carcasses of Mallards. At that moment, the sky began to rain down the bodies of finches, sparrows, and swallows, their bodies hitting the ground with soft, bouncing thuds as they piled up around her like large chunks of feathered hail stones. She stood horrified by all the senseless death that lay at her feet.

"It doesn't have to be this way." It was the little boy who spoke.

She looked down at him and stammered, "What – what's going on?"

"This is what will happen if you keep working on the project for Contitech. All these birds will die. Soon after that, the foxes, the wolves, the deer. Even the pigs. And then the people, most of them – billions of them. Why would you do that?"

That's when she woke up. It was already morning and she'd forgotten to close the window. She shivered as she lay atop the bedcovers and realized she was still wearing her clothes. The report lay on the floor beside the bed, its pages scattered across the smooth hardwood planks.

Morgan shuddered at the retelling of the story and glanced up at Thornton.

"That's it. That's all I remember." She watched the analyst for any sign that he had detected an important detail she had overlooked before.

Thornton began to press the fingertips of the opposing hands together, one by one, and with a slow, deliberate effort. Once his hands had assumed this pose, he said, "The thing that strikes me about your story is the emotional force you display when you talk about the boy."

"And that's significant?"

"Well, for one thing, it suggests that we *are* dealing with an archetype. Encountering an archetype is one of the few things that evokes such an overwhelming reaction when you move from a dream state to consciousness." He nodded, but it seemed more to himself than to Morgan. "Yes, I think we should consider the little boy as a manifestation of the Child Archetype."

"And all the dead birds?"

"Symbols of the world you associate with your own childhood. You did say the setting was familiar to you – a scene from your adolescence?"

Morgan nodded.

"Your unconscious mind may have decided to conjure up a world your childlike self once knew, but one that is now dying because of the actions of your life as a conscious adult."

"And the child itself?"

"A messenger who can link you back to that world." He glanced at the clock on the wall behind Morgan's chair. "That's about all we have time for today." By the time Morgan had made her third visit to see Thornton, she recognized he ended his sessions with the same routine. She speculated to herself that he must have positioned the timepiece where he could check the time without the more obvious action of looking at a wristwatch. But all his attempts at subtlety evaporated by the time a patient had learned to recognize the signs – like now – that the hour was almost over.

Although the doctor seemed pleased with the session, Morgan felt more than a little unresolved. Unlike some of the earlier visits, this sitting felt like a waste of time. Maybe she should consider ending the sessions. What if all the time and money netted nothing more than revealing to an outsider professional information that was very confidential. All she'd seemed to do was pass on her anxieties to a third party – and he looked like the knowledge had shaken him up from time to time on top of it all.

"There's something I want you to try," he continued. "I'm sure the key is the boy. And I also suspect it has something to do with that problematic name you heard him use to introduce himself to you in the dream."

"That seems like such a trivial detail."

"On the contrary, I think it may be important. Humor me. I want you to find a book on origami and learn a little bit about paper-folding."

Morgan couldn't help but roll her eyes.

"Experiential reconstruction often triggers a new awareness about dream images," Thornton persisted. "I've done it myself. All Jungian analysts have to undergo deep analysis themselves before they're certified, and I found it very beneficial."

Great, she thought, *my shrink needed analysis.*

"Morgan, promise me you'll give it a try."

"Okay, if you think it's important, I'll give it a shot," she said, but she had little conviction in her voice. "Anything in particular?" Although she knew what was coming.

"Birds, for starters."

"Yeah, okay."

"And ... chickens especially. That really stuck out as something that took you by surprise in your dream."

"You really think that origami chickens are going to be the break-through?"

The smile he gave her in response seemed genuine, but she couldn't help but wonder how much he was shooting in the dark with this latest suggestion.

Cloak-and-dagger games and paper dolls – well, paper chickens. It was all beginning to make Morgan feel silly. It was as though she were reverting to childish things. She wondered what would be next. On second thought, she wasn't sure she wanted to find out.

Gamma-Ori

Gamma-Ori sat in the council hall beside his mentor as the other Sagittarian priests fell silent. The priests were arranged in a semicircle that faced the seats Gamma and Theta occupied. The Ori was sure he had performed all they'd requested of him, and he was puzzled why no one spoke.

After the craft had returned, Gamma and Beta opened the hatch and then crawled out of the amplification sphere. At the same time, the Sag priests began to file out of the other, larger sphere that hovered nearby. Theta explained to Gamma that the second sphere shielded the priests, allowing them to remain unaltered during Gamma's iterations. It was a precaution, Theta told him, in case the trajectory of changes took an unpredicted turn – unlikely, but always a possibility when dealing with the non-Euclidean geometry of a strange attractor. The entourage of Sag priests led the two Oris out of the cavernous chamber that held the spheres and into the council hall, where they asked Beta to wait outside while they questioned Gamma. Gamma was amused at this request; didn't they realize that he and Beta had entered a simultaneity, a state of consensual shared experience? Gamma had always considered the priests all-knowing, but now he wondered if there were things they didn't understand about the mental capabilities of maturing Oris. Most of the time, he felt awe for the knowledge the priests possessed, but there were moments – like the present – when he found himself questioning their ability to see the things he could. His immediate reaction in the face of such moments of doubt was to redouble his dedication. These were thoughts, he knew, that would distress his mentor, and Gamma still felt a fierce loyalty toward Theta Sag. The Ori would never do anything to upset him.

After the door to the council hall had closed, the priests prompted Gamma to recount the events of the translation from start to finish. But during the debriefing, they had interrupted him at every turn.

Once the Live-ins recorded all the details his inquisitors requested, the Sag priests became quiet. Gamma could sense a shared veil of uneasiness settle over the gathering. He cocked his head toward Theta and piped a surge of questioning anxiety into his mentor's mind.

Even though Theta's face remained fixed on the empty center around which the entire group sat encircled, his mentor subvocalized, *It's all right, Gamma. No one knows quite what to think. You're the only one who's looked on the face of the person who initiated the world we know. And now you've touched her mind and laid the groundwork to start a new trajectory in the strange attractor.*

Gamma scrunched his nose. *But it's what you instructed me to do.*

Yes, Gamma, and you did it without fear. But at the same time, you traveled into a world that's taken on mythic proportions for the rest of us. You're like Theseus, who entered the labyrinth to track down and slay the minotaur – and came away unscathed. We all find that a bit daunting.

Gamma had no idea what Theta was talking about, and for once he didn't seine his mentor's memories to untangle what was no doubt one of Theta's literary references.

Theta continued, *You've done your part – at least, you've begun your part – and now we have to live with those actions. It's, well, it's sobering. At some level, I don't think any of us thought it would ever come true. And, of course, we have to consider how you should proceed.*

As Gamma pondered the thought-words that Theta subvocalized, he watched the priests begin to stir, starting with Alpha Sag.

"That's all for now, Gamma-Ori," the high priest said. "Subject to the will of this council, you can expect to continue plans for the next translation." Then he nodded to Theta Sag.

This time, Theta spoke to Gamma aloud. "Gamma, you've had a busy night. I'll walk with you back to your quarters." And he slipped a hand under Gamma's upper arm, a gentle lift that signaled Gamma should stand.

"And then you'll return here, Theta," Alpha Sag said, "so we can consider your instructions for Gamma-Ori's next translation."

They left the council hall as Beta entered it, and then they followed the corridor that would take them to Gamma and Beta's lodging. Gamma still hadn't gotten used to their new quarters, or rather, their isolation from the other Oris, but Theta had assured him it was more appropriate since their mission had begun.

As they walked along the corridor, Theta said, "By the way, I see from the debriefing you found a way to incorporate at least one of the images from the poem I recited."

Gamma smiled. *Yes. The white chickens.*

"I should have guessed that you'd pick up on that one. However, that wasn't exactly what I had in mind."

I know.

Gamma registered the hint of a surprise in Theta at the Ori's quick admission, and Gamma let himself seep into his mentor's thoughts in time to capture Theta's revelation that his Ori was developing a sense of humor. Of course, Gamma had included the image because he liked the idea of the bird he'd seen in his mentor's mind. But when Gamma had begun to sing the story to Morgan, he drew upon her own memories of a cherished personal landscape. It was then Gamma realized what Theta had in mind with the poem. All Morgan's images of the natural world – a world lost to Theta and never real in Gamma's experience – these were the things that depended on his song. But Gamma was sure that Theta had guessed by now how well his pupil had deciphered the meaning of the poem, and the Ori didn't think he needed to explain his own revelation.

Besides, Gamma couldn't shake the unsettling lack of closure he felt about the debriefing. There were so many things about Morgan he had learned as he stretched into her mind, yet the priests hadn't seemed interested when he'd started to tell them about her. They would interrupt him each time he tried to describe her personality, which bothered the Ori. Although he respected their wisdom and guidance, he still couldn't fathom why they would dismiss Morgan-the-person. Wasn't that part of his mission as well? Gamma thought about the appropriate body language to signal to Theta his concern and decided that a frown would do.

He tugged on Theta's arm and displayed the facial expression as he sang into Theta's mind.

Why didn't the council ask me more about Morgan Johanssen as a person.

"I don't understand what you mean."

I thought I was supposed to help the Order build a portrait of how she thinks.

"Gamma, your account told us what we needed to know. She's susceptible to your storytelling. You were able to place her in a trance and guide her mind. She responded to everything you sang to her, didn't she?"

Gamma remembered to nod. He was pleased how automatic the physical cues were becoming. As they approached a cluster of Commoners who stood near the entrance to an exterior courtyard adjoining the corridor, Gamma projected an illusion that suggested they saw only a boy walking beside the Sag priest. They smiled at the Ori as he passed; but Gamma gave little thought to the ease with which he gave the individual Commoners a different image of a youngster who matched some vague familiarity to someone each knew.

At the same time, Theta began to subvocalize the private conversation between him and the Ori. *And you were able to read from her memories what you needed to improvise.*

Again Gamma nodded.

As they rounded the juncture that led to Gamma and Beta's quarters, Theta continued aloud, "We don't need to know more. Besides, a storyteller should have the freedom to respond to an audience as he sees fit and to adjust the story just as the occasion calls for. You're the one who's on stage, so to speak – not us."

Gamma decided not to press the issue, but he was still troubled. Even his mentor didn't seem interested in what the woman was like. When Gamma had first seen Morgan on the bed, he found himself mesmerized. The resonances in Theta's mind when he spoke of her had led Gamma to anticipate an encounter with someone who was on the verge of becoming evil, and the Ori had steeled himself to encounter a mind that was dark. But when he approached Morgan Johanssen as she lay on her bed reading, he couldn't help but feel amazement. She was just a woman, and a little sad.

All at once, he recognized something else about her: She felt as out of place in her world as Gamma felt in his. He sensed how much she struggled to get along with others, and she questioned why she had so much trouble adjusting the rhythms of her life to the expectations of others. The undertones of her thoughts caught him by surprise, and he searched for some evidence of the evil she was about to do. It wasn't there.

Was it possible the priests had identified the wrong individual? No, he told himself, this was the Morgan Johanssen he was sent to find; a shallow scan of her mind confirmed that she did, indeed, match the statistical profile that Theta had described. When he searched the images embedded in her memory, he found evidence of the research she did, research that would lead to the beginnings of his world. Still, this was no monster. He sensed the genuine anxiety she experienced – as well as the confusion she felt – at his presence. There was nothing hard and sinister about the woman. Even more, he found himself attracted to how gentle she seemed to be at the core of her being. Gamma couldn't help the way his heart had gone out to her, especially when he detected how unhappy she was, deep down. He saw images of one man in particular, someone she worked with, someone she treasured. Although Gamma found it hard to fathom the kind of relationship she hoped to form with this other person, the Ori nonetheless recognized the power of her emotional attachment. It held traces of the sentiments he felt for his mentor, but it was unlike the bond he held with Theta Sag. This attachment pulsed with yearning, and it made her unhappy. Yet she seemed trapped by these feelings, unable to express them. The answer seemed so simple: Why didn't she tell the other person how she felt so he could take away her unhappiness?

Gamma knew he had to sing into her mind the images that would make her reconsider the path she was on that would change the future world. But he also knew that he was going to figure out some way to help her – not in what she did, but in who she was.

These were the discoveries the Sag priests never gave him a chance to share about his experience with the woman in the past. Even Theta Sag showed no inclination to open his mind to Gamma's revelations, and his mentor's disinterest created a certain dilemma for Gamma. As Gamma watched Theta turn to rejoin the deliberations of the council, the Ori knew that he was going to have to find a solution for the dilemma on his own. And it had to be one that wouldn't disappoint his mentor. But at the same time, it had to be a solution that brought this new person in his life some sense of deliverance as well.

Although Gamma knew he didn't need to leave the translation craft to sing into Morgan's mind, he liked to pretend he was in the room with her. He expanded his consciousness and entered her sleeping mind, probing her memories for something he could use. She was dreaming about a playground next to the grade school she and her brother had attended. Gamma allowed the images to wash over him as he stood on the edge of the dream's gravel-covered field, watching her propel the little boy into higher and higher arcs underneath the triangular arms of a swing set. "Faster! Faster!" the little boy called out to her. But Morgan wasn't a little girl in this dream; she looked like her waking self.

Gamma sensed how protective she was of her little brother, Jonathon, and he began to probe the memories that associated the two. Without warning, the gale force of the images Gamma saw were too painful to hold in his mind's eye for long. The Ori felt like an intruder and backed away from the raw memories that Morgan held deep within, and he returned to the dream before him. The first time Gamma had entered Morgan's mind, he had seen this youth as a powerful figure in her life, and he had adopted Jonathon's general appearance as the form he used for his first contact with Morgan. Now, however, Gamma studied the little boy with more care. He was about Gamma's own size, which was a fortunate coincidence. But Gamma had constructed a face for these visits that was much closer to the Ori's own. He didn't want Morgan to think that she was seeing her little brother. After the brief exploration of her hidden memories, Gamma realized more than ever that he wouldn't want to appear to her as her brother. Still, the Ori recognized that Morgan harbored a strong and tender attachment for the little boy, and subtle similarities to the youth could prove useful to Gamma as he sought to establish his own relationship with her. The Ori studied the mannerisms Jonathon used in Morgan's dream, his giggles, his voice.

As he watched Morgan's interaction with her brother, Gamma began to register a new sensation – jealousy. The emotion startled Gamma because it was a hue of sentiment he had never experienced through Theta Sag. It was faint, yet it held a powerful resonance for the Ori. Fascinated by the sudden pang, Gamma tried to sound Morgan's mind for the source of the feeling. The emotion dwindled as he surrendered into her memories, so he retreated to the level of the dream. What was the sensation's source? When Gamma again concentrated on the playground scene, the sentiment pierced him again. Gamma struggled with the confusing feeling, one that seemed to attach more to the little brother than to Morgan. But that made no sense. Morgan's mind contained only her memories and sensations. No one else was present except . . . All at once, Gamma realized that the emotion had to be his own. The realization startled the Ori as he watched the genuine affection that Morgan held for the childlike figure of her memories. Gamma was jealous of a dream child. Not that Gamma wished to replace Morgan's memories of her little brother, but the Ori nonetheless grasped that he wished he could somehow participate in a relationship like that. It was outside his own experience, of course, since the dorm life of the Ori-2s was equal in every way – or at least it had been until the Sag priests had chosen Gamma and Beta to deliver the Iteration. But Gamma had sensed no envy from the other Oris when he became the Storyteller; instead, they had sung songs of support for his mission. Nevertheless, none of the Oris had experienced the love of an older sister for a younger sibling, and Gamma wondered if his own brothers would feel the same twinge of jealousy if they had been here to share the dream. Gamma resisted the sadness that began to descend on him as he observed the closeness of the pair before him. Instead, he focused again on the scene itself.

The image of the brother was, after all, only a dream, Gamma reminded himself, and so he decided to sing himself into the swing set to replace Morgan's brother. For a few exquisite seconds, Gamma basked in the affection that radiated from the woman, but then he felt her recoil at the change the dream was taking. Sadness threatened to overtake Gamma again as he recognized her reaction, but he resolved to make the dream work – both for Morgan and for himself. The Ori sang the dream-story into one that rinsed away Morgan's disappointment at her brother's disappearance, and then he affected some of the mannerisms of the child he had watched moments before from the edge of the playground. Gamma felt Morgan relax into his song, but he sensed her resist his suggestion to push him in the swing.

Perhaps they needed a space of their own, one not charged with these particular childhood memories. Gamma slid off the seat and took her by her hand, leading Morgan away from the playground. Should he take her to the lab? The Ori knew he should be focusing the song on the project Morgan did at work, but he also knew she had to trust him first. Perhaps it was a partial excuse, Gamma conceded to himself, but he was convinced he needed to win her over before he could inspire her change of heart about the lab project. As he scanned her memories, he discovered Morgan had a sweet tooth, a fondness for . . . ice cream cones?

"Let's get ice cream cones," Gamma announced to her, and allowed the playground to dissolve into another scene from Morgan's hometown. He sang the dream into a story in which they were standing in line at a place she called the Dairy King, and he listened as Morgan described why chocolate was the best flavor.

He let her order them each a double scoop, and then they went outside to sit on stone benches beneath the shade of a giant elm tree. Gamma knew from her memories that the Norwegian emigrants of the town had planted that tree – along with hundreds of others – a century before to make the deforested, grassy plains of their new homeland feel more like their native soil. Morgan had grown up in this town, however, and it was home to her just the way it was. As a result, he couldn't plumb memories that explained her family's homesickness, but he wondered if it was anything like Theta's sorrow at the loss of the world he had known before the plagues. Gamma suspected the feelings would be similar.

Then he allowed himself to feel through Morgan how the muggy air would collect under their arms and drip down their sides. Where the edge of the bench creased into his thighs, he savored the way the flat cool stone contrasted with the summer heat. The pleasure of an involuntary shiver rippled through him as he imitated Morgan, licking at the soft, textured chocolate that perched atop the cone in his hand.

As he studied the way the ice cream changed shape with each lick, Gamma found himself wondering why anyone with a childhood home like this could be sad. Even Morgan's home in Colorado was a wonderful world. Yet Morgan was an unhappy person.

He looked up at her and asked, "What would make you happy?"

Morgan didn't even pause. "The man I love."

Grant. That was the name of the man that hovered in Morgan's thoughts, and Gamma stretched deeper into her mind to call up his image even as her dream-self continued to lick at her ice cream. Her vision of him was very detailed – although he had no blemishes of any kind. He was tall, broad-shouldered, and wore collar-length hair, but he was more like an idealized sim-rendered figure, Gamma observed, one who lacked the individualizing characteristics of a real person. Her attachment to this Grant was clear, but he couldn't tell that any of her interactions with him had brought her happiness. But then, he could see that this adult relationship was complex – too complex to compare with his own limited range of human interactions.

Gamma wished he could do something to bring her more joy, but he knew that this idealized Grant was out of reach – unless Gamma deviated from his mission even further than he already had. What if he sang into Grant's mind as well? No, Theta would never approve. In fact, Theta wouldn't approve of what Gamma was doing now. Gamma knew he couldn't make Grant return her affection – and clearly, despite her insistence to the contrary, Morgan knew deep down that he hadn't. But if Gamma couldn't control Grant, maybe the Ori could help her in other ways. That would take time, a series of songs that helped Morgan develop a different sense of self. But if he inserted such a song now and then, Gamma couldn't see how it would affect his mission on behalf of the Sagittarians.

Morgan reached over with her napkin and blotted away some of the ice cream that had smeared onto Gamma's chin. The action surprised the Ori because it wasn't part of the song he was now singing. Morgan had rewritten Gamma's storytelling to add a touch of her own, an act of friendship. Gamma's song-self beamed up at the dreaming woman. At the same time, he felt a wave of understanding for the way other people could affect one's sense of contentment. He knew he had a strong attachment for Theta, and Gamma saw how easy it would be to form a similar attachment for Morgan. Yet Morgan's search for happiness through others didn't bring her fulfillment in the same way it did Gamma.

That much was clear.

Yes, Gamma decided, he would sing into her mind a song that made her less dependent on others in her personal search for happiness. Just as he had made Theta's body whole, Gamma would try to heal the ailing psyche of his new friend.

Theta-Sag

As Theta sat in the circle of the council, he watched the others debate the direction the on-going iterations should take. In the two weeks that had passed since the first translation, the Sag priests had met a total of five times to consider the consequences of their actions. Of course, Alpha had continued to poison the discussions with innuendo. At every opportunity, he dropped the usual hints. "The Order, if it survives the iterations, ...," his observations would begin, or "Should we still possess any influence when this is done, we will have to consider ..." But Theta was dismayed at the high priest's success in undermining the whole endeavor in the eyes of the other Sagittarians. Even more, Theta thought he could detect the resolve of the Sag priests slipping away. They seemed to have lost their nerve. Were they so willing to accept defeat and let the nanos rule their world? Since none of Gamma's translations had produced an effect they could measure, Alpha had begun to insinuate that the project had failed. And the change of strategy seemed to taunt Theta. It was as though the high priest were daring the Ori mentor to play his final trump, and Alpha knew – he had to – how reticent Theta was to endanger his relationship with Gamma.

But in the gathering with the other Sagittarians, Theta dared not mention his own concerns. For one thing, Alpha would be quick to twist to his advantage anything that Theta said to suggest Gamma's developing sympathy for the woman. Not that Gamma had shared this compassion in so many words, but it was evident to Theta from the Ori's timid attempts to defend her, especially when Gamma insisted that she was a good person at heart. Was it a flaw in the design of the Oris? Theta thought not. In fact, it was a trait that made them superior to the first generation of Oris. The Sag geneticists had generated the Ori-2 clones to be more sensitive so that they could be controlled – no, Theta told himself, be honest – so they could be manipulated. That had been the mistake with the Ori-1s, who were more predictable but also less willing to follow the bidding of the Order once they had reached maturity. How typical of scientists to create a generation of clones in their own rational image. But if the Ori-1s were rational, they were also somehow soulless, beings whom the Sag priests had to convince of the project goals through skillful reasoning. Except the Sag priests had begun to suspect that the Ori-1s were forming heretical conclusions. Theta still shuddered at the decision to … phase them out.

What if the Ori-2s also proved unsuited for the project? Theta couldn't bear the thought of their fate if that turned out to be true – not again. No, the Ori-2s would succeed. But Theta had to proceed with care in how he presented Gamma's improvisations to the council. At the same time, he had to figure out a way to assure himself that he still had control of Gamma's actions.

The test with the council came sooner than Theta expected when Alpha challenged the Ori mentor only two weeks after the iterations had begun.

"Why is he so obsessed with birds?" Alpha asked once the rhythm of the discussions in the council had reached a momentary pause.

The puzzled look from the other Sagittarians made it apparent that no one had even considered the question – not yet. Theta was sure the high priest would use the example to show how unpredictable the Oris were. It was a response that Theta had considered himself. And before Alpha could press the issue, Theta attempted to answer the challenge as best he could.

"Surely you had your own fascinations as a child," Theta responded. "Or is that memory too distant in your own past?"

The quip drew a chuckle from several members of the council, and Theta sensed he had the opportunity to disarm the seeds of suspicion Alpha was trying to sow among the other Sagittarians.

"I can remember as a child myself," Theta continued, "being fascinated by dinosaurs. I read about them, I pleaded with my parents to buy me models of the creatures, I obsessed over them like any child at the time. The very fact that dinosaurs had lived in the distant past helped kindle my interest in a by-gone era. And the result was that I turned to science when I became older."

"But the Ori won't grow older – not in the way you have," Alpha countered.

The seat Theta occupied at the table positioned the two of them on opposite sides, and the Sag priests who encircled them turned their heads first to one and then to the other during the verbal exchanges. Theta couldn't help envisioning the scene as a kind of competition between the two Sag opponents, a duel where the other Sagittarians served as spectators, waiting to see who would win. But he doubted that few at the table understood how high the stakes were.

"That's beside the point," Theta said. "The Ori is at a stage of maturity where we would expect to see him interested in a world that existed before he was born."

"Before he was generated, you mean," Alpha corrected him.

It was a slip Theta regretted at once. It betrayed just how much he had begun to think of Gamma as a creature rather than a creation. Theta hastened to make his point, hoping the others wouldn't read as much into Theta's words as Alpha had. "Of course, that's what I mean. But it's his interest in the past that demonstrates how much he's come to appreciate the world we hope to restore through these iterations."

"I'm still uncomfortable with the way he's improvising his

stories." Alpha persisted.

"But we designed the Ori-2s to improvise. That's what makes them effective."

At first, Theta was pleased to see how Gamma had improvised much of the delivery of the storytelling. The Ori was quick to incorporate cherished landscapes he had detected from the woman's own childhood. How typical, Theta mused to himself, that Gamma would select scenes filled with water fowl whenever he could. And the Ori had altered his own image so the woman perceived him in a way that reminded her of the little brother from her childhood – a somehow painful memory that Gamma had finessed into an advantage. Transforming his own image was a nuance that showed just how skilful Gamma was becoming. At the same time, some of his improvisations had seemed too impulsive. Showing her the translation craft had done more harm than good, and the woman had, for a time, become less receptive to him. In fact, Gamma had lost control in that instance as she recoiled at the sight of the craft. Still, it was a lesson Gamma had taken to heart. And to be fair, the Order had taken decades to develop the technology that made translations possible, and their experiments along the way had experienced setbacks of their own from time to time. Theta maintained that the Sagittarians owed Gamma the latitude to feel his way into the best approach.

What bothered Theta more was the way Gamma's iterations had taken a turn that seemed more concerned with developing his relationship with Morgan Johanssen and less with changing the trajectory of her actions. Theta had been patient. After all, the Ori had now become the only one who knew what the moment required. And who was to say that engendering this relationship hadn't increased Gamma's ability to influence the woman's mind? Yet Theta recognized that the rapport could prove dangerous to the Sag's own ability to control the Ori.

Alpha slammed the flat of his palm on the table and

shouted, "But nothing is changing. Perhaps the Laws of Paradox can't be broken and we're wasting our time."

"We don't know that."

"No, we don't." The high priest lowered his voice. "But I suggest that it may be time for the Ori to increase the intensity of his iteration." Nods of approval rippled around the table on the faces of the other Sagittarians. "Will he do that for you?"

"I think it's premature to – "

"Will he do it?"

Theta didn't know. But instead he said, "Of course, he will. But the woman's mind must be ready. Otherwise, the desired trajectory of the strange attractor will be less certain. It's Gamma who must determine the right moment."

"I disagree. The project is ours and the Ori is our tool for expressing it. Nothing more."

It was Epsilon, Beta's mentor, who spoke up. "Alpha Sag, it's true that we mustn't let the Ori control the project, but we must trust Theta to guide the Ori. He's the mentor and is the best judge in determining when to ask Gamma to intensify the story."

Alpha had made his point to the others, it was clear, and he conceded, "For the time being."

When the council adjourned, the Sag priests began to file from the hall. Theta could feel the ice of Alpha's stare on him as the Sagittarians broke into smaller groups, their tangential conversations trailing into the corridor, whispered echoes punctuated by an occasional chuckle as the Sag priests debriefed or added their own informal comments to the outcome of the meeting. Theta was still locked in the horns of his dilemma, so much so that he realized he was still sitting in his chair. As he listened to the receding cacophony of voices, Theta knew he would have to seek out key individuals on the council and try to persuade them to remain loyal to the project. Through the entire council deliberations, Lambda

Sag, for one, had remained silent – not a promising sign. As the council's habitual voice of reason, Lambda often pronounced the final word whenever the gathering became deadlocked. By force of habit, the others tended to acquiesce to his logic. That he had said little suggested to Theta that the venerable Lambda was having second thoughts. Theta suspected Alpha would appeal to him separately, and Theta knew it would be foolish not to do the same.

The Ori mentor felt a hand on his shoulder. Startled from his private thoughts, Theta looked up to see Epsilon standing beside him.

"You look like a man trapped in the gravity well of his own thoughts."

The voice was kind, and Theta recognized the overture as an opportunity to unburden himself. It was tempting. After all, Beta's mentor shared the same enthusiasm for the translation project as Theta did. Yet Epsilon Sag's role was different because Beta's role was different. Theta wondered how much Epsilon knew – or had guessed. Since the two Oris were so close, Theta assumed that Gamma had shared most of the storytelling experience with his clone brother. But had Beta also told Epsilon? Theta decided that he couldn't risk exposing his own weakening control on Gamma if Epsilon didn't already know.

Theta smiled up at Epsilon, although it was a weaker gesture than he had intended, as he determined to hide his real concerns. Instead, he voiced a complaint that he and Epsilon had often shared before. "I thought we were past all this. It seems like such a waste of our energy to revisit the merits of a project we've begun."

"It's the scientific method. Everything is falsifiable until proven otherwise." Epsilon's comment was a permutation of the habitual litany and response of their recurring conversations.

Theta shook his head in slow sweeps from side to side. "In this case, I almost wish we were more than nominal priests. We could use another magnitude of faith in our own ideas."

"It's not over. And besides, you won today." Epsilon seemed to have accepted that Theta was unwilling to share more than the typical topics of their banter, and Beta's mentor retreated from the hall to leave Theta alone.

Today, yes, Theta mused. Not that he doubted his own ability to engage in the council intrigues needed to keep the project alive for the time being. But Theta realized the council's patience would outlast the real challenge he faced. Was it already too late to ask Gamma to intensify the storytelling? The young Ori knew the consequences; that was apparent. Each time Theta looked into Gamma's face, he saw the remorse the Ori felt about the role he had played – unwitting as it was – in Theta's eventual fate. The doctors had told Theta that Gamma's first guided story into Theta's mind had produced a change in the mentor's brain chemistry that would lead to insanity. Perhaps not in the near future, of course, but eventually – and irreversibly. Theta wasn't sure how Gamma had learned the truth; in the days following his collapse, Theta had only vague recollections of what had happened. Maybe Gamma had overheard the doctors talking. Perhaps he had sensed the changes through some direct interaction with his mentor's mind as the Ori had sung Theta back to physical recovery. The event had made them closer – had, in fact, given the Ori a stronger loyalty to his mentor. But was it enough for Theta to ask him to repeat the process with direct intent? With each translation, Theta could see his pupil forming a stronger attachment for the woman.

Yes, time was running out, and Theta could only hope that Gamma would take the final step. After all, it was their only chance to reiterate the past for the sake of the future – a future endangered by the falling numbers of humans left each time the plague reasserted itself.

Theta rose from his chair and walked from the council hall, but with each step he felt the burden of the present weighing him down. He lifted his chest against the weight and made his way down the corridor. It was time to talk to Gamma.

CHAPTER SIX

Morgan

The face that stared out from the computer screen annoyed Morgan. Her features were a little too perfect and her hair a little too blond. But what was worse, each time Grant shifted his head or changed his expression, the face on the monitor did the same.

"Why does she do that?" Morgan asked as she looked over Grant's shoulder.

"What?"

"Mimic you."

Grant smiled. "Affective computing. It's the latest thing." He pointed to a small lens that perched atop the monitor's case. "That's a Web cam, and it's cueing Brittany to follow my every facial cue."

Brittany. Ugh. Morgan found the whole thing a little creepy as she watched him purse his lips into a kiss. At the same time, "Brittany" returned the favor.

"But what's the point?"

As Grant turned his head sideways toward Morgan, Brittany turned hers as well, as though she were carrying on her own conversation with a jealous companion – an electronic one, Morgan assumed. *And keep it that way.* It was irrational, but she was thankful that computers couldn't mix with flesh and blood.

Grant continued, "It's the latest step in making computers more sensitive to humans."

"But it's just mimicry." Morgan tried to hide her irritation. After all, why should she be jealous of a screen full of pixels?

"For now, yes, but someday computers will be more intuitive."

She could tell from his face that her own must have shown the skepticism she was using to hide her true feelings. But they had more important things to talk about.

"Let's get back to the simulation," Morgan said. Before Brittany had filled the screen, the computer monitor had displayed a series of random squares that began to flash on and off, but soon they formed a mosaic that covered the screen in aperiodic but repeating patterns. It seemed to have little to do with viral models so far as Morgan could tell. "I don't see the connection."

Grant shrugged. "That's because you're focusing on biology as a dance between biochemical and behavioral activities. When the normal virus invades the environment of the cell, it's in familiar territory – a programming that's already built into its genetics."

"That's what viruses do." Morgan was pleased to see that she could separate Grant as a love interest from the computer modeler who sat before her. Even though she could feel warmth radiate up from his torso as she leaned over him to point at a pattern on the screen, the project leader in her took over as they perched before the monitor. Years of professional concentration had taught her to disengage her brain from her body when she faced a problem, and – at least for the time being – her training kicked in. "But I don't see anything here that shows me how the virus will react to a real population."

"But that's precisely what you're seeing. Look, genes are a self-regulating network, right?"

She nodded in two curt jerks. He might be cute, but she didn't need a lesson in genetics from him.

"And each cell has the same set of genes, regardless of specialization," he added.

Oh course, they did. All the cells of the body – neurons, muscle cells, bone cells, whatever – they all contained the same code, but cell differentiation depended on different patterns of genetic activity. It was as though neighboring cells influenced which genes turned on in the cell next door. In a sense, everybody on the block wanted to look alike, and so the biochemical activity in the neighborhood gave rise to colonies of cell-types that produced muscle in one community and bone in another. What molecular biology was still trying to figure out was how everybody got their heads together to figure out what kind of community the neighborhood had decided to build. All they could say for sure was that self-organization seemed to be an innate property of biological systems.

"What I've done," Grant continued, "is to create a computer model that strips away your virus's personality. All that's left is a self-regulating system that switches on and off according to the criteria that Conti gave me a few months back." A cloud crossed his face. "Before he told me that the project was back-burnered."

Morgan ignored his darkening face as she tapped on the surface of the monitor. "So you're saying these pixels represent the behavior of the gene sequences that Conti could insert in my virus project?"

"Un-huh. That's my guess. But I won't know until you show me what you've done, of course."

Maybe it was Morgan's insecurity surfacing, but she was still having a hard time sharing with Grant everything she had done. She told herself it was loyalty to Conti that kept her lips sealed, but at some deeper level, she couldn't deny that she was afraid there'd be no reason to continue meeting with Grant if it turned out they'd each been working on unrelated projects. *Was that screwed up, or what?* she confessed to herself. Still, if the two projects were connected, it would make Morgan's job easier to finish. A few clues from Grant about how to queue the transgenics code and the sequencing would advance a lot faster. Which brought up her other dilemma: A self-regulating viral vaccine would also hold the key to a biological weapon since, locked in its code, was the potential of becoming its own enemy. She hadn't devised a trigger that could make the vaccine its opposite, but she knew she could have. Morgan wondered if someone else in the project's history had provided that set of genes already, and Conti was waiting for Morgan to deliver the goods so he could insert those additional genes in her RNA code.

Grant's Brittany screensaver took over the monitor, and he tapped on the keyboard to bring the simulation back to view. "Are you still with me?"

"Yeah, go on."

"Think of your super virus as the carrier. I'm assuming that's a given, so I've taken it out of the equation. What's left is the effects of the gene content." He continued to type. "I'm color-coding that content so you can get a better idea of what I mean. Now, watch this."

Morgan looked on as random red and white blocks flashed on different parts of the screen. Every once in a while, a red pair would flash at the same time when they were next to each other. When that happened, they remained on the monitor while other random firings of white and red continued to appear and disappear. But she noticed that when a white block landed next to the red pair, it also turned red and the cluster enlarged. Firings continued across the screen as other red pairings began to stick, and every time a white flash connected with the established red pairings, the same thing occurred – the clusters enlarged. Within seconds, the clusters began to grow, expanding at an exponential rate until the screen glowed a solid red.

Grant sat back and looked up at Morgan. "Do you get it now?"

Collapsing onto the chair he'd pulled up next to his own, Morgan let out a slow breath. "I'm assuming the white blocks –"

"– are any other activities going on at the same time. It doesn't really matter. Think of it as any competing function."

"Like the flu or the common cold?" She tried to make her example sound casual but, of course, this was the precise competing function she had programmed her virus to assault.

"Whatever your RNA is coded to attack. You tell me."

"And this is what your gene-sequence model was designed to do?" She tapped on the monitor screen, hoping she'd misread the computer modeling. But it seemed unlikely.

"In no time at all, you'll have –"

"– a pandemic." Morgan supplied the only word that fit. A total saturation of the virus throughout the population. Crowd diseases were a topic that had always sent shivers up her spine. The relationship of humans with microbes was ancient, of course. But in much earlier eras, the world's more isolated centers of population had tended to keep things in check. It had taken a new trade route to China to bring the Black Death to Europe and colonization in the New World to depopulate two continents with the small-pox microbe.

"And didn't you say you're making your virus trans-species?"

Morgan decided it was time to come clean. She needed an ally, and Grant at least understood what was at stake. "Yeah, but it gets worse. It'll cross all animal species."

Viruses tended to adapt to new hosts at a surprising evolutionary rate. Under nature's normal rules, however, the process restricted viruses and made them limited opportunists. Rarely did germs wreak havoc beyond the new species they had just invaded. But a nasty virus that could open its own doors between the walls that separated all species was a Pandora's Box that made Morgan cringe. She had devised a way for the virus to cross species while Grant had provided behavioral models that made the germ aggressive. As she thought about it, combining their contributions made the two of them candidates for crimes against humanity, not joint recipients of a Nobel Prize.

Grant let out a long whistle. "Wow, Morgan. No wonder Conti put you in charge."

You betcha, Conti's whiz-kid. But didn't Grant get it? This was dangerous stuff they were playing around with, yet she couldn't detect any sarcasm in his voice. However, Morgan felt free to dish up a heaping helping of guilt all on her own. At the same time she found Grant's nonchalance unfathomable, Morgan was also at a total loss to explain why her boss would undertake such a dangerous project. The specter of Conti's mental instability hovered over her growing fear, and she felt an involuntary shudder ripple through her body at the idea that she might be working for a madman after all.

Grant interrupted her thoughts as he said, "So what we have here is a virus that will permeate all animal life."

"Un-huh, and within weeks – maybe months."

"No, weeks is more like it. That's what the model suggests if this is trans-species. Infected people from the 1991 Peruvian outbreak of cholera spread their microbe to other parts of the world in less than a day."

Morgan could feel her eyes growing wide.

"Courtesy of intercontinental airlines. So what's your prognosis for this little bug? What happens when it hits all its ports of call?"

She scrunched up her nose. "Nothing. At least, not for a while. It's a slow virus, so it could just sit there for years, waiting for a trigger to activate it."

Grant tried to sit straighter in his chair but had to grab the arms to pull himself upright. "And what's the trigger?"

"I have no idea. It could be in the code already."

Grant eyed her with skepticism. "You don't know?"

"The RNA includes genes I don't recognize, but that's not unusual."

"And you didn't get rid of it."

Morgan shrugged. "Lots of RNA code has deactivated or sleeping gene switches. Life is full of left-overs at the genetic level, and tampering or deleting those genes can slow down a project since you don't know if a dormant code supports some later function."

"So the trigger could be in there already and waiting for . . . ?"

"The right conditions, I suppose." But that wasn't right, and she corrected herself. "Or else Conti's invasion."

"Whatever that is," Grant offered.

But Morgan had a pretty good idea. How had she missed it? Yet the real issue to her was why she had continued to work on a robust virus project with obvious ties to military interests. She swallowed hard, realizing that the work had gone far enough that, with her notes and the clones of the latest virus batch, anyone could stumble on the final solution. As she pushed her chair back and stared at Grant, she decided there was a better-than-average chance that Grant's work had led to some of the dormant RNA code she had left in the sequence. But there was no way for her to know which part of the sequence was his without extensive testing. No, years of testing. Of course, she could stall, but not for long if the testing she ordered didn't further the project. All geneticists allowed "junk" to remain in transgenic codes for fear of deactivating a sleeping gene switch that was necessary for the overall functions. Still, she could redirect some of the research to explore dead ends. Without Grant's help, she might have done that anyway. But now, with a clearer idea of the path that lay in front of her – and the path looked pretty certain after seeing Grant's model – at least she might be able to buy herself some time. Morgan knew that the only real solution was to confront the white-haired alpha wolf himself, and in the process to put to bed her fears. Or else confirm them. Yet she still wanted to run a test batch to see if Grant's model would perform on actual lab cultures the way it did on a computer's parallel-processor. She'd have to figure out a way to stall Conti a few more days. But her best defense was an offense, Morgan knew. Better to go straight to Conti and propose some sort of diversion that would buy her a week or two while she decided what to do.

Morgan thanked Grant for the demonstration and, as she slipped out his door, mustered the sudden boldness to blow him a kiss of thanks. She tried to make it look casual, but would he guess how much intention lay behind the gesture?

"We'll talk later," she promised, and ducked out the door before he could respond. She felt confused by how attentive he had become. Not that she wasn't happy to find herself the object of his devotion for a change. Well, maybe devotion was a bit strong, at least for the time being. She admitted to herself that she had used the carrot of the project to entice him, but she was sure there was starting to be something going on between them. More than once she had caught him staring at her, and each time he would pretend to look away as though something else had captured his attention. The irony is that his behavior seemed to describe the same strategy she'd used when he'd caught her doing the same thing back on the Merck project eight months earlier.

She strode down the hall, but the people she passed might as well have been transparent for no more than she heeded them. With each step, she began to refocus her thoughts on what she would say to Conti when she reached his suite. He'd already called three times that morning, leaving messages that he wanted an update. But Morgan felt she needed to see the computer simulation Grant had promised before she reported her progress to Conti. She'd hesitated to break the routine of clandestine rendezvous with Grant, but there hadn't been time with Conti breathing down her neck for the latest details. The alpha wolf had caught her in her office that morning, and she'd promised to brief him later that day. Conti had seemed – well, not frantic – but somehow urgent in his request that she gather what she had and bring him up to speed. But now that was the last thing that Morgan wanted to do.

She made her way through corridor that connected Grant's building to her own and then rounded the corner that led her to Conti's express elevator.

And stopped short.

Had she blurted out "Oh!" first? She'd been so wrapped up in how to approach Conti, Morgan wasn't sure. And it wasn't so much that Sandy was walking out of Conti's elevator as it was the expression on her face as the two of them recognized each other – that was what must have brought Morgan short, she decided. Sandy had the look of someone who had just been caught with her hand in the till, and Morgan could swear that she was the last person Sandy wanted as a witness just then.

Morgan began walking again, but it was too late, of course. Not that anything had passed between them in that instant – woman's intuition had never been one of Morgan's strong suits – yet Morgan sensed that this was going to be awkward.

Before Morgan could say anything, Sandy blurted out, "You're probably wondering why I was upstairs."

"No, not really," Morgan lied.

"I – uh – I just took Conti the updates he's been asking for. I had to tell him I couldn't find you, and he asked me to deliver them. I hope that's all right."

Morgan couldn't bring herself to look sympathetic. Of

course, it wasn't all right. Morgan had held off seeing Conti because she wasn't sure she wanted to show him all the reports, not yet. But now he had them, and he'd know where they stood. There would be no way to bluff much of a delay now. She offered Sandy a tight smile and said, "He's the boss, right?"

"That's the rumor I keep hearing."

It seemed like an odd thing to say, and Morgan only stared at her.

Then Sandy said, "Yeah, well, I better get back to the lab." She hesitated, and then added, "You coming?"

"No. I'd better get up there and see if he has any questions." Morgan turned to press her finger into the pad that gave her clearance. Had she turned away too abruptly? She listened to Sandy's hurried steps recede down the hall toward the lab. Then Morgan stepped into the elevator car piped out a low, slow breath. How was she going to buy herself time now? Maybe she could convince Conti that Sandy had brought up the working notes, prelims that couldn't be trusted. She mulled over the portions of the report that she might point to as preliminary, or too unofficial to take for evidence of success. It might just work.

As she pressed the button and felt the elevator ascend, Morgan realized she didn't know how long she'd been standing inside the car puzzling over the strategy she would use when she reached Conti's suite. When the elevator came to a stop and the doors opened, she stepped out to catch sight of him placing the handset back down onto the phone's cradle. He leaned back in the chair behind his desk, the other hand holding a sheaf of reports – her reports.

"Elsa, you've been a busy girl." His voice sounded distant, preoccupied.

Elsa. Conti had called her by that name before on occasion, and Morgan suspected it was someone from his past, maybe someone related to an earlier phase of the project. There seemed to be some association between this Elsa and herself. Elsa was a good Minnesota name, and Morgan was from Minnesota, so maybe it was nothing. She doubted he had noticed his slip of the tongue, and she didn't correct him.

But he'd also called her a "busy girl," and Morgan's first response was to wonder if she had a guilty look on her face. All her life she'd had trouble lying, and she'd always suspected people could read her thoughts – or, at least, the guilt – tattooed across her forehead whenever she had found herself in a position with something to hide. She studied Conti while she considered how to respond.

"It's not what you think," she blurted out as she strode across the room toward the desk. *Oh no, that's not how I wanted to start out.* She wondered how he took her words, and she conceded to herself that it was a weak denial to offer regardless of the intent of his words. But how much did he know?

A frown spread across his face. "What do you mean?"

She decided to play it safe – as best as she could. "The reports, they're not what you think. I haven't had a chance to codify them, and they're too rough for you to look –"

"They're fine, as is." Conti cocked his head to one side and looked up at her as she approached the desk, ignoring her hands as they reached out to take back the sheets. Instead, he dropped them in an open drawer. "Doesn't matter, as it turns out."

"It doesn't?" Morgan stopped in mid step.

"No. It seems I'm going to have to … backburner this project for a while."

Backburner, the same words Grant had used to describe his own exclusion from the project. Morgan felt her solar plexus begin to tighten into a knot. "You – you can't."

And what would be the plan for Conti's Baby now? At that moment, she realized maybe she didn't know the man before her after all. What had happened to her boss, her mentor? Perhaps she'd misinterpreted his erratic behavior. She'd thought he was losing it, but now she wasn't so sure. It was possible there was more method than madness to the man, and she'd not been able to read the signs for what they were. She only knew that if there was some hidden agenda at work here, she had to find out what it was. Morgan's mind raced, searching for a tactic that would keep Conti from shutting her out of the project. She had to know for sure that her own contribution wasn't going to end up as an element in some military invasion scenario.

"You've been working overtime on this for too long anyway," Conti continued. "And don't think I don't appreciate it. I have plans for you, Morgan. You know, I'm not always going to be around."

She sank into the chair opposite Conti as her legs gave out. *What was going on?* "I don't understand."

"You will."

"But the project."

"You know how these things work. Sometimes what we do gets a green light, and other times our work goes on hold. This one is going to have to wait." As he shoved the drawer holding the reports closed, he added, "Oh, I've taken the liberty of arranging to collect the project material."

"But I've still got to —"

"Morgan, let it go. You've been pushing yourself too hard. Besides, I want you to take some time off. Not too long, but a few days, and then I want you to get ready to ..."

But she didn't hear the rest of what he said. An invisible vortex began to churn between her and the words he spoke. She could see him talking, but his words disappeared into the swirl of her own coursing thoughts. How was she going to find out what would happen to Conti's Baby?

She hardly realized she was on her feet again as Conti walked her to the elevator door.

"It's not your fault, Morgan. You've done all you can." Grant was rubbing her shoulders as she sipped on white wine. Against her will, Morgan's tight muscles began to yield to the kneading action of his fingers.

Even though he had spent two hours trying to talk her down, she still had trouble letting it go. At last, he had seemed to switch tactics, letting his hands work where language had failed. He'd gone into the bedroom and returned with a bottle of lotion, commanding her to sit on the sofa while he poured the oil into his palms. Now her head bent forward against the pressure of his fingers on her neck as she gazed out the floor-length windows of Grant's penthouse apartment. She let her eyes fall on the street lamps that marked the grid of downtown Denver spreading out before her. Further to the west, traffic on the interstate moved at a steady pace, and she found herself envying the vehicles' passengers. She suspected many of them were on their way to dinner, a stop at the mall, a late-evening movie – one of the many recreational rhythms of city life. But none of the conversations taking place in those vehicles, she was sure, focused on a sleeping virus that could one day threaten all living things. She and Grant were the only ones who carried that secret, and the burden of that knowledge made her body feel heavy, listless. Or maybe it was Grant's hands as they massaged her neck and shoulders. Beyond the city, Morgan could make out stationary lights above what should have been the horizon. *Homes up in the mountains*, she mused, realizing that Grant's window showcased the Front Range – something she hadn't bothered to notice earlier in the evening. But then, her focus had been much closer to home.

Morgan shook her head as her thoughts still clenched onto the events of the previous thirty-six hours. At the same time, Grant's fingers gripped her turning head as if to say, "Stop that!" and Morgan obeyed, if only with the position of her neck. But her mind continued to replay what had happened. The previous day, soon after she'd left Conti's suite, Morgan had back-tracked to Grant's office. She hadn't remembered walking to his door, but she did recall the way Grant responded to what must have been the lost-little-girl look on her face. Without hesitation, Grant shut down his work station and ushered her away from Contitech, and they drove to a city park that hugged a small lake. They must have circled the ten-acre body of water twice as she vented about her exclusion from the project. When he insisted she come back to his place, Morgan didn't resist. And then he let her continue to talk on into the night. She'd left around three in the morning, ignoring Grant's entreaties that she could sleep at his apartment that night. He'd only let her leave on condition that she call and let him know she'd made it home all right. Morgan remembered that he had kissed her once, lightly, and stroked her cheek before she left his apartment and made her way back home. It was a side to Grant she hadn't expected. None of her fantasies about him anticipated this kind of tenderness. Although she hadn't felt any better about the project, she had to confess that Grant's continuous attention had given her hope there might be light at the end of the tunnel after all.

The following day, she had clocked into Contitech late in the morning – what else could she do? – and spent the rest of the day watching Sandy supervise the techs who packed and moved the virus samples from the lab. Only twice during the afternoon had Morgan said a word to her, and both times she'd had to stop herself from arguing with Sandy. The woman seemed to be having trouble making eye-contact with Morgan, and Morgan still suspected Sandy had had something to do with Conti's decision to end Morgan's involvement. Morgan migrated over to Grant's office again by late afternoon, and once again, he had suggested she come over to his place.

She was grateful for the company now, as she gazed out the window. Besides, there seemed to be no words left to say.

Morgan realized that he hadn't let her out of his sight for two evenings now, and she wondered why he had put up with her.

Grant reached over to grab the lotion from the table again. She was sitting on the floor in front of the sofa, her back pressing between his knees, and her upper torso leaned back into his legs as he angled and stretched for the bottle. When he sat upright again, Morgan looked over her shoulder and into his face.

He smiled and said, "The massage seems to be doing the trick."

"You've been really sweet to me these two nights." She set her wine glass on the table and twisted in her skirt, repositioning herself by letting her forearm rest on his upper leg. "I don't think I've mentioned how much I appreciate it."

Grant eased down off the sofa and sat next to her. "You just needed to get some perspective. Take your mind off your worries. Besides, there's nothing more you can do. Not right this minute."

Morgan felt a frown knit over her eyebrows. "I know, but there's got to be something I can –"

Grant pressed his forefinger to her lips as he shook his head. "Enough. How 'bout concentrating on us for a while?"

Then he moved his fingers along her face and brushed aside loose strands of her hair until they caught behind her ear. Morgan could feel the warmth of his body against her side as he slipped his hand to cup the back of her head, and then he pulled her toward him. He closed his eyes as their lips met, and soon Morgan closed hers. She could smell aftershave on his cheek and felt just the hint of stubble against his jaw. Her chest heaved as she felt his hand slide down her shoulder to caress her breast. It was what Morgan had dreamed of for months, this moment, but she found herself having to work at surrendering to Grant's foreplay. It was foreplay, she decided, and had been ever since he had begun to rub her neck and shoulders with lotion.

Flashes of the past two days still competed for her attention, but she felt herself yielding to Grant's advances little by little. His hands were experienced, perhaps too much so, and Morgan felt a twinge of jealousy at the lovers he must have known before her. As he worked his hand down her hip to rest on her thigh, her breath quickened. And when his fingers slid up her skirt and between her legs, Morgan moaned as a wave of pleasure surged through her body. Grant was right, she decided, there was nothing she could do about the virus. Not right then. She surrendered to him, determined to push thoughts of work to the light of the next day.

On this, the third and final day of packing up the virus project, Morgan watched as Sandy busied herself collating and logging the last of the reports. Sandy had seemed to take charge while Morgan sat watching the workers dismantle the work she'd assembled for the past few months. But the woman had still scarcely looked Morgan in the eye for three days. Although it wasn't Morgan's nature to be suspicious, she just couldn't shake the feeling that Sandy had had something to do with Morgan's sudden dismissal from the project.

And Morgan was sure that the project would continue. The techs had removed the samples and packed up the apparatuses she had used – but not for storage. No, they were moving the operation elsewhere, she was sure, but Morgan could hardly follow them out to the vans and tail them to their intended destination. For one thing, Sandy – distant as she seemed – was never out of her sight. Or rather, Morgan was never out of hers.

Earlier that morning, Morgan had resolved to reopen the conversation with Conti. But when she arrived at his desk, he had waved his hand in a gesture that made it clear the subject was closed. Oh, he was amiable enough – and continued to tell her how appreciative he was of all her hard work – but he always changed the subject by asking her what she was going to do with her time off.

"You should get outside," he'd told her. "You're too pale for someone who lives in Colorado. Didn't you used to rock climb? I bet you haven't even walked all the trails out where you live."

It was true enough. When she'd bought her dream home, the realtor had pointed out the trail that led to the rock outcropping she used for rappelling. But Morgan knew that she hadn't used the area for recreation. Even when she'd taken breaks to climb or rappel, it was only to help her refocus on work. Hardly the kind of excursions she'd dreamed of when she bought her ranch house getaway.

She'd looked at Conti, not knowing how to respond. He'd never asked her to take time off before, and she suspected he just wanted her out of there until Conti's Baby was secure and underway, without the questions she was sure to ask. But he held all the cards. It was his lab, his proposed project, and he had every right to pull the plug and reassign her.

"Not until I see it all closed down," she'd told him. "After all, it was my responsibility. And if you change your mind …"

He steered the subject to the hiking boots she'd bought the summer before. She'd worn them to work for two weeks, trying to break them in. The techs under her had taken to calling them her "lab booties," which she took with a good-natured shrug. And she had planned to try them out on dirt – once she had the time.

Well, she had the time now. Morgan sighed as the last of the packages left the lab, portered out on the pneumatic wheels of dollies that were as soundless as the veil of silence that had dropped over the project. As she watched the men disappear out the door, she frowned. Ever since the move had started, she'd found herself bothered by something about the workers who carted off the materials – something she couldn't quite put her finger on. In Conti's typical fashion, he'd hired a firm from off-site to remove everything. Just like the cleaning service that tidied his private quarters at the lab. Lone Wolf Conti never seemed able to trust anyone, not quite. It was an idiosyncratic quirk that must have survived from his time in the military.

That's it. The military. She could feel the hair prickle at the nape of her neck as she realized what bothered her about the removal team. It was their close-cropped hair. Short hair was the style these days, of course, which had never appealed to Morgan. Maybe she was too much the product of a rock-music generation, but she'd always found men with long tresses to be the epitome of sexiness. In fact, she had to admit that it was Grant's just-down-to-the-collar hair that had first caught her eye – unusual in this day and age, and unique in a lab filled with scientists and techies who were only a pocket protector away from the stereotypical look. All of a sudden, Morgan couldn't help but grimace; Grant wore a protector in his shirt pocket. Thank goodness for the long hair. But the removal men had hair cropped short enough to blend into the ranks of the Air Force Academy in nearby Colorado Springs. Was she overreacting? She thought not.

She reached for the phone to call Grant but dropped the handset back down even before it cleared the cradle when she remembered that Sandy sat a mere ten feet away. She stood and headed out the door to walk over to Grant's office. Although Morgan had to admit she'd probably blown her "cover" days ago, the pretense seemed less important now than the need to share her suspicion with Grant. The hammer of her heels on the corridor's vinyl flooring beat a cadence that made her feel more confident with each step. It felt like she had found her resolve again and only needed Grant to back her up. She wanted somebody to tell her she wasn't paranoid, that they'd beat this thing yet.

She also wanted to reassure herself that the previous evening with Grant had meant something. To her surprise, their lovemaking hadn't turned out to be what she'd expected. Not the aftermath, anyway. Oh, the bells and sirens went off in her head all right. He was good at it, no doubt about that. But the intimacy didn't last, and Morgan couldn't say that it had brought her the sense of fulfillment she thought it would. Maybe she was still too obsessed with the project to give Grant his due. And maybe she was backing away from commitment; she knew that was a possibility. Lord knew she'd back-peddled out of other relationships when she'd gotten to know her partners better. But never this quickly. Had some sort of bubble popped when she wasn't paying attention? Sometimes Morgan thought she was still the kid who just had to have that new bike. She remembered begging her parents for months, telling them all about the touring sprockets it had to have and the handlebar gear changers. But when they at last presented it to her for her fourteenth birthday, she'd ridden the bike for only a couple of weeks before it lost its fascination. One day she'd parked it in the garage and had never taken it out for a spin again. Now a nagging voice at the back of her mind suggested that she wasn't as obsessed with Grant as she once was. A part of her hoped seeing him again this morning would rekindle what she seemed to have lost. As she approached his door, she hoped his physical presence would remind her why she'd kept the Secrets Box full of his mementos for the past eight months.

Without knocking, she grasped the door knob in mid stride but found herself collapsing against her own momentum when the door failed to yield. Morgan backed up a step and glanced down at her watch. One in the afternoon. When she'd talked to him two hours before, she'd proposed they meet for lunch, but he'd said he was tied up with a meeting and countered that they should get together for dinner again. Dinner and "dessert," his voice had implied. Yeah, she owed it to him to try the dessert part again. What was wrong with her? Then again, she couldn't understand the ease at which he'd coped with the sudden turn of affairs. Was she having trouble connecting with him because he didn't share her passion for the project?

"Sometimes you have to know when to lick your wounds," he'd said that morning. "You'll get used to it. Besides, what can you do?"

"We can find out where Conti's moving the project." At the time, Morgan had felt disconnect with him intensify when she'd reopened the subject after they'd gotten up.

His chest heaved as he said, "Morgan, I wanted this, too – more than you know. But I don't think it's a battle we're going to win. Give it up. Besides, it'll resurface. Mark my words."

Give it up. Those were the words that Conti had used, and she knew it made sense. But perhaps Grant was now too much on the periphery of the project. He'd had time to lick his wounds after his own experience with Conti's Baby; Morgan had not. And she wasn't ready to call it quits. For just a moment, she'd stared back at him, reminding herself that he didn't have to be there with her. The thought flashed in her mind that, if nothing else, he might turn out to be her consolation prize. She could do worse – she had – until they'd starting spending time together. Yet somehow, having Grant didn't seem that consoling. Even as she told him she understood what he was saying, she found herself working his rationalization back into a stance of defiance. It had gone on like that until it was time to go to work, and all the while, he'd let her ... rant. There was no other word to describe it.

Yeah, she was lucky he still wanted to meet with her again that night. Morgan was confused about her feelings for Grant – almost as much as she was about her disrupted status on the project. She stared in the direction of his locked door for several minutes as her mind roiled over what she could do until he returned. She needed to talk to him, and about more than just the project.

This is crazy, Morgan. Get a grip. She wheeled and started back toward her empty lab but stopped short just feet from Grant's door. Why return to the lab? The only thing waiting for her there was Sandy's awkward silence, and Morgan was in no mood for that. She decided she had too much nervous energy to burn off, and besides, she was afraid she'd say something she might live to regret when she went back to her empty lab.

On a sudden impulse, she turned instead and headed toward the nearest security exit. It would be six or seven hours before she met Grant. Lord knew she ought to use the time to do something that could improve the prospects for the evening.

Morgan sat on the concrete slab that served as the step to her front door. The edges of the slab were chipped and worn, grating against her calves as she tugged at the bootlaces. Even in midsummer, she knew the shade of the forest canopy could chill her legs if she stopped to rest along the way, but she was determined to wear shorts. *No more skirts for this gal*, she promised herself. *It's time to find a Morgan I can live with*. As she looped and tied the laces on the ankle-high boots, she glanced over at the forest path. The trail had seen little use since she'd moved into the old ranch house – well, except for "escape rappelling." She noticed for the first time how scattered shoots of grass struggled to cover the rocky lane that traveled into the trees. She stood and tested the boots, which pressed against the thick wool of her socks. The leather felt stiff – hardly broken in from the time she'd spent padding around the vinyl flooring of the research facility in her "lab booties."

Morgan raised a hand to shield her eyes from the afternoon sun and judged that she had at least three hours before she needed to head back into the city. Although she knew she was bound to come home with blisters on her heels, she decided to hike to the base of the ridge, two miles from the house. Starting up the gentle slope, she found herself stumbling at first on walnut-sized rocks underfoot. *That's all you need, Morgan. Twist your ankle out here and you'll have to crawl back on bloody knees.* She made more of an effort to watch where she placed her steps and soon found a rhythm that moved her forward with confidence.

Just like riding a bike – but without the wheels, she told herself, wondering all of a sudden if that childhood bike still sat in her parents' garage.

Soon after she entered the woods, she heard a cracking noise off to the side and glanced over her shoulder in time to see the tell-tale white rumps of two mule deer as they disappeared from view into a dense stand of Doug fir and scrub oak. The deer no doubt thought they had the woods to themselves, and Morgan was sorry she'd startled them. Not because she'd disturbed the pair but because it had been a long time since she'd seen anything that wasn't tethered or straining against a leash. As she settled into her hiking stride, she noticed that the earth all around her smelled of natural decay, and she realized how much she'd missed getting out. Too many long days and weekend shifts at the lab. She remembered when she'd first moved to the Front Range, she'd gone into the local REI store and watched while an instructor showed browsing shoppers some of the basic techniques for scaling an indoor climbing wall. The following weekend, she signed up for a class and soon made her first Colorado friends, twenty-something sisters named Julie and Joanie. The pair showed her the popular climbing haunts – Eldorado Canyon first off, and then some of the other nooks and climbing crannies west of Denver – but Morgan hadn't insisted on enough personal time to give her the mental beaks she had needed. Before long, Contitech had found ways to encumber most of her free days. Morgan wondered what had become of the sisters and made a mental note to call them sometime. She sighed as she walked around a fallen log blocking the trail. She noticed her chest heaving; maybe it was her shortness of breath. Yeah, she really had to start getting out more often – but for the right reasons.

Before Morgan knew it, though, the scenery drifted into

the background of her mind, replaced by her preoccupation with the events of the past few days. When she realized what she was doing, Morgan scolded herself, rationalizing that she'd have a clearer head – maybe even a plan – if she could put aside her worrying for a few hours and try to enjoy the hike. But it wasn't easy. Her mind kept bringing her back to Conti, the man she thought she knew. She had toiled away with the blindness of a worker drone, never comprehending the magnitude of the project. At least, not in time to stop it. She knew that the virus was ready for the final transgenic phase – she'd seen to that. And even a mediocre scientist could add the missing genes. Even Conti could do it. And she still suspected that the triggers were already in place, hiding in the switched-off junk genes that the RNA code harbored. That's what worried her most of all. With all the pieces in place, he could perform the finishing steps, and no one in the lab would be the wiser. What if Conti had already?

Morgan realized that the trees had begun to thin along the trail as she approached a clearing up ahead. She heard a creaking sound that repeated itself at regular intervals. She knew that sound, something she'd heard before but couldn't quite place. She quickened her pace as the noise became sharper, more distinct. Soon the trail carried her around a wall of tall, jumbled boulders, and a clearing opened before her. When she entered the clearing, she recognized the sound.

Of course, I should have known.

She stepped onto the neatly groomed plain of gravel. Everything was just as she remembered as she walked past the merry-go-round and slides and made her way over to the creaking chains on the swing.

"I'm amused," the little boy said. But as usual, his face remained somber. At the same time he spoke, the boy's feet dragged against the gravel until the swing came to a stop.

"I wondered when I'd see you again." What had it been, five-six nights? A week? But not all of his manifestation had brought the nightmare images in the past few weeks. Some had rekindled memories from her childhood that had made his presence a welcome sight. Like a tour guide who led her through the topography of happier times. Still, his appearance always filled her with a edginess, knowing that the lull could shatter at any moment and images of some future horror could intrude just as she let down her guard. *Why can't any of your relationships be simple, Morgan?*

Out of the corner of her eye, Morgan could swear she saw a white chicken strutting near the monkey bars on the other side of the playground. The only thing amiss was the grade school that should have stood beyond the scene, but instead blue spruce and aspen marked the edges on all sides.

She could almost hear Thornton's excitement – if she decided to tell him about the encounter. She knew the single reason the analyst had taken her case was because he hoped she could convince him that she had seen the little boy outside her dreams. In fact, he'd confessed as much – maybe during her fifth or sixth visit – but it had been a slip of the tongue in the glow of his talking about the manifestation of her archetypal child.

"Archetypes are common enough occurrences," he'd said, "but not accounts in the form of waking visions."

The doctor's eyes danced as he talked, and the animation in his voice overtook the normal reserve she'd come to expect.

"So, it's rare," she said.

"Very. But not without precedence, of course. Jung himself experienced archetypes through waking visions, so you're in good company."

Morgan had assumed the shrink was offering her some sort of compliment by suggesting her visions placed her in the same circle as his precious Jung, but she wasn't sure she liked the conditions for membership. Maybe she was the pass key he needed to publish an account in some arcane psych journal devoted to the rare and hopeless. But she wasn't interested in becoming his ticket; to see the child when she was awake had seemed unsettling back then. In fact, the idea that the archetype could manifest itself to her when she was awake – well, it sounded like she was becoming less capable of distinguishing fantasy from reality, and she'd told him so.

"Not at all, Morgan. Actually, it suggests that the meaning of the archetype is so important that the unconscious mind is willing to project it onto the screen of your normal life."

Yet there was nothing normal about it. The first time she'd seen Origami outside of a dream was when she was working in the lab late one night. Sandy had given up on her and left the hour before, but only after Morgan had promised to shut down as soon as she'd logged in the night's findings. She was placing the RNA samples back into containment when she saw the little boy standing beside her. The experience had so startled Morgan that she'd raced out of the lab suite and down the hall without a backwards glance. She found the night security guard on duty and reported a break-in. Somehow she didn't expect the guard to find anyone and, of course, he didn't. By the time she sat in the security office to fill out the paperwork, she'd decided to confess to no more than a shadow that might have been an intruder. What could she say, "I saw the little boy who comes to me in my dreams"?

But to Thornton she'd been more honest.

"Couldn't it have been a hallucination?" she had asked him.

Thornton offered a noncommittal shrug. "Call it what you will. The vision was still a projection you experienced in a waking state."

Yet in the sessions that followed, all subsequent accounts to the analyst could be explained away as dreams, and all of them had been when she was at home.

Until more recently.

And it didn't seem to matter anymore. Morgan was no

longer startled by his unexpected appearances. Sometimes she thought that Origami was a reminder that her biological clock was ticking, a symbol of a child her thirty-something body yearned for. That might explain the affinity she felt for him, and the way he seemed to know her innermost thoughts. Of course, there was also the way he reminded her of her little brother – she pushed that memory aside. Perhaps the little boy was just the force of her conscience, and she couldn't deny that many of the conversations with her little archetype focused on her work for Contitech. She had to admit he'd become a part of her life. If nothing else, the doctor had helped her come to terms with the idea that these manifestations were her way of talking to herself about problems she couldn't reveal to others because of the secrecy of the project. As an analyst he'd earned his keep, to Morgan's view, because he'd given her a way to view the little boy in a way that no longer made her feel like she was crazy.

She wasn't even surprised that he appeared before her now on a swing set – let alone that he did so in the middle of a mountain hiking trail. And she felt certain he was there to encourage her in her setback on the project.

Neither did she worry about the non sequiturs she was so accustomed to making in her workday conversations – something that drove all her co-workers to the brink. But that was their problem if they couldn't keep up. Origami, however, was different; he would follow the transition of her thoughts without the need to explain the link of one idea to the next. Like now, when she assumed he had come to remind her how she'd failed to stop Conti's Baby.

"I tried – you know that."

"But you can't give up. You have to find a way to stop it."

Morgan sank onto the gravel beside the swing, feeling the rocks radiate warmth onto her exposed legs. "I'm not sure there's much more I can do."

As she spoke, a finch fell lifeless to the ground, and then

another and another one.

"Stop that," she scolded and closed her eyes. "You know I hate seeing those things."

When she opened her eyes, the gravel plain was empty again except for the playground equipment. The boy leaned back into the seat and swiveled the seat around and around as the chain wound into a doubled strand that spiraled like a twist of recombinant DNA.

What did he expect her to do? It was too late. She didn't even know where Conti had moved the project.

"It's out of my hands," she said, a defensive tone lacing her lips. "There's nothing I can do about it now."

The boy leaned back in the swing seat at the same time he lifted his legs parallel to the ground. As the twisted chains began to unravel, he stared skywards. Each time his spinning head passed by her, he spoke in punctuated iambic phrases.

"You're wrong … you can … because … it's now."

The action looked playful even though Morgan recognized the intent was serious. But what he said didn't make any sense. *Maybe that's the point*, she thought. Thornton had told her archetypes operated on a non-rational level, unencumbered by inconsistencies in causal thinking. As a result, they sometimes offered solutions that were outside the rational mind's repertory, but it also meant that she might not get a straight answer.

Morgan realized she was standing next to the swing by herself. Where had he gone? She turned to survey the playground. Although she hadn't heard the crunch of his feet on the pebbles, the child now perched on the merry-go-round.

"Push me," he shouted. His voice echoed against the nearby cliffs that formed the base of the ridge just beyond the playground.

It was the same familiar request her brother used to make. Before she realized what she was doing, she stood up and walked over to comply. As she grasped the rungs and tugged the platform into motion, the little boy squealed his delight. She couldn't help but smile, watching his head lean out with the centrifugal force.

"Faster. Faster!" he shouted, and she shoved against the metal piping with a hand-over-hand motion that sped the boy's mechanical rotation. Watching the motion touched a deep memory, the time she had spun her Jonathon around so many times he couldn't walk afterwards. As the older child, she knew it was her job to be the responsible one, but she had watched as her brother staggered off the merry-go-round and dropped to the ground. Without warning, her brother's giggles had ceased. He clutched his stomach and rolled over on the ground, retching up the contents of a peanut butter and jelly sandwich.

She shuddered – *don't go there* – and let the rungs slap at her hands, bleeding the energy from the revolutions to bring the boy to a slower pace.

"See how easy it is to stop, only … ," he hesitated.

"Only what?"

"You won't be able to stop it for long. Not if you don't do something soon."

She didn't think they were talking about merry-go-rounds anymore, but she said nothing.

Then, to her horror, the platform began to revolve again of its own force; the speed of the twirling platform increased and the rungs stung her hands as she groped to grab hold. It was no use. All she could do was watch as the merry-go-round rotated with a gathering intensity. She noticed the wind whipping at her legs and listened to the sound of the straining platform as it gyrated. No, not the platform. The noise was more like the clacking of a freight train when the wheels glided along the joined sections of the tracks – a sound she knew too well. But not from the noise of a train. As the wind lashed at her eyes, she looked up into the vortex that was forming above the merry-go-round. All about her, the force of the wind gathered the ground's debris, which began to thrash around her. The noise became deadening, and the playground equipment started to shudder. Within moments, she watched as the swings and monkey bars tipped over. Swallows and blue jays struggled to flap free of the gale, but were caught in the invisible circle that inscribed her. Morgan bit at her fingertips, which she jammed into her mouth at the sight of the birds striking the toppled monkey bars. She felt more than heard their helpless thuds.

She turned away to focus on the center of the scene, where Origami's small hands clung to the spinning merry-go-round, his body stretched upward into the suction of the vortex.

"Oh no," Morgan said, or maybe mouthed with feeble lips, since she could no longer hear her own voice above the din of the wind's force.

The image of the helpless, suspended child struck her harder than any of the spinning debris. The scene was too close to that awful night of her childhood, the night the tornado had gripped the Minnesota landscape as she and her little brother had struggled across the backyard of their home. Morgan had been all right until she saw the terror in her mother's eyes, who motioned with frantic inward-turning waves to urge them across the void of the yard and to the safety of the cellar. Morgan was afraid to look behind her in the eerie green light that fell over her home, and she gripped her brother's hand as she pulled the two of them toward their mother's arms. She knew the clacking freight-train roar was overtaking them even as they reached the cellar's dark mouth, and she felt her mother's fingers tighten around her waist even as her little brother's hand pulled her arm upward. At first the motion confused her. Was her brother that far above her on the cellar steps? Morgan turned in time to see him slip from her own hand's grasp and into the suction of the vortex that was above them. She remembered that she had watched with a kind of detached fascination as he disappeared, feet first, up into the hollow tunnel of wind.

Her uncles were the first to find him, caught in the branches of an elm tree about a quarter-mile away. Even during her brother's funeral, she couldn't push aside the vision of his rag-doll body as the twister wrenched him from her life.

And now, in the middle of this impossible Colorado playground, tears flew off Morgan's face as she watched the vortex suck Origami's weightless body up into the funnel. This time she felt no detachment, no fascination; all she felt was despair. She sank against the wind and huddled on the ground, sobbing as she buried her head in her arms. She squeezed her eyes shut but she could still feel the thud of the birds that struck the toppled swings nearby.

She couldn't tell how long she sat knotted in the jumble of her legs and arms – or when the wind ceased to blow. But when she felt the pressure of the small hand as it touched her shoulder, she realized that the noise was gone. Everything was calm again.

"I hate you," she muttered, but she was so shaken that she knew her voice carried no conviction.

"No you don't."

Morgan sighed as she admitted to herself that it was true, she didn't hate him. Maybe he didn't look anything like her brother, but she couldn't deny that Origami reminded her of him. And she realized – *why is this such a revelation?* – that talking to her origami archetype had become a way to talk to a part of her past she'd lost. It wasn't an insight she'd shared with Thornton; in fact, she hadn't told him about her brother's death. At least, not yet, and maybe not ever. Some things were just too personal – even to talk about to your shrink. *Morgan, what a number you've done on yourself.*

Origami reached out and took her by the hand as she struggled to her feet. The slide and monkey bars stood once again untouched as he led her over to the swings.

When he slid into the swing seat, she asked, "Why did you do that?"

The boy seemed to ignore her question as he pushed his feet against the gravel, launching the seat into a pendulum of shallow arcs. "Do you want to push me?"

She hugged her arms against her chest. "No thanks, I've had enough surprises for one day."

"Maybe not." But before she could ask him what he meant, he continued, "You have to go. It's getting late."

She looked up and saw that the sun was already touching the edge of the ridge above her. When she looked back down, the playground was gone. She was standing alone, on the border of the clearing. In the fading light, she could just make out the indentation of the trail the led up ahead through the high-mountain meadow. But she had no intention of climbing deeper in the woods. Instead, she turned back toward home.

As she walked, she nodded to herself. And when she spoke aloud, she didn't know whether she was talking for her own benefit or for Origami. Then again, maybe it was the same thing.

"Late, but maybe not too late."

As Morgan approached the outskirts of Denver, she glanced over at the passenger seat. She was certain she'd left her wallet in the car, but she saw no sign of it. Unbuckling her seat belt, she scooted forward and reached across the console to work her right hand under the other seat. Nothing. She glanced up just as her Honda began to wander into the other lane and, with heart racing, she jerked the wheel to correct the vehicle's path. It took her several minutes before she had the courage to try again. Still she found no evidence of the wallet. Not that she really needed it for her rendezvous with Grant, but it bothered her that she'd misplaced the thing. Ever since she'd bought the wallet a couple of weeks earlier, she'd had trouble keeping up with it. So far, she'd left it in a restaurant, a gas station bathroom, and even on the top of her car. She was sure that the style was called a clutch, but it had eluded her grasp for most of the time she'd owned it. Maybe her behavior stemmed from the fact that it was new and she wasn't used to the "convenient" shape.

She'd gotten the thing to match the Short Red Dress, but she found herself about to relent and fish out the tattered old billfold she'd carried for years. Although she wanted to chalk up the new wallet's disappearance to the afternoon hike, she wasn't ready to let herself off the hook that easily. No, with the steady stream of misadventures she'd experienced with the elusive clutch, she had determined to keep it in the car and only take from it, as occasion warranted, what she needed. Only it wasn't in the car; that was clear.

Morgan tried to map out the day's events in her mind – at least, those that had occurred before she'd taken the hike – but she was coming up empty. She was sure she hadn't carried it into the house, and she wouldn't have carted it into the lab facilities unless … *Damn, it's in the lab.* Of course, it was. She swore to herself as she remembered she'd toted it with her because Security had wanted to "update" her ID card, and she'd decided to display it in the little window of her clutch so no one would see the card and ask her to cough it up – not just yet. It was color-coded for a clearance just under Conti's, and she wasn't anxious to surrender that access. Morgan had been stalling because she harbored a suspicion that Security's intention was to give her a downgrade. She hadn't attempted using her thumbprint access to Conti's elevator, fearing confirmation that she had lost her privileges. But the notice from Security had been her proof. No doubt a clandestine order from Conti. But nobody seemed willing to confirm the nature of the purported change unless she surrendered her card, and she'd noticed no one else had received a similar request so far as she could tell.

She'd have heard the grumbling, especially from Sandy – or maybe not from Sandy, given the pall that had descended on their conversations since Conti had swooped in to reclaim his Baby.

Yeah, she knew right where the clutch sat: in the center drawer in her work desk. And next to a sealed envelope she'd received during the day by internal mail service. It had her name on it, scrawled in Conti's handwriting, but she wasn't ready to open it. Hey, what she hadn't read couldn't stop her from doing her job, right?

She hadn't passed the exit to Contitech, so she changed into the outside lane and waited for the approach of the turn-off. It was already half-past six, and she knew she wasn't likely to see many people in her end of the facility, certainly not the security staff who'd wanted her to hand over her ID. By the time she parked the car and made her way into the complex, it was almost seven. She quickened her steps. The last thing she wanted was Grant to think she'd stood him up, and besides, they had some fresh scheming to do.

Morgan was startled to find the door to her lab suite open and the lights on. "Oh great," she muttered under her breath, "another cold-shouldered scene with Sandy." Maybe she could dash in and reclaim the infamous clutch before Sandy had a chance *not* to say anything. On second thought, Morgan decided she would force Sandy to speak. As she passed through the door she began to formulate something snappy to say. But to Morgan's surprise, the person before her was not her former co-worker.

The man whirled around and stammered, "I, uh, I thought everyone was gone."

Same short-cropped hair. Same nondescript uniform the men from the transport service wore as they claimed the contents of the RNA project. But Morgan didn't recognize this man. She noticed that he held a packed box in his hand as he fidgeted from side to side. He looked like he was ready to bolt past her, but Morgan had no intention of giving him that opportunity. If ever someone looked like he'd just been caught red-handed, it was this guy. Morgan decided to apply her best offense to his startled defense.

She mustered her strongest authoritative voice and demanded, "Who the hell are you, and what are you doing here?"

"They sent me over to retrieve a package we forgot." He began to work his way around Morgan, but she blocked his maneuver.

"It's after hours. You'll have to come back tomorrow."

"No," he said, but it was so quick on the heels of her words that she knew he was uncertain what to do. "I have to retrieve this final package."

If he was military, she knew from watching Conti in action that this guy would be easy to intimidate.

"I don't think so," she said as she walked over and wrested the box from his hands. Then she walked around the desk and set the package between them, but kept her hand on top of it. *Let's keep the carrot almost within reach.*

"But I have orders."

When she heard the pleading in his voice, she knew she had him. "Not without some authorization."

"But we just forgot to get this one," he said as he eyed the package. "And it's already been signed out."

"Apparently not, if it's still here."

"Look, it was just a simple mistake. If I don't get this into transit, there'll be hell to pay."

Morgan kept her gaze steady and cool and decided it was time to play the petty bureaucrat. "There's a protocol to follow. And you've broken it. Besides, how do I know the package will get to the proper destination now?" *Come on . . . come on . . . give me something.*

"I just placed the sticker on the package. You can see for yourself."

Morgan glanced down and sure enough, an envelope lay glued to the top of the box. She started to peel open the flap.

"Wait." He stepped forward and stood before the desk. "This is classified material. How do I know you're authorized to check the bill of lading."

Good boy, I guess you are military, and you're learning how to cover your ass. Morgan kept her gaze on him as she reached into the center drawer, hoping that she'd find that damned clutch. She glanced down and, sure enough, there it was. She tried not to let a wave of relief escape her demeanor as she fished out the security card and handed it to the young man. "The blue color means top clearance at this facility."

He studied the card for a moment and then nodded as he returned it to her. "I'm sorry, Dr. Johanssen. I guess it's all right."

"Of course, it's all right." She mustered a tinge of indignity in her voice as she pulled the bill of lading from the envelope.

She made the appearance of reading the slip with care as she prepared to memorize the destination. It was in some sort of shipping shorthand, but when she got to the bottom, she realized it didn't matter. They'd included a zip code, and that was enough to tell her where it was going. *Of course. You sly old wolf.*

Morgan replaced the packing slip and flattened down the flap on the envelope as she stepped back from the package. The young man didn't move, waiting for her to give him a more definitive sign that he could proceed. She wondered if she could get him to check the air in her tires; she had certainly buffaloed him enough. She decided against it, but where she was heading, Morgan knew she was going to need a full tank of gas – and maybe a compass. After motioning to him to take the package, she let herself settle down into the chair behind the desk as he made his getaway.

Once she'd given him time to leave the building, she

glanced at her watch. Seven-thirty. *Grant Winston, you'd better be waiting for me.* And then she stood and walked over to the door to make sure the transport worker hadn't stopped on his way out. Seeing no sign of him, she flipped off the lights and started to close the door.

For the second time that evening, she swore at herself, and then she turned the lights back on and walked over to the desk to retrieve the clutch. Yeah, she needed to find the old wallet. But for once, the replacement had served her well enough. Her mood lifted as she left the building and headed for her car. Her steps felt light. Maybe it was because she wasn't wearing those ankle-high "lab booties." On second thought, she decided she wished she were.

But that would come later, after she talked with Grant.

"This is crazy," Grant said, shaking his head. "What's gotten into you?"

Morgan hadn't expected his response. He'd seemed as concerned as she was about the shape the project had taken. At least, that's what he'd said all along, and she told him so, and then added, "But we have a chance to stop this."

"I thought you'd accepted that the package was over the transom."

Grant often used strange business speak. Strange, at least to her. When they'd first started spending time together, she often found herself wondering what he was talking about. Once, while she waited for him to get off the phone in his office, Morgan had wandered around the room looking at the various diplomas and certificates that decorated his wall. To her surprise, she noticed that one was a degree in business administration. She'd remarked, once he got off the phone, about the diploma. He had shrugged it off with a wave of the hand and told her he'd come into computing through the side door. It was where the future was at the time, he'd said, and so he retooled – another biz-speak term – to flow toward the money.

The transom term was one Grant used all the time, and she'd finally stopped him to ask what it meant. At first, he'd stared at her as though he wasn't sure she was serious.

"You know what that means," he'd said.

"No, I don't."

When he cocked his head to one side and pulled up straighter in his seat, she continued to return his gaze with as much intensity as she could project to let him know she was serious. She came from a research model, but if Grant had a business background, she wanted to understand how he thought. After all, if they were going to have a future together, she determined to learn his lingo so they could communicate on all levels. This transom stuff was as good a place to start as any.

"Well," he'd said after a pause, "it's like slipping something through the transom above old-fashioned doors." He stopped and studied her for a beat. "You know, that little window right above doors in old buildings?"

She nodded. Probably every old high school in the country was built with transoms; hers in rural Minnesota was.

He continued, "Okay, so it's like that. You do your job – add your gizmo to the widget – put it back in the box and slip it over the transom to the person on the other side of the door, and then it's their turn. Get it?"

She did, and now, two weeks later as she sat in Grant's living room, she knew he was trying to tell her that Conti's Baby was out of her hands and into the next phase. But Morgan wasn't willing to let a turn-of-phrase tell her what she could and couldn't do. In fact, she found herself wondering if all that biz-speak was a plot to make workers yield to the thinking of their bosses.

"I'm not giving up."

Grant raised his hands in a gesture of surrender. "Okay, okay. But you have to eat something before you set off on your crusade."

She started to protest, but he cut her off. "How long since you've eaten?"

Morgan's face froze in a blank stare at the way he'd changed the subject. She didn't have time for dinner now; she needed to get on the road. She'd only stopped to see Grant because she thought she could count on him to help her decide how to get into Conti's mountain retreat. It was the zip code on the bill of lading that had tipped her off to the new destination for the virus.

Grant must have misinterpreted the look on her face as her attempt to recall when she'd last had a meal because he said, "That's what I thought. You sit here while I throw together some spaghetti." He stood before she could respond, adding, "And we'll talk this through while we eat."

"There isn't time." Morgan jumped up and began pacing.

"You're wrong. If you go into the night half-cocked, you won't get anywhere." He walked over to her and placed his hands on her shoulders and guided her back to the sofa. Then he walked out of the room without giving her a chance to respond.

When she'd called him on her cell, he had suggested she come over to his condo so they could eat there. At the time, she'd let him believe they were still going to have that meal – and maybe dessert – but she didn't want to get into it over the phone. But maybe he was right.

Morgan glanced around – no, really looked – at the living room for the first time. She hadn't even noticed the previous evening. For one thing, his place was so neat. His office was that way, but so was hers – the lab seemed to dictate that kind of order, or at least Conti had. But her own home was anything but. Morgan found it a bit dismaying that his personal life was as orderly as his professional one, but she held out the slim hope that he'd straightened up the place before she got there. If she'd walked into the bedroom, she hoped she'd have found the litter that usually lived in the living room – certainly the disarray from the tryst of the previous night. But when she stood to examine an odd abstract picture on the wall, she noticed that the frame held no trace of the dust that a quick and careless sweep should have left.

Yeah, you're a tidy-nick, and I hope you're worth it.

When he poked his head in the room, she pretended that the picture – instead of the absent dust – was what had caught her eye. For the first time, she realized that the image was changing at an almost imperceptible pace, but in a way she couldn't quite identify. The picture portrayed a shimmering figure eight against a black background, and the figure bent at right angles where the loops crossed, giving it a 3-D illusion. The frame that held the image must have been a flat screen of some sort. Probably one of those pricey novelty items you could buy at a Sharper Image. She'd only walked into that store once and found herself appalled at all the ways metrosexuals could squander their money.

Before Grant could say anything, she tossed him a noncommittal, "This is interesting. Is it abstract art?"

He chuckled. "No, silly. It's a Lorenz Attractor." When the expression on her face showed no recognition, he added, "A computer-generated graphic."

"Oh," she said, and walked back over to the sofa.

"Dinner is coming right up. Wanna light those candles on the table?" He tossed her a lighter.

Although Morgan recognized that Grant was trying to change the mood of the evening, for once, it was having no effect – well, little effect. *Maybe that's what happens when you've survived a tornado a few hours before.* She'd never bought into the movie scenes where the protagonists fell into each other's arms with undeterred passion after they'd lived through some harrowing experience. Somehow, it didn't seem like the first thing that was likely to be on survivors' minds.

When Grant walked in carrying a bowl heaped with pasta noodles, he observed, "I thought I told you to light the candles."

She gave him a half-hearted smile, and followed him over to the table that rested against one side of the living room, where the flooring dropped to a level one step lower. Morgan guessed the step-down was supposed to create the illusion of a separate room – only without the walls. Grant motioned for her to sit, which she did as he lit the candles. But when she started to talk, he gave her a stern look and didn't let up until she'd dished noodles onto her plate.

She ate with an absent, mechanical action as he talked about the movie playing in the Odeon, a proper theater, he said, the kind that still had the look of the old movie houses. Couldn't he persuade her to go take in a late show with him, and then they would talk about "the other thing" in the morning, after breakfast?

She stopped chewing. Morgan knew, even then, that she wasn't going to spend the night. How much had changed in the past twenty-four hours! In the past four. And she knew that, as much as they needed to talk about them, her mind was elsewhere already. *One crisis at a time, Morgan, one crisis at a time.*

She placed the fork down beside her plate. "Another time."

"What?" he said with a tone that registered more shock than question.

It was clear that he wasn't used to refusals, and certainly not one that came on the heels of the previous night. However, for an instant Morgan saw something else in his eyes. It seemed like a brief flicker of desperation, but the expression disappeared from his features almost as soon as it became visible. *Ah, rejection. Dr. Winston, is that your Achilles' Heel?* It gave Morgan a feeling of power, but she couldn't find the resolve to exploit this sudden, new advantage. It was as though she were in the grips of a stronger intention that couldn't wait, not one second longer.

"I have to go, Grant."

"You – you can't be serious."

She rose and stepped up on the main level of the condo's living room, letting her actions speak for her.

"Wait! I'm coming with you." Before she could tell him that she needed to go alone, he walked past her and grabbed a jacket out of the closet by the front door. "I bet you didn't even bring a coat."

"Yes, I did." Actually, it hadn't occurred to her, and she didn't bother to tell him that she kept one in her car. Morgan had lived in Colorado long enough to know that the elevation in and around the Mile-High City could bring a chill even in the middle of summer, and she'd gotten into the habit of stashing a jacket in the back seat for those nights she left the lab late. But for the time being, she preferred to let Grant think she was more prepared than she really was.

"Okay, then," he said as he pulled on his own black leather jacket, "let's go get it."

She gave him a puzzled look.

"We'll take my Jeep," he continued as he turned the knob and motioned her through the entryway. "We'll need it where we're going."

"Where we're going?" Morgan stopped halfway out the door and turned to face him. She was certain she hadn't mentioned their destination. "You know already?"

Grant gave her a sheepish shrug as he averted his eyes from hers. "I'm pretty sure." He paused, and then said, "Conti's Lair."

Grant used the in-house name for the mountain retreat. Even though everybody at Contitech knew about the place, she'd never heard anyone report more than second-hand rumors. It sat empty most of the time, except when Conti used it to woo clients. The place was made for that sort of thing. Morgan had heard that one of the railroads had built the retreat back in the forties to entertain fat cats; she'd even heard that its dozen or so bedrooms connected to a central secret hallway. High-profile guests of the era could use the passageway to escape into the night if they ever felt in danger of getting caught with the overnight maid service – at least, that's what she'd heard. Morgan had never taken the story as true and, anyway, she couldn't picture Conti using the facility the same way. Fishing, skeet-shooting, maybe big-game hunting. Glasses of port with big cigars fit her image of Conti's style of entertaining better, and besides, she'd never seen him so much as glance at the women in his company. Then she got a sudden image of Sandy coming out of the elevator, the embarrassed look on her face. Morgan was beginning to wonder if she had underestimated Conti all along – and in all sorts of ways.

But at the moment, she was more concerned about how Grant knew about Conti's Lair. "How did you know our destination?"

"You must have mentioned it earlier, while we were eating."

Morgan shook her head. "No. I didn't."

"Look, I've known for a while where he took the project."

"You knew." There was no accusation in her voice – in fact, no emotion at all.

The confession tumbled out of Grant's mouth. "I made some inquiries. Connections, networking, that sort of thing. The point is –"

"And you weren't going to tell me." As Morgan felt her forehead burn with anger, she hoped he could see it in her face.

"I – I thought I could talk you out of this. That you'd cool down."

"But why?"

"Because you can't stop it. No one can, not now."

Morgan continued to stare at him, waiting for the rest of it.

"Conti's got his own lab next to the retreat. The works." He sighed and then added, "I think he's planning to release the virus, and soon."

But that made no sense. Conti had left the metro area and headed away from the center of population. The only thing out that way was local wildlife – what was left in the area, anyway – and . . . Morgan exhaled as a barrage of images from her dreams assaulted her thoughts.

"Birds," she said aloud, although she wasn't really talking to Grant.

"Yeah, that's my guess, too."

Of course, he's going to use birds. Denver was too isolated to serve as an effective point of dispersion. But birds could spread the slow virus all along their intermingled migratory routes, and pin-pointing the point of dispersion would prove almost impossible by the time the sleeping pandemic was in place. Conti had chosen a well-worn path for his dispersion, Morgan mused, since birds were a common source of viruses that caused influenza in humans. It wouldn't even sound an alarm of foul play should someone detect the virus's presence.

"Come on." She hurried out the door.

"You still want me to come with you?"

"I bet you even know which rock to look under to find the front door key."

Grant sprinted two steps to catch up with her. "Let me explain."

She dipped her head and raised both hands to silence him, not even slowing her stride. *Yeah, you've got a lot of explaining to do, Dr. Winston.* But that would have to wait. He'd told her Conti planned to release the virus "soon."

Morgan only hoped they could get there in time.

CHAPTER SEVEN

Theta-Sag

Theta Sag stood in his quarters and felt alarm creep into his mind. He glanced around him, hoping to find some indicator that would remind him what he was doing. Although Theta found it hard to believe that the changes in his brain chemistry could have already created the bouts of memory loss he had begun to experience, he found the episodes unsettling in light of his recent trauma. The doctors had assured him the effects of Gamma's story on his mind would be years away, but Theta had trouble finding an alternative explanation. Had they all underestimated the engineered capacity of the Ori, or his power when amplified by the wearable? So much about the Ori-2s was still a mystery, and he was beginning to wonder if they had rushed the project after all.

Yet the source of Theta's problem might have nothing to do with Gamma. The Sag priest couldn't recall any history in his own family tree that suggested a tendency toward memory loss, but then, Theta had been too young to care about family stories at the time the Nanoplagues had begun to alter life on the planet. Now there was no one left he could ask.

The plague had reached north and south, at first claiming

birds, domesticated animals, pets – anything capable of carrying the invisible enemy into a human host. And then at an ever-increasing, exponential rate, life on the planet began to change. People with the flu, people with long-term dementias, victims of sexually-transmitted diseases – they all fell victim almost overnight and all over the planet. But the Enemy also ravaged the natural world, destroying all but the natural grains and fruits. It seemed that anything that bore the mark of genetic tampering was marked for eradication. In the end, most of the world's human populations suffered death – those who didn't starve or commit suicide. The world no longer harbored diseases like influenza, SARS, or AIDS, but then, their hosts had died too suddenly to allow the microbes to mutate into strains that could survive. The Earth reeled at the imbalances left in the wake of so much devastation, and it took decades for life to reassert some semblance of order.

Order. The Order. Theta shook his head with a slow, sad intensity. *We wanted so much to reclaim the past. Maybe to a fault.* But the alternative was to let the incidence of rogue plagues pick away at their numbers whenever a pocket of the population became infected with symptoms as simple as a common cold. Had they really had any choice?

The Sagittarian paced about the room, still looking for a clue to help him regain his concentration. It was something important, that much he knew, but the intention swirled around the edge of his conscious mind just out of focus. It had something to do with Gamma, he was sure.

At last, Theta surrendered to the necessity to ask for help. He hated the crutch, but he saw no other recourse and turned toward his desk. "Djehuty!"

The Live-in responded with a patience that seemed unaffected by human time. "I'm here."

"Yes, I know that. But what was the last command I gave you?"

"To summarize the Corollaries."

Of course. The Corollaries. The memory of Theta's actions flooded back into his mind at the Live-in's response. Sometimes a computer without a keyboard or screen had its disadvantages. Although Theta could pace about the room and issue verbal commands, he had no visual cues without wearing the stim-band to remind him of where he had stopped. "How long ago?"

"The past four decades."

Djehuty's response stunned Theta, or at least until Theta realized that the computer was giving him the data range collected for the request rather than how long ago Theta had asked for it. The Live-in couldn't read his mind and, despite the computer's ability to intuit Theta's habits of thought, couldn't follow the leaps humans often made from one unrelated thought to the next. Theta reworded his question. "And how long ago did I request the data?"

"Five-point-two-five minutes."

So short a time. And still Theta had lost his concentration. The Sag determined to have the computer collect files on short- and long-term amnesia and its causes, but not at the moment. He didn't want the Live-in to intuit any connections between their conversation and such a request. After all, Djehuty was capable – and entrained – to look for patterns and anticipate requests, but Theta wasn't ready to reveal concerns so intimate, not even with his personal Live-in. Not yet. Not unless the episodes of amnesia persisted.

Once the Sag had regained his focus, he recalled that Gamma was due to arrive at any time.

In the interval that remained, Theta had to decide how much to tell Gamma about the Corollaries of Paradox. It wasn't a question of whether or not the Ori would understand the complexities of the corollaries; quite the contrary, Gamma had demonstrated an accelerating ability to grasp theoretical concepts. Some of that was bound to be the effects of the molecular colonies that had taken root in the associational areas of the Ori's brain. Yet Theta recognized that Gamma had an unexpected and strong facility for abstraction. In just two weeks, the Ori's capacity to comprehend theoretical nuances had increased at exponential rates. Before Theta revealed to the Sag geneticists the extent of that facility – before the scientists had a chance to congratulate each other on this demonstration of the general mental acuity of the Ori-2s – Theta needed more time to assure himself that other Sagittarians wouldn't view Gamma's powers as a potential threat. Anxiety washed over the Order of Sagittarius in unexpected waves whenever the topic of the Ori-1 Heresy surfaced, and Theta needed to be able to assure them that Gamma-Ori was faithful to the Order. Faithful – that would be the euphemism they would use to conceal the real issue. No one would say aloud what they really feared: that Gamma and the other Oris might develop independent patterns of thinking. Heresies. And the reason the Order had lost their control over the first generation of clones.

No, Theta had no doubt that Gamma would comprehend the Corollaries of Paradox, but whether or not he would be willing to intensify his story as a result of that comprehension was another issue. If Gamma understood the loophole the Order had discovered in the laws, would he be more or less likely to comply? Theta had no way of knowing until he put the matter to his pupil. And Theta knew that his Ori's growing insight wasn't the only process that had begun to accelerate; the Sag priest had noticed that Gamma was exhibiting signs of moodiness. Was the child experiencing some kind of hormonal surge that the geneticists had been unable to regulate? Time and again in the early stages of the genetics project, the Order had encountered the surprising ways nature had found to express traits that the Sag scientists had tried to delete, in particular the tendency of the earlier heresy.

On those nights when bad dreams riffled through Theta's sleep, he let himself brood over the decision to phase out the Or-1s. The first Oris had matured at a later stage, of course, close to age fourteen. But the crisis of adolescence gave them the propensity to be quarrelsome, and the clones began to question the authority of their elders. They didn't understand – or refused to learn – how the Order had established a gradual organization in the new world around them, one that had come to give priests and Commoners alike a sense of hope. Yet the Oris represented a group from within that threatened all that stability. And the Ori-1s' enhanced abilities made it harder to outwit them, to destroy them before they could bring the Order down. In some ways, Theta was surprised that the Sagittarians had warmed to the idea of creating a second generation only a few years later. The Order's dream of reshaping the future had been strong, indeed.

Yet that first experiment had colored the data the Order had collected about the nature of the Paradox. In the end, no one could say with certainty that the Corollaries were valid since the earlier Oris might have undermined the first attempts at translation. Those were days when the four-dimensional, non-Euclidean geometry of time was still a mystery. At first, the translations had come in the form of physical messages sent into the past, but they had degraded and disintegrated before eyes living in the past could read them. The next attempts had tried to influence the trajectory of time by direct contact. The Oris could make the translations and observe events and individuals only so long as they kept their distance, but as soon as they tried to approach an individual, the strange attractor's laws blocked such a radical intrusion. At the moment of contact, the Oris reported that their time-states suffered the same fate as the earlier messages. The third phase of experiments failed as well. Even when they tried to effect more subtle, indirect physical changes – tampering with vehicles so engines wouldn't start, removing or erasing key documents in a lab – the strange attractor's trajectory always managed to compensate for these anomalies in ways that nullified the direct manipulations. The first break-through, which came only days before the Or-1s were terminated, occurred when one of the Oris had discovered he could see flashes of the dreams of a sleeping guard on duty at the lab.

In the aftermath, it was Lambda Sag who proposed the first corollary to the Laws of Paradox: The strange attractor of time would not permit direct manipulations by forces outside the trajectory. It seemed like such an obvious statement, but in the end, it led to a discussion of another possibility. To the Ori translators, the events they tried to manipulate were already in the past. Yet to the individuals who lived in the past, actions took place in an unfolding present – in other words, they were still a part of the trajectory and therefore held in their actions the capacity to shape the future. For the first time, the Order began to consider they had approached the conundrum from the wrong perspective. Rather than trying to change the past directly, what if the Ori translators concentrated their efforts on influencing those who could initiate original actions? If direct intervention was not permitted, then the key was to find a way to inspire change rather than attempt to create it. In the end, they had come up with the idea of the Storyteller.

Before Theta had any more of a chance to decide on a tactic, Djehuty announced that Gamma was approaching. Theta instructed the Live-in to allow access and the opaque membrane that covered the door dissolved. The Sag watched as his pupil's lurching steps brought the Ori inside the room.

I'm pleased to see my mentor well. Gamma hesitated. *Or is he?*

Theta nodded. "Yes, just tired."

The Sag motioned for the two of them to sit in their customary arrangement for the catechisms – although catechism no longer described the discussions they had shared since Gamma had assumed the role of Storyteller. Still, the seating arrangement reinforced the illusion of Theta's authority, and the priest knew he needed every advantage he could formulate to coax Gamma into the translation's final phase.

"Gamma, you've surpassed my expectations, and you should be pleased with what you've done." To Theta's surprise, the Ori's face clouded at words meant to encourage. "What's wrong? Don't you realize your accomplishment?"

The Iteration hasn't worked. It's – it's not been enough. Gamma's eyes lowered to the floor as he sang his thoughts.

Theta was surprised at Gamma's direct choice of words to describe the real issue. In the past, the Ori had seemed less attuned to the goal and more focused on the woman. Why the change of heart? Why now? Theta wondered just how much Gamma had read from the minds of the Sag priests. More, Theta had long suspected, than Gamma let on. And certainly too much to hope that Theta could manipulate the Ori's actions by subtleties. Theta realized he would have to speak directly.

"You shouldn't underestimate your success. The earlier Oris were never able to get so far. You've not only contacted her, you've inspired the woman to try to change the trajectory."

Gamma looked up. *The woman has a name. It's Morgan.*

"I know, Gamma, I know." Theta had tried to see the humanity in the woman – had, in fact, come to accept she wasn't the monster he'd once thought. But the reality of what she'd done couldn't bring him to forgive her. "And I know the relationship you've developed with her has made this hard for you. But don't you see? It's also the thing that has allowed you to influence her."

The Ori didn't respond, but his face twitched with the slight flashes of a frown that Theta found alarming. What had they done to this poor child? The mentor's heart sank at the sight of the conflict that must be raging within his young pupil, and he reached over and placed his hand on the Ori's shoulder.

"What's wrong?" It seemed like an unnecessary question, but Theta hoped it would draw Gamma out – or at least keep the Ori from retreating into himself any deeper than he already had.

I can't seem to shake this sadness. It's all so – so wrong.

"You mean what we're doing?"

I guess. I just wish we could find another way to inspire Morgan. One that didn't . . . alter her brain.

"I know it's hard to separate your relationship with this wo – with Morgan – from the larger reasons for what you're doing. But you know the Iteration is for the sake of the future. Her future, our present."

Gamma nodded but his eyes still wouldn't look into his mentor's face.

"Gamma, you've undergone more translations than any other Ori. At least twice as many. Those earlier translation experiments had taken an unexpected toll. Some of your earlier clone brothers had begun to feel the grief of translation for longer and longer periods. Maybe that's what's happening to you. Maybe that's the real source of the sadness."

It was a factor, Theta was sure. Bereavement symptoms had manifested in the later stages of the Ori-1 project, and some of the scientists still maintained that repeated episodes of grief had triggered the Ori-1 rebellion. The confused clone adolescents might have taken their anger – an anger born out of the recurring grief that occurred at the moment of translation – and transferred it to target their Sag superiors. But Theta was grasping at straws. Although translation grief might have compounded Gamma's feelings, the Sag priest felt sure that the real conflict lay in Gamma's attachment to . . . her. The real irony was that Gamma's greatest strength was also the quality that now threatened his potential to succeed.

Theta's chest heaved as he sat watching his young friend. Maybe Alpha had been right all along. Maybe they had no right to try to tamper with the trajectory of time. In a sudden surge of guilt, Theta saw himself – and not Alpha – as the one who was arrogant. Was it possible? The thought was like a sudden bitter tang, and one that, if he accepted it, meant all he'd done in the past twenty years had been misguided. The endless political intrigues and alliances, the deaths of the earlier clones, the fate of the Ori-2s now – all had been the result of his own unbending will to change what was already in the past.

Theta realized that Gamma had lifted his head and now looked into the mentor's face.

Theta Sag, you're not an evil man.

The Sag recoiled for just an instant as he realized how vulnerable he had become before his young charge. He straightened in his chair and said. "No, I'm not. But good men sometimes do evil things."

For the sake of the future.

"Yes, for the sake of the future."

They sat in silence for several minutes, Theta in the grips of an unspoken intensity he could only wonder if his pupil shared. Then he said, "We're at the point where we can reiterate the past – you can reiterate the past. And save what has been lost."

Like the birds.

"Like the birds." It occurred to Theta for the second time he had just repeated Gamma's words. Who was guiding this conversation? Theta determined that it had to be the Sag. To abandon the project because of his own sense of guilt – that would be the greatest arrogance of all. Theta resolved to come to grips with his responsibility to carry the project through to completion. Too many lives had been lost not to try. Before him sat the Storyteller who had the power to make it happen, but would he sing the iteration with the intensity it would take to assure its success?

He looked at the youth as he thought to himself, *Do you love me enough to do this final thing?*

I love you, came the answer.

But is it enough?

Theta didn't wait for Gamma's response. The Sag couldn't bear knowing. It would be a matter of faith, Theta told himself as he stood.

It was up to Gamma.

Morgan

Although Morgan wanted to discuss what to do when they reached Conti's Lair, she couldn't bring herself to talk as they traveled north of Denver on I-25. She felt betrayed by Grant's decision not to share with her what he had learned, and their recent intimacy now felt like a slap to whatever relationship they had – if they had one at all. Morgan wondered if she had sensed Grant holding back from her on some level, and that was the reason she had already felt a disconnection from him. But now was not the time to delve into the rift between them. Besides, she reasoned, the fiberglass top that fitted over the top of Grant's CJ5 didn't stop the wind's howl, and she found it too difficult to talk over the road noise. The light of the metro area receded by degrees, punctuated by the glowing bubbles of light pollution that flumed into the nighttime sky above the distant communities skirting the interstate.

After forty minutes of driving, they turned off I-25 and headed west on Highway 35 to Longmont and then on toward the mountains. Even though Morgan could see little around her because of the dark skies, she knew they were following the course of the Big Thompson River. Every so often, they would cross a bridge and see the name of the river printed in reflective white letters against the turquoise signs. Their pace slowed enough for Morgan to speak, but the short wheelbase of the Jeep had made the trip uncomfortable; the bouncy travel had beaten the spunk out of her. Nevertheless, she still felt the need to punish Grant.

She peered over at the shadows that defined his features,

lighted as they were by the dim green glow of the instrument panel. When she did speak, it seemed less an attack than a plea for reassurance. "Do you know where you're going?"

"In general." He gave her a brief glance – enough to catch the look on her face – and he corrected his assessment, saying, "Pretty close, actually."

"And why is that?" Unbidden, she felt the anger swell again as she recalled the way he had concealed from her the removal location for the slow virus.

"My folks used to bring me up here when I was a kid."

"When you were a kid, huh. Was that before or after you became a jerk?"

Grant seemed to ignore her question as he kept his attention focused on the road. Maybe he hadn't heard her on account of the road noise, Morgan decided.

"My parents both grew up in the south," he continued, "and always thought they'd end up in Colorado. They only got as far as St. Louis, but they vacationed here every chance they got. I think they saw my moving here as the next best thing."

"They gonna retire and move in with you?" Morgan regretted the sarcasm in her voice, but it was too late to do anything about it.

"Dad died ten years ago – just a couple of years after I came. I doubt my mom would ever move out here now without him."

Morgan couldn't tell how much of the story was for her benefit, but she found herself softening a bit anyway. Still, she couldn't bring herself to say so.

The Jeep slowed and Grant rolled down his window, taking in the dark landscape under the light of the waning moon, which had begun to climb into the sky.

"It looks different at night," he said, and then speeded up again. "Did you know that the reservoir above the canyon broke back in the forties? My folks told me that the flood washed out most of the homes down here. When we'd come up here to go camping, I used to notice this old mansion high up the side of the canyon and wonder who'd been smart enough to build a place way up there."

He smiled as he slowed the Jeep once again and turned onto a gravel road. "Conti didn't build it, of course, but he was smart enough to buy the place when it came up for sale."

In the light of the Jeep's headlamps, Morgan could see indentations in the crushed rock that covered the road – recent traffic, and something heavy. Like a transport truck. Grant shifted into a lower gear as they started to negotiate the switchbacks that led them up the side of the canyon wall.

"You don't think they're going to let us in, do you?" Grant's tone was almost smug.

"They?"

"Conti's not doing this alone. Surely that's occurred to you." He slowed the Jeep until it lurched to a halt on the uphill slope of the road. Then Grant set the parking brake and killed the lights.

Morgan hadn't stop to consider the possibility that Conti wouldn't be by himself. But it made sense. In fact, those close-cropped transport workers probably had friends who guarded the entrance to Conti's Lair now that the project lay inside the confines of the mansion.

"How far up the road is it to the property boundary?" she asked.

"How should I know?"

"But I thought you –"

"– had been here before? No, I only said I'd figured out which place was Conti's."

Morgan sat in the darkness, trying to decide what to do. Grant was going to be no help, she could tell. If it were up to him, they'd turn around and head home. No, she was on her own. And she knew that if she sounded indecisive, Grant might turn around anyway. As her eyes began to accustom to the moon's light, she could see thick stands of trees on either side of the road; she could even make out the rough texture of the gravel road before them. And that meant Grant could, too.

"Okay," she began, "keep your lights off and let's try to get closer."

Although Morgan could hear complaint in Grant's exhaled breath, he said nothing. *Good boy. Just do as you're told.* Then he started the vehicle. In the dark shadows under the moon's glow, she could hear more than see him shift into gear as the Jeep lurched forward. Morgan rolled down her window and listened to the tires crunch over hard-packed gravel. When a slight breeze began to tease at the loose strands of her bangs, she reached back and twisted her hair into a coil, which she fasted with a barrette she fished from her jacket pocket.

All the while, her mind stretched, trying to form a plan of action. Somehow she had to get inside and talk to Conti. Morgan couldn't accept she had so misread her boss. And if there were parts of his past she would never know, she had observed time and again through her years at Contitech a man who was, at the core, still compassionate. What could the military have over him that could cause him to resort to . . . what? Secret deeds in the dead of night? Turning his back on his employees? Shutting out those who trusted him? Morgan was at a loss. She only knew that her mission tonight was two-fold: She wanted to stop the release of the slow virus, but she also wanted, somehow, to redeem her mentor. Her second goal was a selfish one, and perhaps had as much to do with trying to salvage her own sense of the man's humanity as it had anything to do with Conti himself. It was a topic she could wrestle with when she saw Thornton – if she decided to see him again. Morgan was beginning to feel like a crusader, not a role she relished. But right now she had to get inside the mansion.

The Jeep snaked on up the road for about a mile before

the terrain flattened to a temporary level stretch. They were still making their way through dense stands of trees when Morgan thought she glimpsed flashes of light up ahead through the trees. The winking light was just past the point where the road made a sharp turn to the right, and she reached over and gripped Grant's arm.

"I see it," he said, and stopped the Jeep.

At first, Morgan thought the illumination came from several flashlights. But as they sat in the quiet of the vehicle, the lights didn't reappear. Stationary lamps of some sort, Morgan reasoned, which only seemed to flash as the aspen trunks blocked the view when the Jeep was moving. A sentry post? That had to be it. Morgan felt a sudden collapse of hope within her. She had clung to the possibility that no one would stand between them and the mansion. But no, the lights suggested that Conti was, indeed, behind a protected gate of some sort.

"Pull the Jeep off the road," she whispered, although they were too far from the lights for the need to muted their voices.

Grant maneuvered the vehicle between the trees that skirted the roadside and parked. "What now?"

What now, indeed. When she stepped out of the Jeep, she could make out the lights of what had to be the mansion, maybe a hundred feet still higher on the hill but on a line further to right and following the bend in the road. The problem, of course, was that the sentry post was between them and the mansion, unless . . .

"We walk," Morgan said and crossed the gravel road.

She started into the trees in a direction, she hoped, would place them on the road about halfway between the sentry and the mansion. She glanced back when she heard Grant stumbling over a broken limb. He was about ten feet behind her.

He swore as he caught himself and called out to her. "Do

you know where *you're* going?"

She couldn't resist mimicking his own response when she'd asked the same question just before they'd found the road. "In general. And lower your voice." She spoke in a hushed tone, but she doubted their voices would carry through the woods very far.

Still, there was no point in taking any chances. If they were entering what amounted to a military reservation, she doubted the natives would be friendly. With any luck, however, the perimeter might have no more than a few "No Trespassing" signs to discourage lost hikers. She pushed out of her mind the idea that the signs might have that other phrase she'd seen on television surrounding such places, something like "Deadly Force Authorized."

Morgan began to struggle over the cross-country terrain, and she made a mental note not to sneer when she heard people talk about following groomed trails. She would settle for a deer trail in these woods. At least she was wearing athletic shoes, she thought to herself, but they were no substitute for her hiking boots. She couldn't remember what Grant was wearing as she heard him thrashing along behind her. Before long, Morgan realized she was losing her bearings, and she decided not to worry about her hypothetical halfway point between the sentry post and the mansion. She was willing to settle for finding the road above them, and she turned to work straight uphill.

Almost too late to stop her hard-fought forward momentum, she came face-to-face with the sagging strands of a barbed-wire fence. *Just as I thought*, she congratulated herself. *They weren't expecting anybody to use the back door.* As she crouched over, catching her breath, Grant struggled to reach her. While she waited for him, her eyes happened to lock onto a line too straight to be natural on the uphill side of the fence. Her hopes fell as she recognized she was staring at the bottom of a second barrier running parallel to the old cattle fence. However, unlike the lower fence, this one was chained link and must have stood ten feet above the ground. She couldn't read the words on the small diamond-shaped signs attached at regular intervals along the fence, but it was easy enough to make out the zigzag lightning bolts. She slumped onto the ground as Grant reached her.

"Are we there yet?" His voice rasped for breath as he turned his back to the slope and dropped to the ground beside her.

"Not even close," she said, jerking a thumb at the new obstacle.

As he swiveled to look at her discovery, Morgan turned her gaze to follow the line of sight of the new fence. She ignored the direction that would lead back to the sentry and instead strained to see in the low light what lay further up-canyon. About a hundred yards away, the fence seemed to run into a large dark mass which Morgan couldn't identify. The weak, milky light of the moon gave the illusion that the fence just disappeared.

Despite Grant's protests, she stood and started walking in that direction, telling him he could turn back any time he wanted to.

"Not on your life," he called out behind her. "But how much farther do you think you can go?"

She smiled to herself. *To the ends of the earth, baby, to the ends of the earth.*

Deciding to stay below the sagging wire fence, Morgan set out to get a better look at the dark form in front of her. She struggled on uneven footing as she traversed the slope, but within minutes she began to make out the near vertical mass of a rock cliff wall. As she neared the natural structure, she could tell how the workers who engineered the fence had abutted the chained link so that it ran up and then joined the cliff, letting the granite face take over the task of keeping intruders out. It was a strategy she'd seen often in the mountains, although usually a design meant only to discourage cattle from straying from their side of a pasture. This wall was far more formidable. Maybe a 5.10 at its worst, if she were scaling the climb for its toughest part – which she was.

Once again, Grant trailed up behind her. She hardly noticed as she studied the granite, trying to trace a route that wouldn't end in a dead end short of reaching the top.

"Huh," he said. "Well, that's that."

"It is for you."

"What? You're going to climb up there? That's suicide."

"Would be for you," she said as she knelt to retie her shoes. The footgear wasn't going to make this easy, but she'd climbed a 5.9 before. With a little luck . . .

"I'm not going to stand by and let you do this, Morgan. Be reasonable."

Morgan stretched back up and turned toward Grant. "Look, you've been a good sport. Really. But I'm not turning back."

"But –"

"I can do this, Grant, but not with you." On impulse, she reached up and kissed him. A quick kiss, and then stepped back just as he started to raise his arms to encircle her. "But here's what you can do. Work your way back down to the road – the safest thing would be to just head downhill to the road below us – and then backtrack until you come to the Jeep."

"And then?"

"And then go home." "

Grant was frowning, but at least he'd quit trying to talk her out of it. For that, she was grateful.

"One more thing, maybe you could come get me in the morning. I'll call."

"That's right. Your car is at my place."

She hesitated, and then added, "And if you don't hear

from me by midmorning, you might send in reinforcements."

"What did you have in mind, the Navy? Looks like the Army's here already."

It was a good question, and she didn't have the answer. If she could only reach Conti, she still clung to the idea that everything would work out. "You'll think of something."

"Morgan, it's not too late to –"

She turned away from him and called out over her shoulder, "I'll talk to you in the morning."

At first, she could hear Grant dislodging an occasional rock as he worked his way down the slope. But as she concentrated on the wall before her, the rest of the world slipped away. Before she could reason with Conti, before she could stop the dispersal of the slow virus, she had forty or fifty feet of rock to climb. And there was only one way to do it.

Very carefully.

Gamma-Ori

Gamma trembled as he left Theta Sag's quarters and walked down the corridor toward his own. The task before him seemed impossible. How could he serve his mentor and yet help his new friend? And he did consider Morgan his friend. As he had entered her dreams and her thoughts, he felt he had come to know her as no one else – except perhaps Beta. Through her, he began to realize how little he knew. Not that it was the fault of anyone around him – least of all the venerable Sagittarians who had shaped his life and his purpose. But her world was rich in ways that his would never be, and he had come to cherish the time he spent with her.

Gamma's mind stretched to form a bubble of perception as he turned into the greater hall that would lead to his own rooms. The action had become such an automatic exercise that the Ori had begun to look for ways to make it more challenging. No longer content to create an altered image of himself to those he passed – those who found his anatomy repulsive – Gamma had taken to singing new stories that could enliven the lives of those around him. To his right stood a cluster of Commoners who were no doubt on break from whatever service they performed for the priesthood, and to these individuals he projected the image of a friend their memories shared. As Gamma passed by them, he sang into their minds that their friend was stopping to chat with the group, but Gamma created a conversation that each would later interpret differently.

You're playful tonight.

Gamma smiled as he heard his Ori clone-brother sing into his own head, sharing in the simultaneity of their consensual vision in the corridor.

But the Ori needed only a part of his mind to nuance the stories that would baffle them later that night, or the next day. *A childish prank*, he sang to himself and to Beta, who waited for his to return in their quarters, *but one that will do no harm.*

Less so than what your mentor wants you to do.

You were listening? But Gamma knew that Beta had shared his earlier experience as well.

However, the mental trick with the Commoners wasn't enough to distract Gamma from the distress he felt over the conversation with his mentor.

How can I serve Theta Sag yet still continue to help my new friend? And he knew it was an honor to be the one who could reiterate the past for the sake of the future, but at the same time, he found himself struggling to find a way that could effect that change without harming his friend.

There may be no alternative. The resonance of Beta's song in Gamma's head was empathetic, but it didn't reassure Gamma.

He knew that Beta was right. Gamma had let Morgan share in the storytelling during the translation earlier that day, but now he wasn't sure she had understood the role he had given her. In fact, she had reacted just like Theta when he was still recovering from his "fall." The Ori had handed over to her the chance to help shape the story he sang when she had met him on the trail above her home, but the images of her own lost brother had twisted the playfulness of the merry-go-round into a dark echo of her childhood pain. Gamma was sorry to see how obsessed she was with her own past, and he wished he could take away her sadness. Why was it that the adults around him always seemed to look for ways to increase their own misery? It was something he could see in their thoughts, but he had trouble understanding why they would do such a thing.

And now Theta Sag wanted him to go further. He wanted Gamma to sing into her mind a story so strong that it would forever alter how she would be able to think. In a sudden panic, Gamma had wondered if he himself had caused his mentor's cruel request. Perhaps Theta no longer realized that the singing could do to Morgan what it had done to him. But Gamma soon sensed this wasn't the case. The Ori had plumbed his mentor's mind deep enough to realize it was a plan that had long rested in Theta's inner thoughts. And Gamma's only consolation lay in the knowledge that his mentor anguished over the idea of asking his pupil to do the same to another human being. No, that wasn't quite the way Theta saw it. Theta didn't care about Morgan, only about Gamma. Even though the Ori basked in the feeling of affection Theta had developed for his young charge, Gamma couldn't fathom the intensity of Theta's hatred for Morgan. And Gamma was sorry he couldn't seem to convince the Sag priest of "the woman's" gentle nature.

Theta had told him that "even good men do evil deeds," but couldn't Theta see that he could have been describing Morgan even as he had talked about himself. Gamma was tempted to sing into his mentor's mind a new song of forgiveness for Morgan, but Gamma had promised himself he would never again tamper with Theta's mind.

Yes, he loved his mentor, and yes he would do as he asked. But first, he hoped to find a solution that wouldn't change Morgan's brain the same way a song had altered Theta's.

The membrane that sealed his own rooms dissolved as he passed through the doorway, and Beta stood before him. For the second time that day, they were to translate to the past, and Beta had already donned his stretch-suit. But not until that moment did Gamma sense that his brother had been shielding him from an anxiety of his own. Gamma felt a rush of shame he hadn't shared in his brother's experience. Beta flooded his brother with what his own mentor had said. The translation ahead of them had a higher degree of risk because of the weather, and it scared Beta. The electromagnetic envelope within which the gravity-well propulsion functioned could be less stable because of the incidence of lightning strikes in Morgan's time.

Never before had the Sag priests asked the Oris to skip into a past that offered a measurable level of danger. The two Oris looked at each other with a shiver of bewilderment. So it was true, the mission had reached its critical point. Gamma and Beta joined in a wash of excitement that resonated through their united minds, an excitement that recognized that their mission was close to success – why else risk everything? And it was an emotion that gripped them with more force than the danger they could face.

Then Gamma broke the bond and retreated into himself to prepare, just as Beta would do. Gamma's exhilaration dissipated into depression once more even before he had changed into his own stretch-suit. He knew the sadness might have been, in part, from the compounding waves of translation grief. But Gamma knew that it was more, much more. Tonight might be the last time he visited his friend, the last time he sang into her unaltered mind.

Morgan

The moon's thin light had shifted enough to give Morgan a sense of the rock's relief as she climbed the vertical surface through her eyes. It wasn't more than a single-pitch climb, she assured herself, but it would be without the security of a roped-up belay – something she'd never done before, and nothing any sane person would attempt at night. Thirty feet above her, she was sure she could make out a narrow ledge at the top of a face she might be able to bridge, but below that she saw no fissures to use for finger holds or fist jams. However, the slab was irregular, and there was no way to tell what she would find until she was staring at it an arm's length away.

Morgan took a deep breath and said aloud to herself, "Controlled motion, controlled motion." It was a mantra her REI instructor had chanted at her as she'd worked up the climbing wall in the outdoor store years before, reminding her to move with an economy of motion that didn't wear her out before the climb was over.

Then she tested the granite by grabbing a jug-shaped jut of rock above her head. The stone felt solid, and she gripped the hold with both hands as she planted her feet against the vertical rock and walked her way up until her hands were at her midriff. Shifting her weight to one hand, she reached with the other for a higher knob of granite about eighteen inches above her head. But without warning, she lost her grip and slipped back to the ground.

Come on, Morgan, you're better than this.

She stepped up to a different spot on the wall and started again. This time she discovered a narrow fissure that slanted up the face about ten feet, and she slipped her fingers, hand over hand, along the length of the crack as she leaned back, letting her grip form a counterforce that let her walk up the rock. When the fissure became too small to jam in her fingers, she changed her tactics and once again reached for this nib or that knob of rock. Then she worked her way higher as she took care to keep three points of contact on the rock – sometimes two hands and a foot, while at other moments two feet and a hand. As her confidence grew, Morgan found her pace, foot by foot and sometimes, inch by inch.

After she was twenty feet off the ground, she reached a dead end – still ten feet below the ledge she'd seen from the view from below. Try as she might, she could find nothing to take her any higher. Morgan's breathing quickened as she realized she was trapped. There was no way that she could see well enough to find her way back down, and nothing above her would let her ascend one more step up the face. She had to force the panic from her mind and she slowed her breathing, trying not to think of the way her hands had begun to sweat fear. She was pushing down with her feet, leaning away from the face as her palms turned up to feel the counterforce of an undercut ledge. She remembered her climbing sisters called the technique an undercling, but she'd rather have remembered what to do next. As she felt the fatigue radiate up her arms, she switched her gaze to the side and saw a parallel set of shallow ridges running away from her. It wouldn't get her higher, but she didn't see much chance of that from where she was anyway.

Yeah, I must be pretty rusty at this.

If Morgan could have spared the breath, she would have chuckled at herself. Of course, traverse, traverse. She shuffled her feet as close as she could manage as she assessed her chances of a two-point transfer – one foot and one hand. *Risky, very risky.* But the bigger problem, she soon realized, was that the parallel ridges were too far from her undercling to stretch her leg enough to reach it. Morgan knew that each moment she delayed she was losing strength and losing any chance of making . . . what? A leap of faith? As good a name as any for what she was about to do.

She sprang sideways to bridge the gap and felt her fingers catch the upper ridge, but the satisfaction of her maneuver was short-lived as her right-hand grip broke away part of the rock ledge. For just an instant, she was swinging on three fingers of her left hand as she clawed with her free hand at the remaining inch of hold. She caught the narrow lip with her curled fingers and at the same time clambered her feet onto the lower ridge, pulling herself erect against the rock face. She could hear a steady knock against her chest and realized it was her own heart.

Knowing she had little strength left, Morgan felt along the ridge and found a new nib of rock to pull her up so she could plant her feet on the higher ledge. Working her way back in the direction she'd leapt, just a body's length below her now, she was able to mantel herself up onto the ledge she'd seen from the ground. Then she rolled over and let herself lie back, panting.

Nothing to it, she lied valiantly to herself.

When she turned back to face the rock, she was relieved to see why she couldn't see what lay above the ledge: The slab raked away from her at a steep angle, but at least it wasn't vertical. And a good thing, too, as she looked up to see a bank of clouds moving in, obscuring the moon. The up-angled slab before her turned into a dark, featureless sheet. Still, the rest of the way was going to be a walk in the park – well, with a pinch here and a cling there.

But for the most part, she climbed up the slab with down sloping footholds, letting the soles of her athletic shoes hold the friction of the rough granite. As she approached the summit, she heard vehicle traffic and guessed the road must pass close to the rock at this point. But as she neared the upper end of the slab, she noticed a steady glow spilling over the ridgeline above her. At first, she couldn't decide what could be causing the diffused light – by now, the moon was lost behind a thick sheet of gathering rain clouds. But before she reached the slab's summit, she knew what she would find when she topped the ridge. While her feet trudged up the last few feet, her upper body began to catch the light source that had caused the glow – the illuminated windows of the mansion. Morgan had arrived at her destination. The mansion stood not a hundred feet away. Conti's Lair.

As her eyes traveled the rooftop, she realized that the building was larger than she thought; the massive canyon wall just beyond had dwarfed the structure. The lighted windows on the second floor seemed much too small, for one thing, unless she were facing a row of a dozen bathrooms, and that seemed unlikely. No, the mansion was the size of a small hotel, which made sense when she recalled the rumored history of the place as a destination for entertaining railroad fat cats. Too many of the upper-story windows glowed with light for Morgan to worry that she would have to wake Conti. But first she had to find out how to get inside. She dropped her gaze to the dark exterior of the first floor, scanning the façade for a front door. It was just possible that it might be unlocked. Why bolt the door when guards watched the gate?

It was then she made out the vehicle parked off to one side. And the man who was motioning her over.

She walked the hundred feet to the vehicle, feeling like a fool, as Grant waited for her by the parked Jeep. He must have gotten lost and stumbled onto the gate on the lower part of the road. And he must have discovered the gate unguarded. She shook her head at how she must have jumped to the wrong conclusion. There must have been a night light on the road, not a sentry, and Grant had driven the remaining way up to the mansion while she risked her life on a fool's errand.

As she approached, Grant stood propped against the Jeep with his arms folded across his chest. She would never be able to live this down.

She could hardly look him in the face as she said, "No sentry, huh."

"Sure there was."

She stopped short, thinking she had misunderstood him.

"What?"

"I said, of course, there was a sentry."

"I – I don't get it."

"You've got balls, Morgan. I'll give you that. But you don't know when to quit."

"But how did you get past the –." She didn't have to finish the sentence as the truth of his actions sunk in. Now she really felt like a fool. "You bastard."

"I've been waiting to see if you made it up the cliff." There was just a trace of amusement in his voice, and it wasn't becoming to him, Morgan decided. He stepped up to her as he said, "Of course, if you hadn't, it would have saved me the trouble."

She was too stunned to resist as he gripped her arm and led her through the front door. As she'd suspected, it was unlocked.

CHAPTER EIGHT

Morgan

Morgan stepped onto the plush rug, its deep pile giving to her shoes as Grant guided her toward the staircase. The stairs ascended from the middle of the room's floor and dominated the entryway. A part of her brain – the part that insisted things were going according to plan – latched onto the lavish furnishings that filled the room. Even in the darkened interior of the first floor, she could make out the forties look of the tables and chairs that decorated the room – Conti must have bought the place lock, stock, and barrel from the original owners. But she didn't have time to notice much detail as Grant steered her toward the stairs.

Morgan tried to wrap her mind around the turn of events. How could she have misunderstood Grant's actions so completely? Had she meant nothing to him? Morgan could feel her heart tearing in two at the way he was treating her.

"What happens now?" she asked, trying to turn back toward Grant.

He gripped her arm tighter and shoved her forward. "My guess is, you've become too much of a nuisance."

As he swung her in the direction of the ascending stairs, Morgan caught a flicker of ruthlessness in his face, and the sight chilled her. Her cheeks flushed at the way she had thrown herself at Grant over the past weeks. And all the while, it was now clear to Morgan, he had been toying with her – using her. A heavy sigh swelled in her chest as she decided she was no judge of men. Not Grant, and not Conti either. As she walked up the stairs, it dawned on Morgan that she might have more to fear than losing her job. A lot more. If she had barged into a quasi-military operation and had become "too much of a nuisance" – well, her prospects wouldn't be bright. A military approach to guarding a threatened secret operation could involve drastic measures.

With each step closer to the lighted hallway of the second floor, Morgan had the impression she was ascending a sumptuous scaffold, and she wondered if one of the doors down that hallway might hide her place of execution. At least she wasn't going to have to sneak around, testing one door after another, to find which one held Conti.

Morgan, you're taking this fairly well, don't you think? she told herself, knowing that, at any moment, the shock would lift and she would realize just how wrong the plan had gone.

When they reached the top of the stairs, Grant released his hold on her arm and motioned her toward the left wing of the house. Even the hallway smacked of by-gone wealth. A wide hall-length runner woven with gold and maroon arabesques covered most of the polished planking of the floor, and dark wood paneled the walls. The air held a faint fragrance of old varnish. They walked to the far end and Grant reached past her to knock. Without waiting for a reply, he opened the door and nudged her through the door's threshold.

At the far end of the room, Conti sat in an overstuffed chair beside a ceiling-high stonework fireplace. He had leaned forward to place a book, face down, on the table before him. Morgan wondered if it was one from the UFO collection in his suite at the lab.

"Ah, thank you, Grant. I see you've brought her safely to

me."

Safe, yes. But for how long? Morgan could feel the pressure of Grant's hand in the small of her back, and she walked deeper into the room.

"Would you like me to stay?" Grant's voice had lost its smugness, and Morgan thought she could make out a hint of groveling in his tone. She turned and realized that he remained standing by the door.

"No." Conti's tone sounded no different from the one he used when he ordered his staff around at Contitech. "I have things to talk over with Morgan that don't concern you."

Morgan couldn't help but feel a certain sense of satisfaction at the way he dismissed Grant-the-Lackey, Grant-the-Bastard, who closed the door behind him as he left.

Morgan turned to face Conti, who was smiling at her. The old smile, the one that had always told her she had done well. But under the present circumstances, she found it disorienting – no, unnerving.

"You've been persistent, Morgan," he said as he motioned her to take a seat in the chair opposite his own. "In fact, you gave me quite a scare with that climbing stunt. But then, it's the sort of thing that's always made me think of you as a cut above the rest."

Morgan studied his face. Conti looked frail – frailer than she'd ever seen him before – as he sat before her in the overstuffed chair. Wasn't soft light supposed to make people look better? The past few days of activity must have taken their toll on him, and Morgan had to resist the temptation to sympathize too much with her captor. At the same time, she also fought the tendency to find a pillow to prop behind his back, or a throw to cover his thin legs.

She was looking for some sign of the stranger she expected to find when she arrived at the mansion, but all she could see was the Conti she knew. She struggled to keep from lapsing into the familiar confidence she used to feel in the man's presence. It had to be a ruse he had learned from those years in military intelligence, Morgan reminded herself, and she promised to keep up her guard. It might be the only thing that could keep her alive. And if he wanted to play the game of old confidants, she would have to try.

"John," she began, "what about the slow virus?"

"What?" Conti seemed surprised at her question.

"The slow virus. It's not ready. It needs more testing before –"

"It's out of your hands." He waved his hand in a dismissive gesture. "In fact, it's out of mine now, too."

"What do you mean?" Morgan couldn't keep the alarm out of her voice.

"They've already taken it."

"They," she repeated. "You mean . . ."

"My contacts, the ones who helped finance the project."

"The military."

"If you say so."

"John, I have to know. This is too important."

He shook his head, but the motion was slow, strained. "It's no longer your concern."

"But if we've been creating – if I've helped create – a biological weapon, I – I can't live with myself."

Conti closed his eyes, and for a moment Morgan thought he had fallen asleep.

"John," she said softly.

And when his eyes opened, he said, "It's not a weapon, Morgan. It's for . . . defensive measures."

"Bullshit!" she blurted out. Conti didn't like profanity – at least, she'd never heard him use it in her company – and she knew that it would get his attention. And after all, what did she have to lose?

"They –"

"The military," she injected.

He shrugged. "They'll do whatever it takes to keep this quiet. I can't protect you if you do something rash."

Protect me! Morgan felt taken aback, bewildered, and angry – all at once. Was he losing his mind? For just an instant, she feared that he might have hidden a dementia all along, and that now her life might hang on the thread of his sanity. It wasn't a comforting idea.

"Why would you want to protect me?" Morgan realized it was a bold question to ask, given the situation, but she needed to know what was going on inside his head.

The response was all over his face. But his surprise was nothing compared to hers when he said, "Morgan, you're the only one I trust to carry on the work of Contitech."

She frowned as she stared at him, trying to fathom what he was talking about, as she found herself repeating, "To carry on the work. But I thought, I mean . . ."

"Haven't you let Security upgrade your ID yet?"

"No, I – I . . ." Morgan realized that her stammering was a way to slow her speech as her mind raced to make sense of his words. The Plan had just taken another twist. Was he really offering to make her head of Contitech? He had made innuendoes, and often, about his "great plans" for her, but this was not what she expected. A promotion, more responsibility, maybe, but CEO? It just didn't fit – not with what she'd been going through the past few days.

"You can't imagine," he was saying, "the burden that's been lifted from my shoulders, now that the project is finished. It's driven me for years – for decades – almost like a demon. And now that it's done, I can stop. I've done all I can before they come."

Conflicting sentiments crowded into her thoughts, but she roused herself enough to ask, "I don't understand, John. Before who comes? The military?"

"No, not the military, Morgan, the aliens. The alien

invasion."

Her hope that he was sincere – or at least, sane enough to be sincere – evaporated with his words. She couldn't decide if it was better to be at the mercy of a manipulator or a madman, but in either case, her prospects looked dimmer. How long would it take for him to regain enough lucidity to call for someone to take her away? She needed to be careful. She couldn't risk the chance that he might interpret her voice as patronizing. Better to adopt the familiar stance she'd always taken the many times they'd argued about the topic of extraterrestrials in the past.

"John, there are no aliens."

"You're wrong. There are; I've seen them. Years ago, back when I was a young biologist with the Army."

Morgan realized it didn't matter if his statement was true. What did matter at that moment was that he believed it was, and that was the level of reality her gut instinct told her to stick with.

"Okay, so you have evidence that aliens exist."

"Not anymore. They disintegrated. Their bodies, their ship – everything. But not before I found out what they were planning." His eyes began to twitch back and forth as he said, "Elsa, I've done it. I've thwarted the invasion."

Elsa? Who was this Elsa? It was the name he had called her two days ago when he had yanked the project out of her hands. Morgan suspected Elsa was someone from his past, someone she reminded him of. He hadn't explained the slip before, and now Morgan wondered if his mistake was more than a verbal slip. Perhaps it signaled a mental one as well. Morgan looked into Conti's eyes, suspecting he was beginning to unravel before her eyes. But she didn't dare correct his case of mistaken identity, not now.

She decided to play along and prompted him, "You said, 'The invasion.'"

"Yes."

"And the virus. It's to stop the invasion."

"No, Elsa, nothing can stop that."

His logic escaped her, but then, Thornton had told her dementia provided its own internal order. She wondered if she could still tease out the destination of the slow virus before it was too late. Perhaps "Elsa" could find out more than Morgan could.

"John, where's the virus now?" she asked.

"I told you. It's gone."

"They've moved it off the premises?"

Conti smiled and leaned back into his chair. "Elsa, it's being dispersed. Even as we speak."

Morgan deflated back into her own chair at Conti's words. She clasped her hands behind her neck and pressed against the headache that was welling up deep inside her head. Then it *was* too late, and she had failed. It was a bitter conclusion. She had risked her life to get there, but that had seemed worth the danger if she stood a chance of blocking the dispersion of the slow virus. But not now, and not if the military had taken charge. And she had no doubt that they were capable of making her disappear if she tried to interfere. All she could do now was wait the ten or twenty years it would take to trigger the virus. She shuddered at the prospects, and she only half-listened as Conti continued his ravings.

"Everybody was running around, scared to death of the technology they saw. And then – I don't know how – I saw it so clearly. The microorganism that would be the real invader. Of course, it was so alien that my mind didn't know how to interpret it at first. I saw jumbled images of the way it would attack the birds, the way it would pass on to infect mammals – anything that carried slow viruses. And then it would even pass into the plant world, eradicating anything that humans had enhanced. And then it hit me, days later, it was just like the smallpox that Europeans brought to the New World."

Morgan tried to concentrate on his words. "What are you talking about?"

Conti's eyes danced, as though he were trying to recapture the long-held vision of a morbid fascination. "The invasion. It's not the aliens we have to worry about; it's the invisible bug. That's what I realized years ago. It's just like the colonists who came to the New World. Invading settlers didn't kill off the Indians; their diseases did. And that's what the aliens are going to bring. I just didn't know if I'd be able to perfect an anti-viral vaccine that could stop it in time." His focus returned to Morgan and he beamed at her. "And you're the one who helped me do it."

Morgan wasn't sure who Conti was talking to. Had this Elsa been an earlier conspirator as well? Was he seeing her before him or Morgan now?

"John, what did I do?"

The old man frowned. "You made the virus trans-species – that was the last barrier."

Morgan's role in the project. Conti was "back." But his words were like a slap to Morgan's face. *Yes, I helped you do it, but I won't be your co-conspirator.* She felt anger flare inside her, but at the same time, a part of her also felt sorry for the old man in front of her. He had made her a dupe in his plans, yet she was beginning to think he was sincere. Demented, of course, but sincere. Thornton had once told her that it wasn't hard for madmen to hide their madness. He'd said that people assumed the world looked the same to everyone else. It was only when individuals couldn't keep their visions to themselves that others called them mad. Well, Conti had kept it to himself – until now. If only she had seen the signs. If only she had recognized his obsession for what it was.

Then a new hope sprang to mind. What if he did plan to pass his authority at Contitech on to her? After all, he had issued an order to change her security pass. "John, you said you're making me CEO."

Conti studied her for a few moments as though he wasn't sure who she was. Morgan wondered if he was struggling to see her instead of Elsa. Then the words tumbled from his mouth as he seemed to click into the present moment again. "Yes, it's all arranged. I informed the advisory board that I'd been grooming you as my replacement. They all agreed you were tailor-made for the job." He cocked his head to the side as he said, "Didn't you get the note I sent you?"

The letter in her desk. Morgan kicked herself for not opening the envelope. The change in her pass, the letter – it was all there. A *fine spy you'd make, Morgan Johanssen.*

She started to speak, but he rushed on, as though he didn't want to give her a chance to protest. "I know, I know, I should have told you myself. I did hint about it the last time we met – when I took back the project. Surely you'd guessed. Anyway, I told Sandy earlier in the week, and I asked her to help you make the transition – she's been involved in so many things I've engineered through the years."

Conti appeared lucid again, and Morgan wondered if she had better make the most of it.

"So I can leave here now. You won't stop me."

"Of course not, Morgan. Why would I do that?"

"No reason." It almost sounded like it might be true.

"Just have Grant drive you back."

Oh yes, Grant-the-Lackey, Grant-the-Bastard. "How long has Grant been keeping you informed about my . . ."

"Your persistence."

She shrugged, embarrassed and still puzzled that Conti was willing to overlook her determination to thwart his project. Now she wondered just how much Grant had really told him.

Conti seemed to guess her train of thought because he continued, "You didn't know the real goals of the project – I hadn't planned to tell you – and besides, you delivered in the end." His face creased into a smile. It was that familiar smile again. The alpha wolf to his cub. "And then it was time to kick you out the nest."

Or the den, Morgan mused.

"And let you fly on your own. But first I had to reclaim my project."

"And Grant?"

He shook his head, disdain spreading across his features. "He was trying to get ahead and thought he could finagle his way back onto the project again if he kept me informed about what you were doing."

"How long had he been talking to you behind my back?"

Conti pursed his lips at first, and then said, "I suspect from the beginning. Anyway, as soon as he thought the project was going to take him to the top. He thinks he's going to profit from this, but if you want my advice, Morgan, I'd get rid of him. He has no loyalty."

"And you still believe I do?" Morgan was feeling humbled by the sincerity in Conti's voice.

"You may have had misgivings, but at least you came here to talk to me about them."

Morgan nodded. She still didn't know how she felt about the whole thing, but she wasn't ready to confess to him that she hadn't given up on the notion of thwarting the virus. Conti was too obsessed by his anti-invasion plan, and she realized she was in no position to be defiant.

She stood. "Will you be back to the lab?"

Conti shook his head. "Not to work. Maybe to see you installed as CEO."

She stood and looked down at the frail man in the chair before her. She had trouble converting the anger she felt earlier into a kinder emotion, but her rational mind told her that John Conti was not her enemy. Conti didn't see his actions as betraying her – that was clear to Morgan. In fact, he must have thought he was taking care of her. Of course, she was still determined to stop the effects of the slow virus.

But if what he had told her about becoming CEO was true, she realized that she had the time – and perhaps the resources – to launch her own countermeasures. Morgan's Baby – maybe that's what she'd call it. And if she couldn't stop the dispersion, it was, after all, a slow virus; at least she knew how it worked. As she looked down at Conti, she realized he might not live long enough to see her counteract his dream.

Just as well, she thought.

She walked across the study and opened the door to find Grant standing a few feet away. Had he eavesdropped? The door looked solid and her conversation with Conti had been in quiet tones.

She called out to Grant, who still hovered in the hall. "Have you heard the news? John just made me head of Contitech?" Her words were tinged with spite and, yes, scorn, but Morgan didn't care. They tasted good at that moment.

The look on his face told her all she needed to know.

He stammered, "Wh – what? You've got to be kidding?"

Conti rose and said, "I think congratulations are in order."

Morgan watched as Grant's face flipped through a range of micro-expressions she couldn't begin to register. Gratifying. Very gratifying. He might not like it, but what could he do?

"I guess we can go," she said as she brushed past Grant and headed down the hall.

As she descended the staircase, Morgan marveled at the strange course of the night's events. She couldn't decide what had shocked her more, Conti's announcement of her promotion or Grant's betrayal. She heard Grant stumble down the steps to catch up with her.

"We need to talk," he called out.

She didn't even break stride, and she sure as hell wasn't going to give him the satisfaction of an answer.

"Wait up. Morgan!"

When she reached the first floor, she came to a halt and then turned to watch as he approached her.

"We need to talk," he repeated, but the tone in his voice sounded less assertive this time.

Her gaze was cool. "There's nothing to talk about."

"But –." Grant stopped short, and then he started again. "Is it true? Did Conti really make you head of Contitech?"

"You think Conti would joke about something like that?"

Grant stared at her, the disbelief in his face melting away as he returned her gaze. "So where does that leave me?"

She turned her back on him as she said, "You figure it out."

When she felt his hand take hold of her arm, she spun around. "Take your hands off of –." But Morgan couldn't finish her sentence because Grant had clasped his hand on her mouth and ushered her backwards out the front door.

She struggled out of his grasp as they reached the overhanging porch and spat back at him, "How dare you! You're through. Don't you get it?"

Even in the shadow of the light shining through the door, Morgan could see his face had darkened. *Not smart, Morgan.* What was she thinking? This was the man she was going to have to sit beside all the way back to Denver. But he deserved it, and she didn't feel like holding back, not to Grant-the-Lackey, Grant-the-Bastard.

"You can't do this," he began. "This project is going to make millions – maybe even billions – and you can't cut me out like this."

Morgan had expected him to say something like that. It fit the way she was beginning to see him. Conti was right: He wasn't to be trusted, and the sooner she got rid of him, the better. But there was something about the way Grant was talking now that was all wrong. He wasn't groveling; instead, his voice – his whole demeanor – had taken on a kind of smoldering rage. When he began to clench his fists, Morgan realized her words might have gone too far – at least, they'd gone too far for that time and place.

Only then did she remember what he'd said to her before they'd gone into the house. Something about saving him the trouble if she hadn't made it up the cliff, and the thought made her shiver. Grant had already scratched her off his list – in fact, he had assumed Conti would want her out of the way.

The wind began to whip around her legs and she could smell rain. On any normal evening, she would have delighted in the scent of a coming storm, but the storm gathering in Grant's face was all she had time to think about at the moment.

Only a half hour earlier, Grant had forced her into the mansion, but now she started thinking about how she could maneuver past him to get back inside. She inched to the side of the porch, hoping he would reposition himself in response to her movement.

At the same time, she tried to distract him by saying, "Look, the project's not what we thought. It's Conti's personal project, and none of us are going to get anything out it."

"Liar!" He didn't move as she shifted another step to the side.

Okay, that didn't work. Try again.

"Let's go back inside and you can ask Conti yourself."

"I bet the two of you have decided to shut me out."

Morgan backed up as he took a stride toward her.

"That's not true, Grant. You were right earlier when you said it was out of our hands."

"But it wasn't. I made that up so you'd back off. You're ruining everything."

Morgan jumped when she heard a crack of thunder, but Grant must have thought that she was going to bolt because he lunged forward and grabbed her by both arms, pinning them to her sides. She struggled to free herself when he began to force her backwards again, but this time toward the Jeep.

"Grant, what do you think you're doing?"

"You're not going to stop me from getting my fair share." His voice seethed with anger. Still clamping her arms, he swung her around and marched her to the passenger side of the four-wheel-drive.

Not knowing what he had in mind – or maybe not wanting to guess – Morgan's thoughts flashed from one action to the next, searching for a way to get away from Grant. She could try to call out to Conti, but the wind had started to swell in intensity and he'd never hear her. Besides, her old mentor was too far away for him to hear her shouts. If she agreed to get in the Jeep, maybe she could signal to the sentry that something was wrong. The notion didn't sound promising, especially since it was nighttime, and she had no idea whether or not they'd stop to check an out-going vehicle. Security at Contitech didn't. Of course, she could try to make a scene, maybe even jump from the Jeep before they got to the road. But Morgan had the sick feeling that once she got into the vehicle, no one would see her again. The forest around them was a very big place.

When they reached the passenger door, she stopped short; after all, she could hardly grab the handle while he had a firm grip on her forearms. He was either going to have to loosen his grip so she could open the door, or else open it himself while he held her other arm. Either way, Morgan decided this might be her only chance. She had to get back inside the house and try to get to Conti before Grant could catch up.

As she felt his hold on her loosen, she leaned toward the Jeep as though she were reaching for the handle. At the same time, she raised her leg and kicked down, dragging her shoe along his shin and dropping her heel to stomp as hard as she could on the top of his instep. For just an instant, he let go his grip on her as he howled aloud. Morgan wished she had on her hiking boots; the athletic shoes were designed to absorb shock, and they didn't inflict the level of pain she had hoped for. But it was enough.

She darted clear of Grant's swiping arms as he tried to catch hold of her again. Morgan knew her mistake even as she made it. She had jumped toward the rear of the Jeep – and away from the front door. Even as she dashed to circle the four-wheel-drive, Grant made his way around the front of the vehicle to head her off. Her plan wasn't going to work.

She considered making a run for the sentry, but she knew she'd never be able to outdistance her pursuer fast enough to get the attention of the guards down the road. She wasn't even sure how far around the bend the sentry post stood. A dash into the trees would mean the same thing – eventual capture.

That only left one option.

Grant was rubbing his shin as he watched her shift first one way and then the other. Morgan knew she had to give herself as much of a head start as possible, so she worked her way around the back fender toward the house. Grant matched her movements, poised now at the front bumper closest to the house as well. She faked a jump toward the house and he followed suit, lunging along the driver's side. But Morgan positioned herself just clear of the Jeep's rear end as she feigned her lunge toward the house, giving her a precious second or two of straight-out running time away from the mansion while Grant would have to circle around the back of the Jeep to give chase.

Morgan sprinted with all the might she could muster. She was afraid to waste any effort by turning to see if Grant was closing the gap, so she concentrated on her goal ahead. As she ran across the flattened pad that formed the parking area before the mansion, she could hear her feet strike into the crunching gravel. It wasn't the surest footing, and not the fastest either, but Morgan could only hope that the ground would slow Grant's progress as much as it did hers. A storm wind came up from behind her and almost lifted her off the ground, feeling so tangible that at first she thought it was Grant breathing down her neck.

Another twenty feet, she thought to herself, as Morgan pumped her arms to drive her legs forward. It was then she began to hear the sound of a syncopated crunch of gravel behind her, filling the pauses between her own steps as they hammered at the ground. It was Grant's own pace, and the sound was increasing – closing in on her.

Just as she sprinted over the remaining feet of the pad, she felt his hands groping to gain a grip on her back. He caught a strand of her hair and tugged, and Morgan winced as the strands broke or tore from her scalp. He was much closer than she had thought. But she was going to make it, she realized, and reached the summit of the granite cliff that she had struggled to scale less than an hour before.

Morgan didn't hesitate – she had no time to think about what she was doing. Before Grant could catch hold of her, she leaped forward and over the summit, plunging into the black in a somersaulting free fall.

Gamma-Ori

Gamma pinched his eyes shut as the amplification sphere hummed, generating and locking in the quantum states that determined the skips to send them back in time for the final translation. But this time, he knew the skips were more important than ever.

Theta had told him that one of the more daunting behaviors of the skips concerned the way the attractor reacted to certain points in the past.

"We call these points translation nodes," Theta had said, "and this time you'll experience a larger number of skips to be sure you arrive at the precise node."

Gamma sensed a mental dissonance surrounding Theta's words, and the Ori traced the anxiety to an unspoken fear deeper in his mentor's mind. Gamma glimpsed how the Sag priests found themselves baffled by these nodes because they seemed to connect in mysterious ways to other points in time, points the scientists couldn't always fathom.

Why do I need the extra skips? Gamma asked, shrinking at the prospect of the heavier burden of translation grief he would experience.

For just an instant, Theta had chewed his lip and frowned before he responded, and Gamma found the mannerism fascinating. The Ori noted the facial expression and made a mental note to practice it. It telegraphed a nonverbal message that Gamma thought he might be able to use the next time he sang into Morgan's mind. But at almost the same moment, Gamma had recoiled at the association with his friend in the past. His next encounter with Morgan would not be a happy one for him.

Then Theta had answered, "Do you remember the street intersections in the sims?"

The Ori nodded.

"When you walked through an intersection, you had several choices at that point. You could walk straight through the intersection, or you could turn and walk a different direction. The nodes are a bit like that, except the other directions in a strange attractor connect to points that have some causal meaning to that intersection."

Gamma listened to the thought-flow behind the words, and the Ori also let himself hear what Theta hadn't wanted to say: that earlier translation experiments had sometimes led the Ori-1s to nodal points that were different from the ones the priests had selected. These unexpected translations made everyone nervous because the further back they traveled in time, the greater the risk to influence more than just the event that was closer to their own time – or at least, that's what they'd feared. But that was before they had discovered how the Corollaries of Paradox seemed to prevent the Ori-1s' attempts at direct intervention. So far as the Sag priests could tell, the underlying laws preventing paradox had erased these bolder Ori-1 translators. However, Gamma's own translations had avoided attempts at direct intervention, and as a result, he'd avoided the paradox disintegration that his predecessors had experienced.

As he listened to his mentor's explanation of nodes, Gamma realized that the analogy to the intersection wasn't sophisticated enough to capture the nuances of the four-dimensional non-Euclidean geometry of time's strange attractor, but the Ori couldn't tell Theta that without revealing that he had plumbed his mentor's thoughts. Too often, Theta still treated him like a child, not seeming to recognize that Gamma had developed a much higher capacity for abstraction. A better analogy, Gamma decided, would be to envision nodes as points where invisible causal forces intersected with the attractor's unfolding lines of time, and the nodes were a recognition of the affinity of one point in time to an earlier one. During the conversation, Gamma had instead pretended to listen to his mentor's outer voice while the Ori learned from the inner one.

Now, however, as Gamma waited in the amplification sphere for the coming translation, all these theoretical nuances fell away while he waited for the crushing waves of grief. The Sag priests had added twice the number of skips because they were sure that this final window of opportunity was a major translation node, and they were taking no chances that Gamma and Beta might skip to the wrong node.

But Gamma felt an even greater burden, and before the translation had begun. Tonight he had to sing into the mind of Morgan Johanssen, and it had to be a song strong enough to inspire her for the rest of her life. A song that could reiterate the past for the sake of the future. Gamma felt a terrible sadness at the task that lay before him, but he had found no solution that could satisfy his mentor yet save the sanity of his new friend. The thought of what he was about to do made him tremble even though he knew that Morgan would be long dead when the translation returned him to his own time. Zero time would seem to elapse by the time Beta and Gamma returned to their world, but all of Morgan's life would have marched by at a subjective pace, her body weathering through old age. And with each of Morgan's passing years, the proteins in her brain would eat away at her thoughts until she surrendered, at last, to insanity. All this would be history when the Oris returned, of course, but that knowledge would do little to ease this new kind of grief he knew he would feel. The loss of a person dear to him, destroyed by him, and he missed her already, even before he'd begun to sing his final song.

Gamma couldn't seem to shake the glum mood that crowded down upon him, and the moment of translation took him by surprise. The two Oris shuddered through the cascading skips that created and destroyed version after version of their temporal selves. And as soon as the final skip had carried them to their destination, Gamma felt the transitional slip from the Earth's pull to a suspended sensation of rocketing through its gravity well. They were on their way to Morgan's home. It was after midnight, the corresponding time when they had begun the translation, and Gamma expected Morgan to be on the verge of sleep. He knew her frame of mind would make her even more susceptible to his song. As the craft's opaque surface seemed to melt away, Gamma focused on what he would sing. He felt no joy in watching them glide southward in their transparent craft along the Rocky Mountain's sudden up thrust above the plains. From time to time, he trembled as he saw the sky over the ragged jaw of mountains flashing with electrical energy – the nighttime storm that Beta's mentor had warned his own protégé about – and Gamma didn't need to glance over at his brother to feel his anxiety at the lightning's proximity to their craft. Instead, Gamma looked up at the concave sliver of light that defined the moon above them. Transiting the glare of the Front Range cities took a few brief minutes, and then the craft approached the ridges that described the southern extent of the population density, and the forested cranny where Morgan's home lay nestled. In total silence, the craft accepted the vertical vector that dropped them to an elevation just meters above and beside the old ranch house.

And that's when Gamma recognized that something was wrong.

He couldn't feel Morgan's presence, and his first reaction was that they had skipped to the wrong transitional node after all. Had the strange attractor of time pushed them into a different moment of causal affinity, one with unknown resonances with the present moment? Despite the possibility, Gamma doubted they had arrived at any other than the proper moment – the priests had calculated the skips for the trajectory with great care. So he stretched his mind, searching for any residual evidence of Morgan's thoughts. Gamma knew he could detect his own Ori brother even at great distances, but then, the two Oris shared a consensual plane of entangled mental simultaneity that operated outside the bounds of proximal space. Gamma had never tried to attune himself with someone other than Beta – the experience was, after all, a mutual exchange, and non-Oris lacked the facility to construct such a simultaneity of mind. Still, the signature of Morgan's mind had become very familiar, very personal to him, and it was just possible he could intuit her presence if he knew where to start looking. He concentrated, hoping to feel a trace of her awareness, but after a few moments had to admit he felt nothing.

It stood to reason she could only be somewhere among the lights of metro Denver, which he flash-shared with Beta. They considered why she might be out so late, and what that might mean.

Perhaps she's with Grant Winston, Beta hypothesized.

But Gamma was less inclined to accept the notion that she would spend a second night with her love-interest. He had plumbed the event from her mind as he'd created the playground scene earlier that day. At the time, Gamma had also sung to her the final undertone of a medley designed to help her strengthen her sense of independence from that coworker. Perhaps her possible return to him that night was something, Gamma conceded to himself, that he didn't want to imagine. Although he couldn't yet understand these pair-bonding relationships, he had sounded Morgan's emotions and saw little to suggest that her maturity in such matters of the heart was any more advanced than his own. In this, Morgan was a child like him, and he couldn't see himself surrendering to the continued vulnerability of another overnight stay. No, he doubted they would find her at Grant Winston's home, and Gamma suggested to Beta that they sweep the area – the gravity-wave propulsion system of the craft would make it easy to cover the area in a nominal period of time.

But you didn't sense her when we crossed the Front Range before, Beta observed.

I was . . . preoccupied with formulating my song. I might have missed her presence as we passed overhead. Gamma knew how transparent his mind was to Beta, who shared Gamma's shaken resolve in the face of the lightning that flared in the western sky.

So long as we avoid sweeps that bring us too close to the storm cell. Beta's mental tenor was adamant on this point. The Ori brother projected to Gamma a series of images that explained the consequences – flashes that described the craft's vulnerability to electrical surges. *Our trajectory to the current coordinates managed to skirt the mountain storms, but the electromagnetic envelop around the craft can't risk a closer sweep.*

But it's our mission. What else can we do?

They weighed their options in a further series of flash-exchanges that brought them both to the same conclusion: Unless they were willing to abandon their final window of opportunity, they had little choice but to search until they found her – regardless of where that led them.

Beta lifted the craft and reversed its trajectory as Gamma

tried to focus his mind on collecting any trace of Morgan's presence. As they passed over the lights of metro Denver, Gamma struggled to ignore the competing resonances of the city's many inhabitants. At so late an hour, Gamma was puzzled by the many minds below him who remained active. They made their way first to hover over Contitech, but Gamma was sure he detected no sign of her there. So they continued north, cutting sweeps that brought them ever closer to the gathering storm that hugged the mountains to the west. A part of Gamma was disappointed he might not have a final opportunity to share time with Morgan, but another part felt an immense release from the terrible task before him.

As they left the concentrated pockets of the population behind, Gamma relaxed his focus and allowed himself to open into emotional channels of thought – less accurate in deducing direction but sometimes stronger in determining presence. And it was the last thing he could think of in order to honor the promise to his mentor.

As soon as he tuned his mind into the emotional terrain, they made two more sweeps along the length of the Front Range without success. But when they turned to make a closer pass by the mountains, he sensed her presence. Gamma knew that Beta had sensed it as well – not the direct sensation, of course, but through Gamma's own spike of recognition.

Although the physical action was unnecessary, Gamma turned his head to look at his brother. *She's somewhere in the mountains beneath the heart of that storm cell.*

Gamma reeled from the anxiety his clone-brother felt at the news, but he was proud of the way Beta vectored the craft to head toward the mountains without protest. As they approached the Front Range mountains, Gamma once again shifted the stretch of his mind to search for her location. Morgan's mental signature began to emerge, and Gamma felt his Ori brother respond to the information, changing the craft's vector to carry them to the edge of the approaching storm as the sky filled with electrical discharges.

All the while, Gamma focused his mind to guide them to Morgan's precise location. The closer they got, however, the more he realized that her thought-flow tinged with agitation – no, alarm. Her thoughts flashed through a chaotic array of conflicting sensations, and she was running from some perceived sense of danger. Gamma knew he had to sing to her his final song, but he knew that first she had to survive the present moment. His reaction was quick, appealing to Beta to bring them in close so Gamma could help her. Through her mind, he realized she was fleeing – Grant? That made no sense to him, but he didn't have time to plumb the details as he began to focus on what he could do to assist her. Even for Gamma, the events unfolding below him gave him little time to formulate a new song because she was running toward a cliff and –

Gamma's contact with Morgan broke as a blue-white flash resonated through the craft's cabin. The craft began to vacillate from one vector to another, like a high-speed leaf that slipped and wheeled from one supersonic current to current. Gamma heard the overtones of Beta's frenzied thoughts as his clone-brother fought to regain the craft's guidance. *A lightning strike, a direct strike . . . disruption, unstable . . . must flow my mind into the guidance, must – oh no, oh no. . . . we're . . .*

In the disorienting moments that followed, Gamma lost all sense of Morgan. He felt Beta struggling to regain control of the craft as it careened toward the south at a high velocity.

Beta, we have to go back, we have to save Morgan.

Beta was babbling. *unstable systems . . . can't go back . . .electrical amplification interfering with . . . not even there anymore . . .*

Gamma couldn't sort through the barrage of thoughts that intermingled the tech reports with Beta's attempts to answer his questions. Gamma felt panic build inside him. He had no idea if there was still time to save Morgan; he only knew that he had to try.

Gamma asked again, *What do you mean? Beta! What's happening?*

Beta responded in a voice of unexpected calm. *We're already skipping to another node.*

Gamma couldn't make sense of Beta's reply. *What are you talking about? What node?*

It was clear they were still in danger, and Beta didn't have control of the craft. And what about Morgan? What would become of her? But in that same instant, Gamma realized what Beta was saying. They had their own problems now.

Beta, where are we going?

The craft emerged into the new node even as Gamma was flash-asking his final frantic question. At the sight that emerged around them, all he could do was sing out a single, feeble stream of thought.

Oh no. This can't be happening.

Theta-Sag

As Theta and the other Sag priests sat in the second amplification sphere, he realized how weary he felt. All the years of experiments – all the losses of life – had come down to this final moment. Although the subjective time that the Oris experienced during the translation might last for hours, the Sag priests would see no more than a slight flutter on the polymer screen that filled one concave side of their own sphere. The screen produced the illusion that they were peering into the adjacent sphere that held the Oris. And that's just what the Sagittarians were doing now as they all waited for the completion of the mission.

If everything went according to plan, the Sag priests would emerge from their own sphere into a different world, one that was unaltered by that woman's fulminating plague. But not all of the priests had elected to join them in the sphere – Alpha the most noticeable of those absent. In fact,

Alpha Sag was adamant that he wanted no memories of a parallel world that no longer existed. Theta couldn't help but smile to himself at Alpha's comment. The high priest had championed the status quo and lost. Although Alpha had never said, in so many words, that the priests stood to lose all their power if the translation project succeeded, Theta knew Alpha well enough to recognize ambition when he saw it. And besides, did they live in a better world if the likes of Alpha Sag were in control? Theta was willing to take his chances in an alternate future.

But of course, no one knew, not really, what would happen to any of them. The Sags' amplification sphere should lock all those within its curved walls into their current states of being, and they would remember the world as it now was. In theory. But none of them knew how the strange attractor of time would react to a world whose future held little or no similarity in a modified trajectory.

Only in recent days had the debate among the scientists shifted to formulate the possible outcomes – now that their various conjectures had an end point. *How like this band,* Theta mused. *Always the academics when it comes to fashioning a new experiment.* Some maintained that the new trajectory would change them all, regardless of any attempt to hold on to their present memories, and they reasoned that a new corollary of Paradox might emerge, one that asserted how an alternate future wouldn't waste resources – not even mental ones -- on events that no longer retained relevance. Others maintained that the attractor might tolerate the anomaly of their own existence since the sphere would exist, in the event of a successful new trajectory, the same way that singularities exist. In effect, their lives would become the time-bound equivalent to a black hole. Theta was uncomfortable with the analogy since a black hole was unknowable, and he didn't relish sharing that fate. Still, he was hopeful of the outcome, and he still preferred a world without the Nanoplague.

He listened as the hum of the amplification generator

searched for the series of time-evolving states that would plot the Oris' skips back into Morgan Johanssen's time. Gamma hadn't told him that he would sing the intensified song, but he hadn't needed to. His protégé had smiled at him as he entered the sphere and flashed him a private, focused thought-flow: *I love you*. It was enough to convince Theta that Gamma had resolved the conflict in his heart enough to follow the prescription of the song. And he was glad to see that the young Ori must have come to terms with the attachment he had formed for the woman. In a few moments, it would all be in the past anyway.

"We are approaching a complete set." It was the proxy voice for the community of Live-ins who guided the translation. The computing power necessary to identify and stabilize the time-evolving states for the Ori and their craft was staggering. Sometimes Theta was still in awe of how much society had recovered from the devastation of the plagues. In only a handful of decades they had reclaimed so much science. He had only nursed one regret through those years: that humanity would have come so much farther during that period of time had Morgan Johanssen not fulfilled her own project. He had often likened the disaster to the Roman burning of the Alexandrian Library in Ancient Egypt. How much knowledge had humanity lost? He had once read that the library may have held inventions and instructions for everything from electricity to computers when the library was intact. The Sag priests hadn't lost that much knowledge in the wake of the plague, but until their rekindled biotech research had been able to make the advances that led to the Live-ins, Theta had felt like they were still teetering on a second coming of the Dark Ages.

"The set is complete," the proxy voice announced.

Theta scrutinized the polymer screen so he wouldn't miss the flicker that would tell his senses the translation had occurred. Even if he blinked, he might miss it. But as he watched, he soon realized that a flicker that was not the issue.

Instead, he witnessed the craft vanish.

The Sag priests sat stunned, sat speechless, and Theta felt the moment stretch into a full minute.

Epsilon, Beta's mentor, was the first to speak, requesting data from the Live-ins. "Were there any anomalies in the time-evolving states sent with the Oris?"

"None," came the proxy's reply.

"We knew the risk," Epsilon said, glancing around at the others in the sphere.

"What are you talking about?" Theta frowned as he spoke, but all at once he realized the context of Epsilon's remark. They had sent the Oris to a date when weather records indicated a concentration of electrical disturbances. The Lector Priests had offered alternative dates for all the previous translations as a safeguard for the Oris, but this final journey had no such alternative. It was the final window of opportunity, and they had all voted that the translation was too important to forego. The risk had been nominal, and Theta had heard Epsilon remind his protégé to take precautions against the storms they might encounter. It seemed unlikely the Oris would endanger themselves, but what other explanation could explain the craft's disappearance?

"Perhaps they'll return in a few minutes – a miscalculation of the return time-state." Although Theta couldn't see who was speaking as the Sag priests began to stand, the voice might have been that of Delta. But no one responded to the suggestion. The Live-ins had embedded the return time-state, and the proxy had already confirmed that none of the states held anomalies. There had to be another explanation.

The outcome they all avoided mentioning, Theta knew, was the Balanced Equation. Some of the early Or-1 translations had also failed to return, which had caused endless rounds of debate until one of the Sag scientists pointed out that all the missing Oris had remained in the past for subjective periods longer than twenty-four hours. The attractor, it seemed, might have some sort of built-in time limit for translations. Maybe the Ori travelers couldn't remain in the past because their presence created a temporary imbalance in the equation between past and future, tolerated for short durations, the Sag argued, but "balanced out" by the attractor if translators overstayed their welcome. The notion seem to accord with the universal law of uniformity – physical properties should be the same everywhere, so why not in every time? Differing pressures struggled to equalize, opposing forces counteracted one another, what went up would come down – Nature's other laws all balanced inequalities. The idea had gained support – if nothing else, as a precaution – and subsequent translations had taken the Balanced Equation into account. The circumstance had never occurred again, and translators had always returned after a flutter of absence. Until now. That Gamma and Beta had not returned suggested that they couldn't – and worse, that the attractor may have balanced them out of the equation. Translation disintegration.

Theta filed out of the sphere along with the others, walking in disbelief that he had lost his young Ori. Theta had reconciled himself to the possibility that an altered future might erase his own existence, but this turn of events was unsettling. It lacked any sense of closure. Even more, Theta had to admit to himself that the Ori child, engineered or not, had become a part of his life. If Gamma had altered Theta's brain chemistry in a way that would one day lead to insanity, the Ori had also given Theta a second chance when Gamma had helped him recover from his dream fall.

Theta glanced up as he left the Sag sphere to see if he could detect any changes in his surroundings, but he held out little hope. The mission had failed. The future still belonged to Alpha Sag and his ilk after all.

But the intrigues of the Order would also persist – or at

least so long as someone survived the rogue attacks of the nanos. In the meantime, political intrigues would ignite like brush fires. At the moment, Theta couldn't give himself permission to grieve the loss of his young friend. There was too much damage control to consider, not the least of which were the machinations that Alpha Sag would begin – had perhaps begun already. Theta knew that he had to begin rebuilding the confidence lost in the Ori-2 project. What choice did he have – other than to accept eventual extinction from the nanos?

No, Theta Sag would have to set aside all else for the time being, reserving his personal feelings for future days, or for private moments late at night when he could grieve over what had become of Gamma-Ori.

Morgan

As Morgan leaped over the summit of the granite cliff, she heard a crack of thunder that sounded too close for comfort. But a rogue lightning strike was the least of her worries as she tucked her head to summersault down the steep angle of the slab that formed the backside of the cliff's pitch. At the same time, she stretched out her arms, hoping that the slab was as smooth as she remembered it when she'd struggled up its face not an hour before.

She fell through space for what felt like an eternity. But when her palms touched the surface, the angle felt steeper than she expected and she spun head over heels three times at an alarming, increasing rate. She knew the slab couldn't extend more than forty yards before the face changed its grade to a near vertical descent. In the dark, she couldn't begin to calculate how far her summersaults had carried her, but it had to be at least half that distance and probably more. In only three spins, she could tell that the grit of the rock had peeled the hide from the heels of her palms, and she heard the knees of her pants shred as they grated against the rock. But she felt no pain – at least, not yet. Perhaps it was the adrenaline, perhaps shock, but Morgan was alarmed at the missing signals her body should have given her about the state of her injuries.

As she entered a fourth spin, she stretched out her legs, hoping to slow her revolutions. But the momentum catapulted her body up and then down as she arced toward a belly flop against the rock. She had little time to push out her hands as she collided facedown with the slab. The unforgiving surface knocked the breath out of her as her chest slapped the stone, and then gravity continued to drag her toward the drop-off. While the texture of the rock abraded her face, pain began to streak up her arms – no, just the left one. Something was wrong about the way her arm was turned, but Morgan tried to ignore the sensation. She continued to slide down the slab on a bed of talus and pebble-sized rocks. Morgan had the illusion of hydroplaning across the tiny rock debris as her torso yawed to the left. What would someone call it, she found herself asking – pebble-planing? Yet she was also slowing, and her body came to a sideways halt.

She tried to extend her left arm – *ouch!* – as she spread-eagled her legs to keep her from rolling and realized that her foot had found the edge. She was no more than a foot or so from the drop-off. She didn't know whether to feel relieved or horrified, but at the moment, it seemed she had escaped Grant. The cure already felt worse than the disease, but hey, she was alive, right? Or, at least, more alive than dead. She scooted closer over to the drop-off, hoping she had calculated her jump to place her near the ledge that should lie a few feet below the edge. If she could lower herself onto that ledge, Morgan hoped she could conceal herself should Grant discover that the leap wasn't to her death. But she could see nothing beyond the edge, and in the dark she had no way of knowing whether or not she had plunged down the slab anywhere near the route she'd taken up. Perhaps if she lay without moving, the blanket of darkness would lead Grant to think she had died from a fall.

Above her, she heard more pebble debris cascading down the steep slab and thought at first they were the tail end of the minor rockslide she had dislodged by her acrobatic descent. But the cascades were almost rhythmic, punctuated by the sounds of sliding shoes. Grant-the-Bastard was working his way down the slab to determine her fate.

How sweet, Morgan thought. *Maybe he'll break his neck on the way down.*

She tried to quiet the ragged breathing that still escaped her throat and listened as the sliding shoes moved down the rock slope. It occurred to her that he only had to follow a straight downhill path to find her, and she was in no condition to stand – let alone creep away with anything approaching stealth – so she waited for him. With her luck, he would stumble over her and they'd both tumble the rest of the way down. And Morgan wasn't feeling very lucky.

She realized she was right about her luck when veins of lightning flashed across the sky and illuminated the rock surface. She saw that he was only twenty or so feet above her, and what was worse, he had to have seen her lying there the same way she could see him. Although she was having no difficulty lying still – any movement was going to take effort – she wondered if he might think her unconscious. It might be her only advantage.

As she listened to his awkward steps try to negotiate the slab's steep pitch, she found herself wondering what it was that she had ever seen in Grant. He was good looking, of course. Anybody could see that. But as she thought about it, she couldn't recall a single thing he'd said or done that showed they had much in common. He hadn't even been nice to her until there seemed a chance he could weasel his way back onto the project. She decided to add weasel to his list of names: Grant–the-Weasel. And he was too sharp of a dresser. *Baby, don't you know you're gonna get those designer slacks all dirty climbing down here to check on me?*

She felt the first pebbles roll up and strike her side with the gathering force of gravity. He was getting close.

But above all, Morgan decided, he was just a nerd in sharp clothing. Anybody with half a brain could tell it from a distance. He wore a pocket-protector, for Christ's sake, bulging with assorted pens and markers. If that didn't shout nerd, she didn't know what would. She let herself visualize his city-slicker progress down the slope. *I bet he's never set foot off a groomed trail – well, before tonight, that is.* She had to stifle a derisive chuckle as she thought about the way he'd struggled to keep up with her on their approach to Conti's mansion from the road. The closer he got, the more she searched for ways to build up her anger; she'd need it when he reached her.

She had no trouble hearing the skid of his steps now. And each time he placed a foot lower on the slope, the delay of pebbles that collided with her body grew shorter.

And then the noise stopped.

He could only be a few feet away. What was going on? She had turned her head so that she could see him, but they were both in the slab's deep shadow and there was nothing to see except during the occasional flash of lightning. Morgan began to feel little pings hit the length of her body, and at first she thought he must be throwing tiny rocks at her. Ashes to ashes, dust to dust – some sort of weird ritual before he let her lie in peace. But when a rain drop splashed on her cheek, she knew she was feeling the beginnings of a nighttime mountain shower. Morgan figured that was bad news and good. Pretty soon that rock was going to get slick and she was awfully close to the edge – that was the bad. But on the good side, Grant wasn't going to have very good footing either. And he had a lot less practice, she hoped, at keeping his footing when the conditions deteriorated.

"Morgan? Are you all right?"

The sound of his voice so startled her that she must have flinched, but she doubted he saw it. He could only know for sure where she was because of the lightning that continued to flash at intermittent intervals. The sudden flares gave the scene a kind of surreal, unpredictable strobe effect. She didn't answer him.

"Morgan, I know you're faking. Let me help you."

She heard the gravelly shift of his feet as he stepped down to stand right above her. Then he tapped her with his foot. A soft tap at first, but then a harder, steady nudge. Although she still didn't respond, her body tensed as the force of his foot tried to push her toward the edge of the slab. But when she felt both of his hands start to roll her over, she knew he must be squatting over her.

She tightened the muscles in her downhill limbs against the pressure he started to exert; he was trying to roll her over the cliff's edge. His touch repulsed her – a reaction she hadn't expected somehow. *You know, you're a lousy lay, too,* she thought as she readied herself for her desperate final act. In the darkness, Morgan doubted he could figure out why he couldn't budge her more than a few inches up off the rock. Since she still hadn't moved, she also hoped he was beginning to let down his guard. *Come on, Grant. Grant-the-Bastard, Grant-the-Weasel. Do it, do it!*

It took him half a minute to alter his strategy to the one she had been waiting for, and she felt him shift his weight forward to reach past her body, searching for whatever was obstructing his attempt to leverage her over the cliff. Morgan wasn't sure how much control she would have over her left arm, which by now had begun to throb with pain, but she knew it might be her only opening. As she sensed his body overarching her own, she jerked her arm up next to her body at the same time she retracted her spread-eagled legs, and then she twisted and rolled over on her back. The roll took her so close to the edge that, for an instant, Morgan thought she was going to slip off the cliff by her own actions. But the effect also unbalanced Grant, and she felt his arms shoot down to find enough rock to steady his own pitch forward.

While Grant's arms tried to grab at the granite slab, Morgan reached up and groped at his chest, searching for the pocket protector she was sure he wore. Her fingers found the thin tube of a mechanical pencil, and she hoped it would be sharp enough. She pulled back her hand just as a quick succession of lightning strobes lit both their faces. She found herself staring into his startled face, but she thought she could see recognition in his eyes about what she was doing. His arm flinched to block her next move when she tried to drive the pencil into his throat. The after-flare of the lightning was enough for her to see the pencil-stiletto stick in his jaw, and she felt a warm spray hit her own face. She knew it wasn't rain.

Grant squatted on his haunches in a rage while he tugged the writing tool from his face. She felt her lungs collapsing from the struggle. Not now, not now! She couldn't fight if she couldn't breathe. Morgan clutched at her pocket to bring out her inhaler. Curling into a ball, she tried to bring the tube to her mouth, but she felt Grant scrabble over and again try to roll her off the cliff. One turn, two. Her free arm flailed at the rock as he rotated her to the edge. On her back again, she brought a feeble fist to his face and pumped the inhaler as many times as she could.

Grant struggled to his feet, trying to wipe at his squinting eyes, but he was too close to her and his actions only made him stumble forward. The drop of his buckling knees drove into her ribs, and she convulsed so hard she feared she was passing out.

And then he was gone.

It took her a second to realize that he had stumbled over her and then off the cliff. Wheezing, she looked over the ledge.

Her inhaler was still in her hand. After two quick squirts, Morgan squirmed to roll back onto her belly and away from the edge, but her damaged arm wouldn't cooperate, and she had to settle for scooting her shoulders and hips as far uphill as she could manage. She turned to look up the slab. Her eyes had begun to adjust to the dark, and she could just make out the outline of the summit above her, described against the diffused glow from the mansion's lights.

She decided to lie there for a few moments as she gentle sheaves of mountain rain began to wash over her body. The crawl back up to the summit could wait. For the moment, all she wanted to do was feel the cool, wet rock beneath her.

Gamma-Ori

The craft vectored across the nighttime desert sky at high speed as Gamma shuddered through wave after wave of grief. Before his eyes, the same scene repeated itself – no, not the same. Each time it was slightly different. The muscles in his cheeks tensed but only a silent scream could push against his residual mouth. Gamma felt the panic in Beta Ori's mind as well. Gamma didn't want to distract his brother, but still Gamma reached out with his mind to get some of sense of what was happening.

Through the maelstrom of Beta's thoughts, Gamma saw that their time-evolving state refused to stabilize and, like a stutter in time, they retraced their careening descent over the desert again and again. And then he saw another of his brother's revelations: *Fifty years!* They had translated more than fifty years deeper into the past. Gamma wondered what the affinity to this place, this time could be.

He turned his attention back to the closed-loop world that replayed itself around them. Through the transparent skin of the craft, Gamma could see that each time the scene of the craft's path recurred, the moon appeared to jump a little further across the sky. And then he realized what was different: They were skipping through the same time on one night to the same time on the next, and the next, and the . . . But just as he began to understand the repetitions, the scene on the subsequent night darkened as they plunged into a giant thunder storm, its crackling electrical energy surging all around them. Before Gamma could register his horror, a blue-white flash crackled though the craft. Another lightning strike. Gamma expected to see them translate once again, but instead the craft slipped past the stutter as they rocketed forward through the storm.

The time-evolving states must have stabilized, he sang to his brother.

Before Gamma had a chance to feel relieved, another overtone from Beta's mind pulsed through him: Beta couldn't regain the craft's guidance; they were accelerating on a vector that had already carried them a thousand kilometers to the south. But now they were headed for impact.

The craft clipped across the desert landscape like a high-speed rock skimming the surface of a lake. The first time they glanced off the ground, the friction eviscerated half the cabin's bottom and the craft's power began to fail. Gamma knew it immediately because his stretch-suit began to lose its energy field and gravity began to tug at his body. Even before he glanced over at Beta, Gamma had sensed the life force slip from his brother's mind. The sense of loss that wrenched through Gamma was different from translation, and more intense than he thought he could stand. But there was no time to grieve as Gamma's body flew free from the dais at the center of the craft. He tried to push himself away from the rear of the hull, hands flattening to meet the contoured surface as he braced himself for the next impact.

Each bounce bled away the craft's velocity and by the third impact with the ground – or was it the fourth? Gamma was no longer sure – the craft began to carve a continuous, raking groove into the ground. A thousand meters later, it lurched to a sudden stop. At the same instant, Gamma's body catapulted forward and crumpled in a heap in the forward end of the tiny cabin.

He was dazed but still alive, trying to focus on what had happened, on what it was he was supposed to do. *Where was*

Beta? His mind searched for the undertone of his brother's presence, but there was nothing. For the first time in his life, Gamma-Ori felt totally, utterly alone. He also sensed that something was amiss in his body – a broken bone, perhaps several. Gamma had trouble understanding what could have happened to overcome the elasticity and strength of his limbs.

He had no idea how long he lay in the ship as his mind hovered near the edge of consciousness. At last, he struggled to crawl through a hole in the hull and then tumbled to the ground. Then he half-dragged, half-pulled himself a few meters from the craft before he collapsed, his down-turned face resting against the roughened texture of a caliche cliff wall. In the distance, he sensed the throb of birds twittering a tentative song. *Birds!* As he lay there, a realization started to swell inside him: the Iteration, he had to sing the final Iteration.

Then he sensed that he was no longer alone, that a growing number of human mental signatures had begun to swarm through the area nearby.

"Oh my god," he heard one articulate with astonishment, and probably aloud. "This one's alive!"

Moments later, Gamma-Ori felt strong hands take hold of him and turn him over. Gamma sensed amazement flooding the thoughts of the figure who leaned close over his face. The Ori saw the man's close-cropped white hair bristling through the aura of spotlights that backlit his head. There was a familiar resonance in the man's mind, Gamma thought. Something or someone they shared; Gamma was too dazed to focus on what it was. Yet even as Gamma felt the life force ebb from his own body, he found the strength to sing into the mind of the white-haired figure above him. Not as passionately as Gamma had hoped, and not as fully. There seemed to be parts to the story he couldn't recall, but he sang as best he could. He sang of the plague, of its coming – or of its having already come? He no longer knew for sure.

Gamma sang of the birds that would die, of the people, of the invisible invasion that would infect the whole of the Earth. He sang as long as he could, letting the Iteration fill the mind of his listener.

And as his song dimmed, Gamma-Ori felt his silent voice merge into the throbbing, warbling chatter of morning songbirds, alive to the first early shafts of desert light.

EPILOGUE

Morgan

Morgan dropped into the chair behind the desk, deciding she looked good in black.

It wasn't a color she kept in her wardrobe – in fact, she'd had to make a special trip to a LoDo boutique to find the outfit she wore to Conti's memorial service that morning. He'd appointed her executor of his estate, which surprised her since she hadn't seen him much since "the incident" – the way she'd come to think of Grant's death. Oh, Conti showed up when the board of Contitech confirmed her as his replacement, but he seemed to have lost interest in the facility. As an almost eighty-something he was entitled to slow down, she conceded, but she knew how hard it had been on him when he moved into a posh assisted-care facility. She'd gone to see him there. During a brief lucid moment, he'd told her he had accepted that his mind was failing, that he was no longer competent to live alone. Morgan had seen it coming, of course, and she found she was more disturbed at the way all public memory of the alpha wolf had faded from the thoughts of researchers at the lab once he'd put Conti's Baby to bed.

With an action that required no thought on her part,

Morgan pulled a sheet of computer paper from the desk drawer and creased it into a valley fold as she mused over the way things had turned out. Out of respect for Conti, she had kept her plans to herself – for Conti's sake, and for the sake of the occasional unmarked van she spotted following her in those early months after her promotion. Conti had told her that night at the mansion that "they" wouldn't hesitate to stop her if they thought she were meddling in the slow virus project, and she suspected "they" had allowed her to see them tailing her. She couldn't be sure, of course, but the driver and front-seat passenger both had closed-cropped hair. Not that they did anything; it seemed more a display of continuing interest in her affairs rather than an overt threat.

She glanced down at the paper. Its texture felt too slick for her tastes, she realized, and she made a mental note to order more rice paper as she doubled the corners over into a squash fold.

Although her close-cropped guardian angels kept their distance, she also knew she owed them. After all, no one had ever questioned her about Grant's death. No one, not even her co-workers. It was as though the circumstances of his demise had ceased to hold relevance. But the cold efficiency by which Grant's death was rendered mute was a reminder that the same thing could happen to her; she knew she had to be cautious. Cautious yet diligent.

She leaned back in the chair as her fingers fashioned the paper corners into a petal, and she knew the next step, the inside-reverse, would make or break the eventual paper chicken that began to take shape in her hands.

Careful, Morgan, be very careful, she reminded herself. But she knew she wasn't talking about the folded paper in her fingers.

She sighed as she added two more inside-reverse folds. Behind her on the bookshelf stood an array of large and small paper chickens. She'd cleared out the space where Conti had arranged his assorted UFO books, and replaced them with a growing flock of paper still lifes. It had become Morgan's ritual, and almost every week she fashioned a new bird, sometimes a crane or a chick, but most of the time her creations were chickens. At one a week, she guessed she'd filled the shelf behind her – together with all the flat surfaces inside her house – with close to a hundred paper birds. It had started during her convalescence after "the incident," when she'd taken to heart Thornton's suggestion that the art might help her understand the child-archetype of her dreams. She didn't know if she bought Thornton's premise – let alone his explanation – but she had to admit that she hadn't experienced the dreams or visions since she'd adopted the hobby. Part of her suspected that it had become her private superstition, but viewed another way, the paper-folding was a tangible reminder of the promise she'd made to her inner child. Either way, folding sheets into chickens kept her focused on her goal: finding an antidote for Conti's Baby.

Morgan had found a way to reconstruct her research, and she passed pieces of her project around to various scientists at the lab – a trick she'd learned from the alpha wolf. The virus had shown surprising resistance to tampering, and she still hadn't come up with a strategy that would counteract the microbe. To her chagrin, the virus seemed to possess an almost sentient cunning in its ability to dodge the vaccines she had tested against it. This survival trait was, in part, a testament to the hardiness she'd helped engineer into the slow virus, but she was still determined to neutralize it before some unforeseen agent triggered its genetic programming. Conti had said it might be years, but Morgan felt the clock ticking.

As she rocked the chair forward to the desk, Morgan finished the final inside-reverse folds and began to open the wings. She'd made better, she decided, as she studied her handiwork. Then she placed the bird on the desk beside the stack of duplicate reports.

Yes, the reports, she thought. Morgan had a meeting that

afternoon with the board, and she hoped to convince them that Contitech should acquire an interest in the company featured in the reports. Although the company would be good for Contitech, Morgan's real agenda was the potential she saw for her own secret project. She was intrigued by the technology they were developing: molecular-level machines capable of enough autonomy to engage in self-organizing tasks. According to the company, the little machines functioned like a swarm of bees or a colony of ants, achieving things together that no single unit could accomplish alone. They might offer a way to launch a sneak attack on that damn virus, and Morgan hoped the technology would be the new approach she'd been looking for. What were they called? The term always escaped her, and she flipped open the top report to look at the company's name.

"Oh yeah," she said to herself, hoping that by saying the name aloud she would ingrain the term in her mind. "Nanofacture, Inc. They produce nanos."

I need to call in Sandy to brief me on those little –. Morgan caught herself in mid thought. *That's right, Sandy won't be helping me with this stuff anymore.*

Not that Morgan could complain. Sandy had been a woman of her word – at least, to Conti – and she had assisted Morgan just as she had Conti all those years. But when the alpha wolf died, Sandy had come in to tell Morgan she was tired of administrative work. And she issued Morgan an ultimatum: Let her go back into research or she'd retire. Despite her annoying quirks, the woman was a damn fine scientist, and Morgan had acquiesced to her wishes. Now Morgan had a new administrative assistant – Rebecca, was that her name? Something like that.

Morgan buzzed the outer office. "Rebecca?"

"Becca," the voice on the intercom corrected.

"That's right, sorry. Could you come in here, please?"

Morgan had converted the outer office in Conti's lab suite

into a reception area, and she had taken Conti's study as her own work area. Although she'd vowed not to sleep in the lab, in the end she'd had to compromise by placing a sleeper-sofa in the inner office. In some ways, she was still Conti's Cub, she had to concede; if nothing else, he'd bequeathed her his work ethic.

When Becca came in, Morgan asked her to collect the reports and take them into Contitech's main conference room on the first floor. Morgan noticed Becca eyeing the paper chicken standing beside the stack of reports.

"Isn't that . . . what's it called? Gamma something?" the admin assistant asked.

"Origami."

"Yeah, origami."

The assistant stared at the bird and seemed to wait for more of an explanation. After all, why would the head of a biotech research firm sit in her office folding paper chickens? That's what she really wanted to know, Morgan figured.

"It amuses me," Morgan said, but she knew she didn't find the exercise amusing. Maybe that was the point. "And it reminds me of a promise I made." Morgan let a small, enigmatic smile crease her mouth, and then thought but didn't say, *and I never break a promise.*

Becca nodded, collected the reports, and left.

As Morgan picked up the origami chicken with an absent gesture, her mind traveled miles away – or rather, years. If the nanos proved the best solution for beating the slow virus, that's what she'd use. And she'd never stop, she told herself. Not until the nanos found all the birds, all the animals, and all the humans that carried the viral strain. Even if she had to spread the nanos until they covered the Earth.

Morgan placed the origami chicken on the shelf behind her as she stood, and then she gathered the report into her arms. She headed toward the door to meet the board, determined to sell them on the new acquisition. And she would win, she knew. After all, it was for the sake of the future.

THE END

AUTHOR'S NOTE

For current research on the future influencing the past – at least at the quantum level – see the article by Xiao-song Ma, et al., "Experimental Delayed-Choice Entanglement Swapping" in *Nature Physics* 8 (April 2012): 480–485.

The time translation machine in this novel is based on theoretical models developed by Yakir Ahanoronov, Jeeva Anandan, Sandu Popescu, and Lev Vaidman (AAPV). See most recently Ahanoronov's paper, "Time and the Quantum: Erasing the Past and Impacting the Future," *Science* 301:5711 (February 2005): 875-79; and much earlier, Lev Vaidman's paper, "A Quantum Time Machine," *Foundations of Physics* 21:8 (August 1991): 947-58; and AAPV's joint paper, "Superposition of Time Evolutions of Quantum System and a Quantum Time Translation Machine," *Physical Review Letters* 64 (1990): 2965-68. John G Cramer provides an excellent summary of their work in one of his The Alternate View columns, "Quantum Time Machine," *Analog Science Fiction and Fact Magazine* (September 30, 1990): AV-45. All I had to do to make their time translation machine tractable was provide sufficient computing power, which I solved with an organic computing system.

For an introduction to fractal geometry, see Manus J. Donahue's "An Introduction of Chaos Theory and Fractal Geometry" (Fall, 1997): http://www.duke.edu/~mjd/chaos/chaosp.html.

ABOUT THE AUTHOR

In his checkered past, Mark Todd lived consecutive lives as a mortician, a mountaineer, and a musher. These days, he's a simultaneous professor, poet, and stage performer. He's penned two collections of poetry and co-authored a speculative fiction series of novels with wife Kym O'Connell-Todd. He directs the graduate creative writing program at Western State Colorado University. He and Kym argue constantly over what really happened in Roswell.

You can contact the author at mark.todd@gmail.com.

Also by Mark Todd

NOVELS
co-written with Kym O'Connell-Todd
The Silverville Swindle
(Ghost Road Press)
and soon to be reissued as
**Book One of the Silverville Saga:
Little Greed Men**
(Raspberry Creek Books)

Forthcoming in late 2012
**Book Two of the Silverville Saga:
All Plucked Up!**
(Raspberry Creek Books)

POETRY
Wire Song
(Conundrum Press)
Tamped But Loose Enough to Breathe
(Ghost Road Press)

GUNNISON COUNTY LIBRARY DISTRICT

gunnison county
Libraries
connect ● discover ● imagine ● learn ●

Gunnison Library
307 N. Wisconsin
Gunnison CO 81230
970-641-3485
gunnisoncountylibraries.org

15497253R10155

Made in the USA
Charleston, SC
06 November 2012